IT ALL COMES DOWN

ARE YOU AFRAID OF THE DARK?

The Cove has fallen. Leonardo and the survivors return north to where their journey began, in search of allies to fight The Dark—a tangible nightmare in search of blood. But when they reach the Darkwoods, they find it even bleaker than they had feared. Any semblance of clan life has crumbled in the aftermath of the Dark, and the woods are collapsing.

In an effort to unite the woods, Leonardo leads a party deeper into the shadows, to the distant Redwoods, where they face a race against time. An ancient and bizarre game takes place high above the ground, ruled by a ringmaster who calls himself *the general*. The Redwoods kids care more about their rivalries than the impending Dark, and Leonardo is forced to join the game to dismantle it from the inside.

Every plan is dashed by a new setback, and the Dark draws closer by the day. Leonardo must outthink both the general and the Dark, or the woods—and all of its children—will vanish.

THE LOST BOYS TRILOGY

Lost Boys
The Cove
The Dark

THE DARK

THE DARK

BOOK THREE OF THE LOST BOYS TRILOGY

RILEY QUINN

For permission requests, contact:

pr@rileyquinnofficial.com
www.rileyquinnofficial.com
www.westbaypublishing.ca

ISBN 978-1-7771298-5-9 (pbk) — ISBN 978-1-7771298-6-6 (epub)
ISBN 978-1-7771298-7-3 (mobi) — ISBN 978-1-7771298-8-0 (pdf)

354 pages
Text set in Baskerville

Map design by Sofia Soria

First Edition
1 2 3 4 5 6 7 8 9 10

For Kirsten,
who patiently listens to the voices in my head.

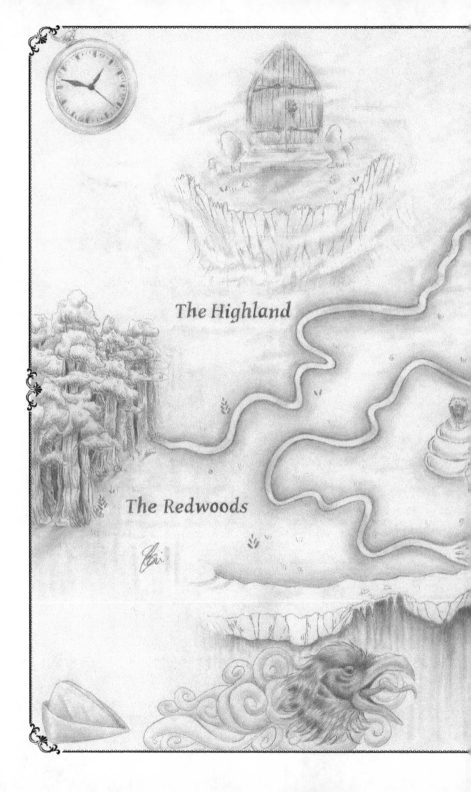

The Highland

The Redwoods

The Darkwoods

The Cove

"Second star to the right and straight on 'til morning."

—*J.M. Barrie*

CHAPTER 1

Tension crackled as Leonardo gripped the stem of his longboat. Oars clunked in precise rhythm, and sweaty faces squinted at the shadows along the bank. Four boats plowed through the river behind them, piled with colorfully robed Cove kids, their expressions tight.

They cut through the Backwaters, a marshland on the edge of the Darkwoods, and not a single living thing broke the silence. It was as if this entire corner of the woods had frozen in time.

"Everything's dead," said Moth, breathless from working his oar. His flushed cheeks turned pale as islands of charred grass slid past.

"I know." Heaviness weighed on Leonardo's chest. He studied a withered stand of reeds, cattail tops drooping for the surface. Around the Backwaters, previously lush aquatic trees had blackened, their branches shrunken.

"Like *dead* dead," said Bates.

1

"It's so quiet," said Viola softly, her gaze fixed on another island of scorched grass. She glanced at Leonardo. He met her grim eyes.

They had traveled a week to get here, chased from the Cove by the Dark, the all-consuming presence that spent its days ravaging the woods.

"Did you expect green gardens?" Kate sat cross-legged in the boat, a salt-stained coat draped from her shoulders and a skull-and-crossbones trilby resting cockeyed on her head.

"When we left, this place was untouched." Leonardo shuddered. The Darkwoods were never quiet.

"Raven Clan territory was dying fast, though," said Nym, clipped and impatient. "It was only natural for it to spread."

Leonardo frowned at him.

He's not...right.

Nym had been battling the Dark inside him for weeks now, but he'd *changed* since the last attack. He was thinner, sunken, bitter. His deterioration was a reminder to all of them, the sand racing through an hourglass.

Leonardo eyed the other three clans of Cove kids, regarding the miles of rotten trees with apprehension. They were all veterans of the Dark, yet they knew so little about it.

They knew the heart of it lay in the Cove. They knew its reach extended across the entire woods. A small group of them knew it was a nightmare, let into the dreamworld by the woods itself. And they knew that sea monster venom could hurt it.

That was all. And they were a long way from any sea monsters.

We're on our own. Viola's people—the guardians of the woods—

2

were gone, and the sirens had abandoned their post as guardians of the Cove.

"The Hawk Clan patrol is still sitting at the border," said Viola, eyes shut as she searched ahead with her mind. "They're not moving."

"Then let's introduce ourselves," said Mishti. Leonardo's co-leader of Lion Clan, she stood atop the captain's platform of her boat, with its gold lion head and silk sail. Days of travel had disheveled her black hair, her gold robes smudged and stained, but the knife-edged throwing rings around her wrists glinted as sharp as her eyes.

A few girls in her boat leaned closer, whispering quickly. Leonardo watched them out of one eye. For all of Mishti's bravado, her clan weren't fighters. Leonardo's boys had told them stories of Hawk Clan's ferocity, and he recognized the hesitation on the girls' faces to confront such a formidable enemy.

Formidable or not, we have five-times their numbers.

"I agree," said Leonardo. "But this is only a fly-by. We don't stop."

"What?" Pinch twisted back to look at him. "Why?"

"If we attack a border patrol," explained Leonardo, "we'll have a second fight on our hands with the rest of the clan. Instead, we'll scare Hawk Clan, let them gather all their numbers, then we'll capture them as one."

He held no illusions that Gallus would listen to logic. He was the new Aleksander, and they would waste precious time trying to convince him to leave the Darkwoods. Tying up Hawk Clan and dragging them in front of the Dark would be the only way to gain their allegiance.

3

"Imagine when Gallus sees all of us," laughed Bates. "The halfwit's going to curl up and cry."

Leonardo grinned, despite himself. He'd be lying if he said he wasn't looking forward to the expression on Gallus's face. They slipped past a blackened tree, its branches sagging like rubber. The amusement turned sour in Leonardo's mouth.

We can't waste time here. They needed the imaginative power of all the clans in the Darkwoods, as well as the Redwoods and the Highland, if they wanted to save the woods and survive the Dark.

He eyed the boats beyond his stern, filled with Lions, Tigers, Dragons, Snakes, and pirates. They were weary, tattered from their escape. He hoped they were ready for the fight Hawk Clan would bring.

"There's the river," called Pinch. He pointed over the prow to where the sprawling delta of the Backwaters narrowed into the mouth of a waterway, laid bare by the flattened, dead vegetation.

The river. They'd been on 'the river' for a week, but this leg was different. This was home.

How much has changed? Has died, he corrected himself. He wondered if he'd recognize it once they rounded the rocky stretch of Hawk Clan territory and entered Raven Clan's boundaries.

The five boats slipped out of the Backwaters and through the bottleneck of rotten banks, single file, to the steady splash of water sloshing off paddles. The current strengthened, impeding their progress and spraying around the tip of the prow. Leonardo's heart pounded. They were in Hawk Clan territory now. They had returned to the Darkwoods.

"I never imagined five clans could be so quiet," said Moth. Sweat matted his curls, and a partially healed scab marred his cheek, earned during a fight with demonic freshwater sirens a few days earlier. The journey north hadn't been any easier than the one south.

No one replied, punctuating his point.

Their surroundings became sandier as the banks gave way to large outcroppings of rock. Leonardo tugged the rudder, guiding the boat left, around a bend in the river, and down the final stretch toward where the water funneled through a massive cleft in the Tree Cliffs. The silhouette of pines atop the ruddy stone set his fingers twitching on the stem, dry wood flaking under his nails. Those trees leered down, sinister now. Leonardo had become a trespasser. An intruder in his own woods.

A hawk cry split the air, and Leonardo jumped.

At the far end of the tunnel, a longboat floated near the Raven Clan border. He drew a sharp breath.

Calm down, Leonardo told himself. His clan needed him in control.

His clanmates glanced at one another, but they uttered no raven cry in response. They weren't Ravens anymore.

The Hawk boat rotated to face them, and Leonardo wrapped his fingers around his sword's leather grip. A pudgy figure on the stern platform lifted a hand, shading his eyes.

Viola glanced back at Leonardo, her brown eyes scrutinizing his. It was Gallus's ploy that started Raven Clan's demise. Memories of the ambush played through Leonardo's mind. Of Hawk Clan, Bear Clan, and Fox Clan storming the clearing below the treehouses. Of the treehouses burning as he watched helplessly.

Leonardo's boat passed into the cleft between the cliffs and closed on the Hawks fast, oars churning under anxious hands.

"Oars up," called Leonardo. His clan responded instantly, oars clattering out of the water.

Gallus's face came into focus, all apple cheeks and baby-fat. His mouth dropped open at the sight of the ex-Ravens.

"You!" His gaze darted past Leonardo to the four packed longboats in his wake. He focused on Leonardo again, his eyes wild. "What the hell are you doing here?"

CHAPTER 2

W e're not here for a fight," called Leonardo. Even with the oars raised, his boat closed rapidly on Gallus's. Hawks glared at the Lions and Cove kids.

"No?" Gallus drew his sword.

"The Dark is growing," said Leonardo. "We need to unite."

"The *what?*" demanded Gallus.

"The Dark, idiot," said Pinch. "Look around you." He loaded his slingshot under the lip of the prow as they edged alongside the Hawk boat.

Gallus swung his head around, eyes wide and exaggerated as he feigned searching for something in the murky water. Beyond his boat, ranks of black trees and underbrush slumped together, as far down the riverbanks as Leonardo could see. His stomach constricted into a knot.

"It's daylight," said Gallus.

"No shit," said Pinch. "And all that,"—he waved dramatically at the trees, "is the Dark."

"It's a living thing," said Leonardo. "It's what's killing everything."

"It already destroyed the Cove," added Mishti.

"Who are you?" demanded Gallus, bewilderment slackening his face. He glanced from one boat to the next, laden with kids in gold, red, blue, and grey robes.

"Mishti," said Mishti, as if it were the most obvious thing in the world.

"Ok…" Gallus shook his head, focusing back on Leonardo as their captain's platforms glided toward each other. Rowers spat insults from both sides as the flanks of the two boats passed.

"I appreciate that you brought this…circus here, Leonardo," said Gallus. "I really do. But please…get out."

Leonardo frowned at the silent woods. A breeze whistled through the blackened branches, carrying a rotten stink. He'd smelled it in the Cove a week earlier, when the Dark laid waste to everything.

"Gallus, you need to leave with us. There's nothing left of the—"

"Oh, no-no-no-no. You are mistaken, my…not-friend." Gallus waved around grandly, drawing a deep breath of the stench. "This is fine. Actually, it's better than fine!" He laughed, then winked at Leonardo. "I'll bet this is Aleksander's worst nightmare."

Suddenly, Cyrus stood up from his bench in the middle of Leonardo's boat. He straightened his grand, purple-feathered pirate's hat, and all at once, he was a perfect twin of Gallus.

His magic hat gave him a disturbing talent for changing his appearance.

Gallus blanched and staggered backward. He made a choked noise and nearly tripped over the edge of his boat, stubby arms pinwheeling before a Hawk jumped up and caught him.

Damn. Leonardo would've liked to see Gallus take a plunge into the river.

"I'm Cyrus," said Cyrus, in Gallus's voice. He stepped closer, eyes locked on the real Gallus.

Gallus pushed away the boy who'd saved him. Terror covered the kid's face, along with every other Hawk, as they gaped at their leader's doppelganger. Gallus swallowed hard, fingers shaking as he gripped the edge of his boat for support, and visibly mustered his bravado.

"I don't like this one, Leonardo," he declared, with a thin veneer of joviality. He shivered. "I don't like him at all."

"Well, I don't like you either," said Cyrus. "A friend of mine was from the Darkwoods. He's dead now. But if everyone here is as annoying as you, I can see why he left."

"Right. Well," Gallus smacked his lips together. "I choose to ignore you." He drew himself up and faced Leonardo as the boat's momentum carried Cyrus past him. "This has been a *lovely* chat. But you all must leave my kingdom now."

"*Kingdom?*" Leonardo raised his brows. "Okay…fine." They came side-by-side. "Oars down."

His boat jumped forward under the push of the oars, across the Raven Clan border and away from Gallus.

"Hey!" Gallus whipped around to watch them over the stern. "I said get out!"

"We are out." Leonardo twisted to see him. "Raven Clan territory isn't part of your 'kingdom' anymore."

Mishti eyed Gallus as her own boat glided by, then Caliban passed Gallus on the opposite flank.

"You're crazier than me," said Caliban, one blue eye and one green narrowed as he regarded Gallus.

"Who are you?" demanded Gallus. Then, "Get out! All of you! I'm the ruler of the Darkwoods!"

No, you're terrified, thought Leonardo.

The five boats slipped around an indignant Gallus, and he made no move to stop them.

"That went...better than I expected," said Viola. She returned her slingshot to the leather loop in her dress. Next to her, Charley did the same. Next to Charley, Pompey still gripped his too-big sword, eyes narrowed as the Hawk boat grew smaller in the distance.

"They'll start preparing for war," said Puck.

"Which is exactly what we want," said Mishti, as she brought her boat alongside Leonardo's.

If we topple Hawk, Fox and Bear will follow. If everything went to plan, they could be out of the Darkwoods by sunset. But capturing Gallus wouldn't solve all their problems. First, they needed to pay a visit he'd been dreading since they left the Cove.

"Good job, everyone." Leonardo drew a breath. "Now for the real challenge."

"Raven Clan," said Moth.

***

The rest of Raven Clan territory was just as bleak as the first hundred meters. If Leonardo had to guess what had happened to the trees, he would say they melted. They leaned against each other, branches drooping and trunks warped at unnatural angles. The dappled sun glinted off white shapes in the underbrush.

"Those are crocodile skulls, aren't they?" called Mishti. She squinted at the bank, drawing her dark brows together.

"Oh, they're croc skulls alright," said Pinch from his fore-watchman's bench. He said it grimly, too quiet for Mishti to hear, but everyone in Leonardo's boat tightened their grips on the oars, half-rising from their benches to see better.

Everywhere the Dark went, it left crocodile skulls.

That's how it sees, Viola had told him last time they were here.

The boats rounded a bend, past the raised bank and the old oak tree where Leonardo and Viola first met. It was as dead as everything else, its vast canopy like a sad carnival ride, all the branches drooping around a twisted trunk. Viola blinked slowly at Leonardo, and he squared his jaw, a silent emotion passing between them. They'd been through a lot since that tree was alive.

Seeing it didn't make him sad. He'd accepted by now that his home was gone. The oak tree was just another reminder they needed to act.

"So, Raven Clan," said Sophie, Mishti's second-in-command. "I suggest we try to negotiate with them. We don't have room for two full clans of prisoners."

Half the ex-Ravens laughed.

"Good luck negotiating with Ajax," said Pinch.

Sophie crossed her arms. Her red hair was pulled back in a severe bun, and her freckled cheeks didn't offer a hint of a smile.

"We may have no choice but to fight," Leonardo told her. "The Darkwoods are very different from the Cove."

"So we fight," said Mishti. "We'll tie up every clan here and drag them to the Dark if we have to."

Sophie tightened her lips. Leonardo watched her from one eye. Until recently, Sophie had been pulling the real strings behind Mishti's façade of leadership. Even Juliet had manipulated Mishti's devotion to the woods to steer decisions. With Mishti's newfound confidence and Leonardo's support, she'd grasped the full reins of her clan, and Sophie didn't appear to be taking it well.

"Remember," Mishti turned in her boat to get all five clans' attention, "priority number one is to spare as many lives as we can. We need them to defeat the Dark."

The boats glided through bars of sunlight, thinly filtered by the sparse canopy.

"Defend yourselves," added Leonardo. "But fight to disarm."

Then the old Raven Clan beach came into sight.

Leonardo caught his breath.

The trees were gone. They'd burned before the Dark arrived, in a wildfire that destroyed Raven Clan's original camp, but when Leonardo left the Darkwoods, the burnt trunks were still standing. Now, the rest of the forest looked how those trees had, and that stretch of woodland had collapsed to ash under the force of the Dark.

"Camp's gotten worse," said Pinch dryly.

"Do you think they're still living across the river?" asked Nym.

Leonardo eyed the span of woods opposite the old beach. It looked like a tar pit had exploded.

"Well," said Moth. "It's no worse than anywhere else."

"Take us to the edge," said Leonardo, tugging the rudder.

"We're not going ashore, are we?" called Cleopatra from the Tiger Clan boat. She picked up her tiger cub from the footwell in front of her, holding it against her chest. Neither she nor her girls wore the white makeup they had donned in the Cove. Formality was gone within the clans. They were one alliance now, just trying to survive. And Cleo's youth was plain in the hesitance of her expression as she studied the grim banks. She was the youngest of the leaders—maybe thirteen.

"A few of us will have to," replied Leonardo. "Raven Clan will be hostile—"

"Duck!" shouted Pinch.

A pebble whistled past Leonardo's cheek.

Dammit.

He dropped to the boards, scrambling for a shield.

"Shields up!" yelled Puck.

Sophie yelled the same thing from Mishti's boat.

Kate shoved one at Leonardo. He grabbed it and climbed into the footwell, breathing fast and crouching low as a shower of pebbles popped against the sides of the boat, pinging off the gold embossed shields. They'd taken every weapon from Lion Clan's fortress before leaving the Cove.

"I think we found them," called Bates.

"Ow!" snapped Moth, clutching his arm beside Bates. A pebble clattered to the footwell. "Keep your shield up, halfwit."

The attack wasn't as strong as he'd expected. Maybe a dozen slingshots.

Are their numbers that *depleted?*

Leonardo straightened from behind his shield. Moth and Viola looked at him sharply.

Shapes moved between the trees, their faces indistinguishable in the shadows.

"Ajax!" yelled Leonardo. "Stop shooting!"

He dropped behind the shields again. Three pebbles whisked over his head.

They haven't lost their aim, at least. When Puck used to run battle practice, he'd force them to spend hours shooting at targets on trees under Aleksander's orders.

"You think he'll listen?" Viola crouched two benches over from Leonardo, her shield in one hand, slingshot in the other.

The pebbles stopped. Viola frowned.

Leonardo shrugged. "Maybe."

He straightened again, hesitantly. For a second, nothing happened. The Ravens in the underbrush kept still. He squinted through the shadows for Ajax's lanky form. But it wasn't Ajax who stepped out into the sunlight.

"Leonardo?" Soot smeared the boy's face, his tailcoat torn and dishevelled, but Leonardo recognized him immediately.

"Jack?"

"What are you doing here?" Jack let his gaze travel over the five boats. "Who are all these people?"

"Where is Ajax?" asked Leonardo.

"Ajax is gone," said Will, stepping out of the trees. He looked older than Leonardo remembered. His bloodshot eyes were too small for his soot-covered face, and his brown hair was hacked in an uneven fringe. Any youth he'd possessed had hardened and weathered. "The Dark took him."

Gasps rippled across the boat. Leonardo stared at Jack and Will on the bank.

He's gone? A surge of relief flooded through Leonardo. Without Ajax, the Ravens might actually be reasonable.

"And Cato?" asked Pinch.

A hulking figure lumbered out of the forest, covered in more soot than a firepit.

"I'm still here, dumbface," bellowed Cato. He grinned, and Leonardo grimaced.

How did he get soot on his teeth?

"Right," said Pinch. "Great."

"Are you here in peace?" Jack's eyes glinted, searching for answers in Leonardo's.

"We only left because Ajax forced us to," said Leonardo. "We're not here for a fight. Are you leader now?"

Jack drew a deep breath. "Closest thing we have to one." He eyed the four other boats again. "Come ashore. I think we need to talk."

CHAPTER 3

Leonardo's boots thudded against the dirt. Darkwoods soil back under his feet.

In truth, part of him felt like he'd never left. If he didn't think too hard about it, the Cove and everything there could have just been a strange dream. But then again, everything in the woods was a dream, wasn't it?

A world of imagination.

The other four boats angled up along the bank, and a parade of kids in colored robes jumped over the side, shattering any illusion that he'd just imagined the Cove.

"Follow me," said Jack. Up close, Leonardo realized it wasn't soot but a thick, tacky substance the Ravens had smeared across their faces.

Why?

Leonardo ducked under branches, jogging to keep up with Jack's brisk pace. He pushed a bush aside, and his fingers came away coated in a syrupy blackness. He grimaced and paused to rub it off in the dirt.

"It's harmless," said Jack over his shoulder. "The Dark is holed up downriver, in Fox and Bear territory. All of this is just deadness."

"Why are you wearing it?" Caliban ran a finger across a coated branch and drew a symbol on the back of his hand, his expression pensive.

Can you harness its power, was what he meant. Leonardo and Mishti tightened their lips.

"Camouflage," said Will. He stopped and peered into the rotten vegetation. Leonardo spotted something white poking through the black, and Will climbed toward it, unceremoniously stomping the crocodile skull, so it shattered into dust.

"If we blend in, it can't see us as easily," said Jack. "That's how we survive."

They stepped into a clearing. Sleeping rolls were arranged like a sort of carpet on the tarry grass. Spare shirts and clothing had been stitched together and stretched into makeshift lean-tos. A pile of swords and shields lay against a rock, most of them blackened and warped.

Leonardo's jaw dropped. He'd fought the Dark before, but seeing the state of Raven Clan's weapons brought the severity of their situation into a new light.

The thirteen surviving Ravens gathered in a cluster as a hundred and fifty Cove kids poured into their camp. Aside from Jack, Will, and Cato, Leonardo recognized Snout and Rugby through their camouflage soot, along with several other kids he'd known from his Raven Clan days. There didn't appear to be anyone new.

17

Have the woods stopped bringing new kids here?

"I'm not going to sugar-coat it," said Jack, his voice soft. "Things are bad. We need help."

Leonardo glanced at Mishti. She moistened her lips. Optimism sparked in the eagerness of her raised brows.

Careful, he thought. All these Ravens had turned their backs on Leonardo's clan once.

"Where's Page?" asked Bates.

Jack swallowed. He met Bates's gaze, his lips white, then blinked slowly at Leonardo.

Gone too.

"I'm sorry," said Moth.

The pain on Jack's face confirmed what Leonardo already knew—Jack and Page had been a lot more than friends.

"We need help too," Leonardo told the Ravens warily. "Everyone's help. In every corner of the woods. Together, we can defeat the—"

"Ok," said Jack.

Uneasiness spiked Leonardo's nerves.

Jack shrugged. "We'll die if we stay here. Whatever you want to do, we'll join you."

Leonardo analyzed him.

Jack met his gaze plainly. *This is our reality,* his expression said. *Welcome back to the Darkwoods.*

Leonardo bit his cheek. *It's too easy.*

Jack scanned the other Ravens. "Anyone disagree?"

Heavy bags weighed under their eyes. Several blinked rapidly as if struggling to stay awake. Will lost his balance and stumbled sideways, stopping himself against a tree. The wood gave way under his hand, compressing like a sponge. Black tar oozed between his fingers, and Leonardo resisted the urge to gag.

"There," said Jack. His voice bore the bleakness of the entire clan. "It's decided. However, as leader of Raven Clan, I do have one condition."

That didn't take long.

Leonardo hadn't realized how little he trusted the Ravens. These kids used to be his friends, but that felt like a lifetime ago.

"Ok," he said slowly. "What is it?"

"You be the leader."

"What?" The ground shifted under Leonardo's feet. He looked from Moth to Pinch, to Viola, and the rest of the Lions. Their faces fell slack with shock. Pinch started to say something, then closed his mouth, then opened it again, deepening his frown.

Jack crossed his arms. *You heard me.*

Yes, Leonardo had heard him. *You be the leader. Of Raven Clan.* Never in his life had he expected to hear those words.

Leonardo eyed Cato. Cato had nearly killed him the last time they saw each other, for the exact thing Jack was now proposing. But even Cato didn't react to the suggestion. A few Ravens exchanged looks, but no one seemed ready to argue.

All eyes were on Leonardo. The blood rushed in his ears. Dizziness set the world pitching around him.

"We made a mistake choosing Ajax," said Jack. "He wasn't Aleksander. Not by a longshot. We need a real leader." He gestured to the army of kids behind Leonardo. "Clearly, you know what you're doing."

Leonardo didn't know how to respond. He and his clan had

risked everything to become Lions. But they were Ravens first. Nothing would ever change that.

Are you actually considering it?

His own reaction surprised him. The proposal was so absurd, he wanted to laugh, but he could see the hollow desperation in his old clanmates' faces, and that was as sobering as anything.

"No way," said Mishti, plowing into his scattered thoughts. "Not a chance."

"Excuse me?" Leonardo turned on her. Hearing Mishti insist that he *stay* leader of her clan was one more absurdity than he could handle. Yes, they had been cooperating lately, but—

Mishti faced him, hands on her hips. "Did you forget the sign? The lion head in Juliet's quarters? The Lostwoods want you to be a Lion. We cannot dishonor—"

"I faked that sign," said Juliet quietly.

"What?" Mishti whirled on her.

Shit. Now? Leonardo glanced at Moth. They both knew that already. Moth drew himself up, stepping closer to Juliet as Mishti advanced on her.

Leonardo's heart pounded. The last thing they could afford was a fractured alliance, but the cracks were spreading fast in the raw light of the clearing. Caliban leaned closer to Demetrius, whispering something in the other leader's ear. Demetrius brought his fist over his mouth in half an attempt to hide his grin.

Enjoying the show? Leonardo scowled at them.

"Say that again," said Mishti.

"I faked the sign," repeated Juliet. Her voice shook slightly, and she clasped the hummingbird feather around her neck. "I could see we needed to work with them, and I knew that you wouldn't unless—"

"You lied to me?" Mishti's voice came out razor-edged, but her eyes glistened. The same as when Thaisa betrayed her.

Dammit. Do something, Leonardo swore at himself. But he hadn't the slightest idea how to right their keeling ship.

Mishti never wanted a co-leader in the first place. If I step down as leader of Lion Clan, I could take over Raven Clan and still lead the alliance.

But that wasn't true. He needed Lion Clan to cement his authority.

"We don't have time to argue." Moth stepped between Mishti and Juliet. "We can deal with hurt feelings later."

Leonardo winced. *Hurt feelings* were a trivial choice of words.

Mishti spit out a laugh. Leonardo placed a hand on her shoulder, and she shoved it off, spinning to face him. "Did you know?"

Leonardo caught his breath. The veins stood out on her neck, her muscles clenched tight. An insect zipped past her ear, and she whacked it hard enough to kill it on impact.

"Mishti," he said, as calmly and steadily as possible. "We can't be emotional about things. This is all too important."

Mishti worked her jaw. She balled her hands into fists, then swore under her breath.

"Fine," she hissed. "So there was no sign. We were never supposed to be co-leaders at all. Are you giving me back my clan then?"

Leonardo dragged his hands through his hair, fighting the urge to snap at her.

"No one's *giving back* anything," he said carefully. "This is *our* clan."

Mishti raised her eyebrows. "You've been a Lion for how many days?"

Leonardo stepped closer to her. He could feel a hundred and sixty-one pairs of eyes trained on them, but he never broke contact with Mishti's.

"You were living in the shadow of a hundred-year-old legend. We made this clan powerful *together*. And we're staying together."

He closed his eyes. A gentle hand closed on his arm, and he recognized Viola's touch. It was a steadying force in the chaos, and Leonardo leaned into it, drawing a slow breath and releasing it.

He blinked at the uncertain faces around him, then focused on his clanmates—the seven remaining survivors who had stood by him since the beginning.

"But," continued Leonardo, "that doesn't mean we can't be Ravens too. It's time we made our own rules."

Bates and Puck looked at each other. Moth slipped his fingers into Juliet's. Nym stared off into space, either oblivious or aloof to all of it. That troubled Leonardo more than Mishti's reaction.

Will we lose him completely? A week ago, he was still Nym. Now…Leonardo wasn't sure how much *Nym* was left in the shell of a boy standing before him.

Charley looked at Viola, and Viola kept her gaze locked on Leonardo's. Intelligence glinted in her brown eyes as she pieced through the recent developments, but she didn't say a word.

She was never a Raven to begin with, he thought. Knowing Viola, she would hold her opinion until those it truly affected spoke first.

It was Pinch who broke the silence.

"Fuck yeah," he said. "Let's be Raven-Lions."

A smile tugged at Leonardo's lips. *Can it be that simple?*

Moth, to Leonardo's surprise, was the first to start nodding. Then Puck, Bates, and finally, Nym, though he had a faraway look.

"Ok," said Leonardo, still watching Nym. "That's six of us. Viola, Charley?"

"Hey!" Cato narrowed his eyes. "Raven Clan is only boys."

"*Was*," said Leonardo. Cato crossed his arms, but Leonardo ignored him. He had plenty of experience navigating Cato's pigheadedness. "What do you say?" he asked Viola and Charley.

Viola took Leonardo's hand. "Of course."

Charley nodded, echoing her.

"Then we're Ravens," said Leonardo, a little lightheaded. "And Lions. Welcome back, everyone."

CHAPTER 4

Raven Clan streamed upriver, oars churning, with the rest of their alliance behind them. The raven figurehead was disfigured into Moth's attempt at a Lion. Part of Leonardo now regretted that decision, but if nothing else, it represented the trials they had endured. The carved raven was damaged but still standing.

If he'd learned anything, it was to stop predicting how things would play out. He could count on one hand the times he'd been right.

"Gallus is going to be ready for a fight," shouted Leonardo. "We don't want to lose numbers, and we can't afford to vanish Hawks who could be helpful in the real fight. We take prisoners unless forced to do otherwise, understood?"

Heads nodded across the boats.

"Mishti?" prompted Leonardo. "Are we clear?"

"Excuse me?" Mishti placed her hands on her hips, standing

rigid atop her captain's platform. "Just because you lead two clans now doesn't mean—"

"Your throwing rings are the most dangerous and unpredictable weapon we have," Leonardo interrupted her. "I need to know you won't vanish half of Hawk Clan."

"Fine." Mishti rolled her eyes. "You have my word."

He didn't entirely believe her, but he knew it was the best he'd get.

"Their advantage will be ambush," he shouted. "We don't know where they'll be waiting—"

"They'll be on this side of the fork," said Jack. "They've been guarding the border day and night so no one can escape Gallus's 'kingdom'."

"Ok." Leonardo nodded to Jack. The other boy had washed the tar off his face, and his skin looked sallow underneath. He was wire-thin in his tattered coat, his hair hanging scraggly, but a renewed flicker of life glinted under the grime. Raven Clan was rising again, shaking off the ashes.

This side of the fork meant the sandy expanse just beyond the cliffs.

"If we take away their time and space, they'll crumble fast," said Leonardo. "That means we're out of the boats as soon as we get through the tree cliffs. If they're behind the rocks, we'll be on them before they can take more than a few shots."

"Jack," said Puck. "What's the news with Fox and Bear clan? Are they still with Gallus?"

Jack shook his head, surprising Leonardo. "No one has heard from them in weeks. If you saw their territory…" The trauma playing behind his eyes painted a clear enough picture of the

Dark that Leonardo's blood went cold. "They're gone," finished Jack.

The news knocked the wind from Leonardo's lungs.

Why didn't he say anything before?

Because you never asked, Leonardo answered himself immediately. There were too many moving pieces. And with only half the information, Leonardo had mistaken this fight for something very different than it was.

Jack's twelve soot-covered Ravens and Gallus's Hawks were all that remained. They weren't toppling a make-believe king; they were capturing the only remaining survivors.

How many more kids are left anywhere? When they first decided to 'unite the entire woods,' he'd expected them to quadruple their alliance numbers. Now, he wondered if they would even reach double.

"Tree Cliffs," called Pinch.

Leonardo's chest tightened.

"Here we go!" he shouted, stooping to lift a shield from the footwell. It was more vital than ever that they survived this fight with no casualties.

The rowers dug in, and the five boats jumped toward the cleft in the cliffs. They plowed up the waterway, smooth stone walls flashing past. Ruddy veins of rock and mineral passed Leonardo's face while he stared ahead, gaze fixed unblinkingly on the bright end of the passage, drawing closer by the second.

Then they burst into the dry territory beyond the cliffs, and Leonardo yanked the rudder, driving the prow hard into the bank.

"Move, move, move," yelled Puck.

Someone let out a raven cry as Pinch vaulted over the prow, followed by Bates, Nym, Puck, and the rest. Leonardo ran across the benches, drew his sword, grabbed the bulwark, and launched himself down to the sand.

A pebble glanced off the side of his head, and Leonardo flinched, stumbling sideways. Pain blossomed above his ear, but he ignored it and swung up his shield, deflecting another shot.

He yanked his sword from his belt and sprinted after the others.

Hawks charged out from behind the rocks, blades ringing as they collided with the Ravens. Gallus screamed battle cries somewhere in the throng, his shrill voice piercing the crash.

Leonardo swung his sword at a Hawk with long, greasy hair. The taller boy deflected it, lunging at Leonardo, just as a second Hawk charged him from the side.

Dammit. Leonardo bashed away the tall Hawk's sword and twisted as a throwing ring whistled past. The second Hawk threw up his shield. The ring buried itself in the wood as an army of Lion, and Tiger girls flooded the bank.

Leonardo yanked the ring out of the kid's shield and took a wild swing at the tall Hawk. The boy staggered back, stumbling over his own ankles. Leonardo spun and lunged at the shield kid, Mishti's ring in his left hand while his sword cracked against the wood.

Across the river, the blue robes of Dragons, the grey cloaks of Snakes, and the mismatched patchwork of pirates crashed the opposite bank. The Cove kids weren't exceptional fighters, but they outnumbered the Hawks by such an overwhelming mass that

Gallus's clan never stood a chance. A shimmering wave of colored robes smothered their rush.

Leonardo threw the shield kid onto his back, then disengaged as Pinch and Rugby grabbed the boy from behind, knives at his throat. The Hawk dropped his sword, eyes wide.

A few feet away, Cato smashed his way through attackers. He disarmed a Hawk and raised his weapon two-handed.

"Cato!" shouted Leonardo.

Cato glanced at him.

"Prisoners," said Leonardo. He'd lived this moment before. A lifetime ago.

This time, to Leonardo's surprise, Cato listened. He eyed the Hawk, then shrugged and punched him so hard the kid dropped flat on his back. Unconscious, but alive.

Maybe Cato can change after all. If nothing else, Cato had been loyal in the old days.

The fight ended as quickly as it started. Mishti and Sophie ripped a boy's shield and sword from his grip, forcing him to his knees as Kate and Cyrus skillfully disarmed their attackers on the opposite bank, swords flashing like a choreographed ballet.

"Enough!" yelled Gallus, suddenly jumping atop a rock. "Get up here," he snapped at someone Leonardo couldn't see.

Then Pompey cried out in pain, stumbling onto the rock as one of Gallus's cronies shoved him. Gallus grabbed him by the collar, pressing his sword to Pompey's pale throat.

Shit. Leonardo's chest constricted. *Shit shit shit.*

Leonardo pushed around a trio of Tiger girls, then past Cato and Snout.

"Hey!" yelled Charley. "Let go of him!"

No! New panic charged Leonardo's blood.

She sprinted through the crowd, sword raised, before Sophie grabbed her in a bear hug.

"Hey!" Charley jerked to a halt and tried to yank herself free. "Let go of me!"

Thank you, Sophie. Adrenaline pinpricked his skin. Heroics wouldn't save Pompey.

"Gallus," said Leonardo carefully. He stepped into the clear space before the rock. Pompey breathed heavily, Gallus's blade glinting in the sunlight.

Leonardo scowled. *Why was he in the fight? Why was Charley?*

Because you never told them not to, he answered himself. He had too many people to coordinate.

"Leonardo," replied Gallus, grandly rolling the 'r.' "You want him back? I'll offer you a dealio." He paused, laughing at his own wit. "A dealio! Get it? A *deal, Leo!*"

"We set all your Hawks free?"

"Astute guess! But I will also require you to swear loyalty to me, king of the Darkwoods, and—"

A bowstring snapped, and an arrow slammed into Gallus's chest. He gasped, staggering back a step to the very edge of the rock. Pompey ducked out of his grip and jumped down, sprinting to safety. Gallus looked at his chest as a red stain spread around the feathered shaft. The thick leather vests that Darkwoods kids wore as armor had shifted to expose his heart.

Cleopatra stepped out of the crowd, a bow in her grip, a second arrow already nocked.

"Cleo," said Mishti.

Cleopatra loosed.

The arrow struck Gallus an inch from the first. He vanished instantly.

Gasps were cut short as the Cove kids tightened their grips on the prisoners.

Leonardo's heart raced. Blood pounded hard in his ears.

No casualties. That was their plan. But Cleo had possibly saved Pompey's life. And Gallus was gone.

Cleopatra regarded Mishti, then Leonardo. Her young eyes were cold and unruffled. She eyed Pompey, shaking between Charley and Viola, then looked back at Leonardo.

"You're welcome. I don't swear loyalty to anyone but the Lostwoods," she added.

She nodded to a crocodile skull half-buried in the sand. "The Dark is watching. Let's keep moving."

"Wait," called Kate from the opposite bank. "Where's Cyrus?"

Leonardo frowned, squinting across the sparkling water. Cyrus was typically hard to miss in his giant purple-feathered hat. Dragons, Snakes, pirates, and captive Hawks covered the bank, sweat glistening on their faces, but Cyrus was notably absent.

A pit of dread clenched in Leonardo's stomach.

"You didn't see?" Caliban blinked his mismatched eyes, his hood flipped back from the fight. "He was vanished."

Caliban said it as simply as if he were speaking of the tide.

"What?" Kate's voice came out strangled. "But…"

"You're not safe anymore." There was no sympathy in Caliban's tone. In fact, he sounded pleased. "You're the only one left."

"Who was it?" demanded Kate. A wild energy possessed her, her chest rising and falling as if she'd just run a mile.

"Kate," called Leonardo. He had no idea how to console her.

"Who vanished him?" snapped Kate.

"I believe it was this one," said Demetrius. He strolled over to a young Hawk, still on his knees. "He looked quite surprised before he vanished."

Leonardo hadn't realized how much enmity still existed between the clans and the pirates.

"It wasn't me, I swear—"

"Oh, you're sure?" Kate leveled her sword. "Tell me what he looked like."

"I…" the Hawk's gaze darted anywhere but her blade. Leonardo held his breath as Kate advanced on the kid.

"He was tall," said Kate. "His coat was purple, and he had a hat…" She paused as the kid blanched. "Ah, I see the recognition now. Get up."

The Hawk boy heaved a sob.

"Kate," called Leonardo. "We need numbers—-"

"Shut up, Leo." Kate never took her eyes off the boy.

Across the river, Leonardo clenched and unclenched his sword. He couldn't do anything but watch as she stopped in front of the kid, who nervously climbed to his feet.

It happened faster than Leonardo could blink. Kate's sword flashed, the boy vanished, and she was already walking toward the boats before Leonardo's mind caught up.

Dammit, Kate. Leonardo swore and jammed his sword back in his belt. *He was a kid.*

Things were spiraling fast. Leonardo squared his shoulders.

"Everyone in the boats," he shouted, one eye on Kate, the other on Cleopatra. "We're done here."

CHAPTER 5

No one spoke of Gallus, Cyrus, or the Hawk boy. But Leonardo knew all three were at the forefront of everyone's thoughts. He couldn't stop seeing Cleo's arrow, Kate's sword, John and Pip's vanishing because now Cyrus had joined them.

You're all that's left, Caliban told Kate. Just like Viola.

And yet, they still couldn't stop to regroup. The Fox and Bear Clan borders were the last unknown factor in the Darkwoods.

"So, no one has entered this half of the river since we left?" he asked the Ravens.

They rowed toward the fork at the opposite end of Raven Clan territory, under a canopy of dead branches that met over the water.

"You'll see why," said Jack, as Leonardo used the rudder to steer them down the Fox Clan fork.

"What does that mean?" asked Puck.

Long, claw-like shadows stretched across the faces of the clan kids and their Hawk prisoners, tied up on the middle benches of the five boats. They twitched and tugged at their restraints, terror plain in their trembling fingers. Their faces paled as they peered downriver. The Ravens were no different. Free or bound, all the Darkwoods kids radiated fear.

Can it really be that bad? wondered Leonardo.

Of course it can, he answered himself. *It's the Dark.*

"This is a bad idea," said Nym flatly. He studied his hands again. He'd been checking his hands a lot lately. Leonardo shivered at the iciness in his voice. Nym was a lot of things, but cold had never been one of them.

None of them had seen the Dark since barely escaping with their lives. This would be their first encounter since, and Leonardo had no idea what to feel.

Nym's arms were bound in rags soaked with river water, and Moth and Juliet had healed the rest of their Dark marks, but still…

We faced its heart in the Cove, he assured himself. *This can't be as dangerous.*

Right?

The Dark had fled out to sea after they burned it, but that didn't mean it stayed there.

They rounded a bend in the river and slipped out into a wide bowl at the top of a jumble of rocks. In the old days, they'd called it a waterfall, but after living in the Cove, the idea seemed absurd. Lion Clan's fortress was full of towering waterfalls, crashing from underground rivers into deep rock pools. A little effort and muscle could get a boat over these rocks without much delay.

Not that Leonardo had any intention of traversing the rocks

today. A wall of blackness swirled over the waterway beyond, weaving through the woods at the edge of Fox Clan territory. Crocodile skulls covered every tree branch, like a flock of long, pale birds. More faded into the distance, just visible through the haze.

"What the hell..." Leonardo stepped onto the first bench, picking his way around kids and prisoners as he walked toward the prow, gaze fixed on the Dark.

"Reverse," he said. "Hold us in place."

The rowers shifted, backpaddling to keep them stationary above the waterfall.

The other boats drifted up alongside. Kids leaned over the water to see better, and grave voices stirred the air, almost whispers, afraid to wake whatever hid behind that blackness.

The atmosphere was dry, charged with static. The hairs on Leonardo's arms stood on end. He stopped on the bench behind Pinch, squinting into Fox Clan territory. At first, he thought it was as silent as the rest of the Darkwoods; then, he noticed a low hum. It vibrated his teeth. And the river was behaving strange, as if the water that flowed over the rocks evaporated instantly upon reaching the pool below, leaving the surface as flat and undisturbed as a granite slab.

"We should go," said Nym. He sounded a bit like himself.

"I think so too," said Moth. "And that's not me being a coward, Pinch. Something feels really wrong—"

"I agree," said Pinch. He glanced at Leonardo, his eyes deathly serious under his tricorn hat. "I don't like this."

A screech split the woods. Leonardo jumped, grabbing for his sword. The noise stretched out, incredibly loud and grating, like metal on metal.

"What the hell is that?" shouted Bates.

"Let's go!" yelled Mishti, barely audible over the noise. "Retreat!"

A blast of air slammed into Leonardo, as rough as sandpaper and hot enough to scald him. He cried out, stumbling back, and fell awkwardly into the footwell between Cato and Bates.

The next bench struck him hard in the ribs, and Leonardo twisted, shouting in pain. He blinked hard, focusing on a wooden shield half-buried under supplies. He grabbed for it, his shirt billowing and hair whipping across his forehead. Leonardo yanked the shield out and forced it up, sheltering himself from the wind. Everyone scrambled around him, hunching low and shouting words that were torn away.

Hunkering behind the shield, Leonardo glanced at Mishti's boat. She yelled something. He didn't catch any of it. But he could guess the sentiment.

We need to leave now.

Every kid present knew what followed a wind like this.

Leonardo grabbed Cato and yelled "Row!" in his ear, then he pulled Bates closer and shouted the same thing. He waved to get the other kids' attention and pointed at the oars.

If we stay, we die.

He peered around his shield, squinting into the wind, just as a deep, thundering rumble ripped over the water. The swirling blackness took shape, rearing into a giant mouth that gaped at the five boats.

Leonardo's stomach dropped.

"Oh shit!" Nym swore, a few feet from Leonardo. Leonardo twisted, the image of the Dark etched into his eyes, as Nym spread his hands. Black veins raced across his skin. The soaked rags weren't enough.

"Move!" yelled Bates, shoving Jack aside and tackling Nym. He forced the slighter boy's arms over the side and plunged his fists underwater.

"Snakes!" yelled Pinch.

"What?" Leonardo spun to face the Snake Clan boat, but Pinch was pointing at the Dark, and Leonardo's heart stopped as a wave of inky snakes spilled from the giant mouth and into the water.

Leonardo choked on his breath, yelling, "Row!" The word was ripped from his throat, strangled and ragged.

Kids jumped to the oars, stabbing the paddles underwater in a panicked, uncoordinated scramble. Viola sprang to the captain's platform, forcing the rudder over as they churned into a turn. Leonardo threw his shield aside and gritted his teeth as the wind blasted his face. He clambered onto Nym's bench and took the oar. Meanwhile, Bates kept Nym's hands underwater, his fedora rolling around the footwell.

The five boats picked up speed, the wind at their backs as they retreated upriver. Leonardo fell into rhythm with the other rowers, propelling the boats away from the Fox Clan border. The wind howled after them, rippling the surface of the river and throwing waves against the banks.

They navigated a bend, but the onslaught didn't let up. Leonardo hunched his shoulders, his fingers like a vice on the wooden handle as water splashed over the sides.

"We're not out of it yet!" Viola crouched on the captain's platform, peering over the stern and gripping the rudder in both hands.

Leonardo leaned out to see an army of black snakes pursuing them.

"Nym," he shouted, his throat raw. "How are your hands?"

Bates let Nym pull them out of the water, and Leonardo silently thanked the woods. The black veins were gone.

The river still works.

For now. Weeks ago, it had been powerful enough to dispel the Dark completely. Now, the Dark could travel over its surface. Before long, it would completely infiltrate the river.

We can't let it get that far. If the Dark actually entered the water, nothing would be safe anymore. He would die of thirst before letting the Dark enter his body.

Leonardo dug his fingernails into the wood. The waves rippled slick and oily behind the snakes as they gained on the splashing oars.

We won't outrun them.

"Wait!" shouted Pinch. "I've got this."

He closed his eyes, adjusting his hat.

The rowers hesitated, and Leonardo shot a look at the snakes again. He couldn't distinguish individual serpents in the rush. They twisted and wove in a thrashing mass of blackness. He pictured them slithering over the sides of the boats, overwhelming the clan kids in seconds. They wouldn't win this fight.

"Keep rowing," he shouted.

This had better work, Pinch.

"Got it!" said Pinch. He squared his shoulders and slowly lifted one hand, then snapped his fingers.

Instantly, hundreds of blood-red fish shot past the boat. They streaked toward the snakes, jumping and frothing in the water. Leonardo watched, wide-eyed, as they collided with the dark mass in a vicious, splashing frenzy.

"What are they?" he asked, alarm tingeing his relief.

"Piranhas," said Pinch, with a grin in his voice.

"But...piranhas already exist here," said Bates. Pinch's hat only allowed him to create new things, which didn't currently exist in the woods.

"Not these ones," said Pinch. "These have one eye, and it can't see anything but those snakes."

Leonardo nodded slowly as the school of piranhas destroyed the Dark snakes. The boats pulled further away, and the wind died.

We need to learn more about that hat. So far, it was their most effective defense against the Dark. But a defense wasn't enough. *We need to use it as a weapon.*

Each of Pinch's inventions had been disturbingly sinister in its own unique way.

"What now?" called Caliban from his boat.

"We regroup," said Leonardo. He wasn't taking another step until they examined everything and weighed their options. He was done with reacting and improvising. "Let's go ashore somewhere...*better* than Raven Clan's camp and make a plan."

"I know a place," said Viola. "I want to see my old camp."

CHAPTER 6

L eo." Puck tugged his sleeve as they trekked up the trail to
the clearing. "Can I talk to you?"

"Of course." He frowned at Puck's troubled expression. The cover of dead branches filtered a checkerboard of sunlight on his face and shirt.

"Remember when we first became Lion Clan?" asked Puck,
licking his lips. "And you named me and Pinch your se-coms?"

Leonardo nodded, frowning deeper.

"Well…the thing is…" Puck studied the muddy ground; then
he drew himself up. "I don't really feel like a se-com."

Leonardo didn't blink. His clan's strange concerns no longer
surprised him.

"What do you mean?"

"Well…" Puck kneaded his hands. "It's just…You consult
Pinch on everything, and he saved us from the Dark with his hat,
and he's point-watch in the boat…"

Leonardo inclined his head. *Is Puck jealous?*

It wouldn't be the first time. It was also the last thing he needed right now. He was exhausted to the breaking point, and—

"All that is great. Pinch is great," Puck added quickly, shooting a glance over his shoulder. "But it would be nice if maybe I could contribute something too…to, you know, feel like a se-com too."

Fine. Then contribute something. No one's stopping you.

A fly zipped past, and Puck clumsily swatted at it. He nearly tripped on a root, and Leonardo caught his arm.

Leonardo reined in his tongue. He drew a weary breath and released it.

"Of course," he said instead. "What do you have in mind?"

In front of Leonardo, Mishti bent a branch aside and stepped around it, then unceremoniously let go. It whipped back and whacked him in the ribs before he could react. He sucked in a breath, silently swearing at Mishti as she marched onward.

"Well," Puck puffed his chest. "I *was* the battle master at the old Raven Clan. Maybe I can teach the Lion girls to fight, and anyone else who wants it, and the kids too, Pompey and Charley, and that girl from the full moon ceremony in the Cove. She's still with Dragon clan. Did you see her? And you know, the Ravens looked pretty rusty; they could use some practice—"

"Great," Leonardo interrupted him, holding the same branch so it didn't strike Viola. "I think that's a great idea."

Weary or not, he appreciated that Puck was in a tough position. Immediately after being appointed se-com, their clan had merged with Mishti's. There was only so much room in command,

and he felt bad that Puck's authority had fallen casualty to the expansion.

"Really?" Puck's eyes lit up.

Leonardo chuckled, then his mood soured as he stepped over what might have been an ant hill once. Now it was slick with black goop. He tried not to inhale the stink. The air hung heavy with the rancidness of it.

"You're still my se-com, Puck," he said as they neared the top of the trail. "If you're willing to teach these kids to fight, it will only improve our odds of surviving the Dark. One thing though…"

"Anything." Puck jumped ahead to hold aside a branch for Leonardo. "What is it?"

"Be tactful," said Leonardo. "Do me a favor and don't get under feathers."

"Of course." Puck nodded sincerely. "I'll dial it back."

He's grown a lot, thought Leonardo. The old Puck wasn't even aware of his more…abrasive tendencies. Not only could he see them now, but he was mature enough that Leonardo trusted he wouldn't cause any problems.

He slapped Puck on the shoulder, then followed Mishti through an opening in the sticks into Viola's old camp.

***

"Cyrus and Gallus are gone," said Leonardo.

"Beautifully said," remarked Kate. A deep loneliness pooled in her eyes.

You're all that's left.

The clans stood on the edge of the perfectly round clearing. The cooking fires and tipis were long gone, but Tokala's presence remained. The place felt as safe as anywhere could in the gloom of the dead Darkwoods.

"The rest of us will join them," he continued. "Unless we work together."

Viola plucked a seed pod from a stalk of long grass, her gaze traveling around the barren clearing. Leonardo took her hand. All of them had lost friends and loved ones.

"Cyrus could have helped us," he continued. "Gallus could have helped us—"

"Are you serious?" Pinch scoffed.

"We don't have the luxury of playing favorites," said Leonardo. "The woods did that for years, and look what happened. Each of us is equally important. We need to band together and defeat the Dark together."

"Fine." Cleopatra placed her tiger cub on the ground. "I'm sorry for vanishing that fat kid."

Leonardo chewed his lip. He wasn't optimistic about her sincerity, but it was a start.

"Don't look at me." Kate crossed her arms, shaking a lock of brown hair off her face. "I'm not going to apologize."

He'd never expected her to.

"Work with us," said Leonardo. "No more rogue moves. That's all I'm asking."

Kate nodded, biting her lip hard.

A heavy silence fell over the clearing. All six clans stood in the shadow of the trees, regarding the total emptiness the Dark left behind. A dry leaf fell from a branch, seesawing through the air before it settled on the crispy black grass. Cleopatra's tiger wandered in Charley's direction, gently tugging its gold chain. Charley hugged her hamster basket tighter, edging back into the trees.

"So, what's the next step?" asked Mishti.

"Redwoods or the Highland," said Leonardo. "We need to decide."

"We know nothing about either." Moth scratched his chin. "Flip a coin?"

"I can imagine one," said Pinch, whipping off his hat.

"Not yet." Leonardo wasn't ready to put their fate in the hands of an imaginary coin. Besides, he wasn't sure if the hat came with any limits. He didn't want to max out their uses before they truly needed it. "We could start with the Highland," he suggested. "Hawk Clan territory connects to it, right?"

"That's what the stories say," agreed Jack.

"Aleksander never let us travel," explained Puck, in response to the Cove kids' furrowed brows.

Heads nodded, their expressions pensive in the filtered light. Even the Hawks were listening. He hoped they would realize sooner than later the value of shedding rivalries.

"But we'll need to go to the Redwoods eventually," continued Leonardo. "And the only way we know of is through Fox Clan territory."

Pinch slowly placed his hat back on his head. "Tell me you're not suggesting we go back to Fox."

"I'm not. You're from the Redwoods," Leonardo addressed Kate. "Is there another way to get there?"

She shrugged in her heavy coat. "I walked along the side of

the river. It took me straight to the Darkwoods. 'Fox Clan territory,' I suppose. I don't remember any rivers branching off."

Over to Leonardo's right, Pompey and Charley leaned close, talking. Charley raised her hand.

"What if we go *around* the Dark?" she suggested, pointing to the northwest. "We can walk that way, then that way,"—she made a wide arc with her arm—"and end up behind it."

"If there's only one river," added Pompey, "we'll just walk until we find it."

Jack was already shaking his head. "You don't want to go into the trees."

"We've fought off the Dark every time," called Cleopatra. She tugged her tiger back and moved into the sunlight. "We might be able to survive the woods."

"*Might* isn't good enough," said Leonardo.

"Besides," added Mishti, joining them in front of the alliance. "We wouldn't have the boats."

"It's a long walk on foot," agreed Kate, shadowed below a stand of dead birch trees. Their brittle branches twisted like claws. "Although, when you have forever, it doesn't feel that long."

"We don't have forever," said Leonardo. "We need to unite the clans *now*."

This was an entirely new dilemma. Without the river, their odds of success plummeted.

"Sorry," Kate shrugged. "I don't make the rules."

But you can help us solve them. Annoyance pulsed under his skin.

She's all that's left, a voice reminded him. Before, she and Cyrus had each other for support. Now, she was the last of the ancient kids. She looked completely out of place, even surrounded by her pirates.

Leonardo pinched the bridge of his nose. The pressure in his skull was building by the second.

"Let's find something to eat," he said. "It's been a hard morning. Jack, are we safe here from the Dark?"

"As safe as anywhere," said Jack. Despite everything, he looked lighter. The weight of leading a doomed clan no longer rested on his shoulders. Leonardo had taken it, and now he needed to find a way to get them out.

***

Twenty minutes later, Leonardo found Pinch seated in the Raven Clan boat, gaze fixed intently on the bench in front of him. He said something under his breath, then swore and yanked his hat off, glaring inside. He whacked it and jammed it back on his head, fixing his gaze over the river again. Viola sat at the opposite end of the boat, on Leonardo's steering platform, head tilted as she watched him.

"What's he doing?" asked Leonardo, picking his way down the bank. The four Cove boats and Hawk Clan's longboat lay in a tidy row alongside Raven Clan's, their prows buried in the shale.

Viola held up a finger. *Just watch.*

Pinch refocused on the bench ahead of him, then straightened and said, "Elephant."

Leonardo raised an eyebrow.

"Elephant," repeated Pinch. He snapped his fingers.

Nothing happened.

"Dammit. *Elephant.*"

"Pinch," said Leonardo, climbing over the side. He swung his legs into the boat and dropped to the footwell with a thump.

"What?" Pinch whipped off his hat and peered inside again as if the elephant might be hiding there.

"If that works, you'll destroy the boats."

"If it works, we'll have an elephant," countered Pinch. "We won't need boats."

Leonardo ground his palms into his eyes.

"Maybe you're dreaming a bit big?" suggested Viola mildly. "Try something smaller. And less destructive."

"Fine." Pinch snapped his fingers. "Whiskey."

Leonardo's eyes widened as a crystal decanter appeared on the bench.

"Hey!" Pinch laughed out loud. "It worked!"

Viola was on her feet in an instant. She walked across the benches as Pinch picked it up, then snatched it out of his hand.

"Hey! What the hell, that's—"

"We need you sober," said Leonardo.

"Fine." Pinch rolled his eyes. "At least let me smash it then."

He grabbed the decanter back from Viola and weighed it thoughtfully, then gripped the narrow neck of the bottle and hurled it at a rock, where it exploded with a crash and a spray of amber liquid.

"Are you done?" asked Leonardo. "Because I need your help."

Both Pinch and Viola perked up.

"What is it?" asked Jack. He picked his way down the bank, Will and Bates behind him. Flies buzzed around their heads, dipping and weaving as all three boys swatted at them.

46

Leonardo smacked a mosquito on his arm. "I think I have a plan. But I don't know how to get through Fox Clan territory."

"We're going to the Redwoods first?" asked Viola.

"Yes. And no." Leonardo drew a breath as the three boys hoisted themselves into the boat.

"Damn flies." Jack swatted at another circling his head.

"Did all the friendly bugs die?" Pinch scowled at the insects.

"*Everything* died," said Jack. "We can barely find a rabbit to eat anymore."

Leonardo's mind churned while they spoke.

"We need to split up." He watched a raven skim low over the water. Its black wings flapped powerfully as it set down to a landing further up the bank. "Half of us to the Highland, half to the Redwoods."

"Are you sure?" asked Viola. "We'd be safer as a group."

"We can't gamble with time." Leonardo traced his finger through an old gash in the wood. "The Dark is moving too fast."

The dead forest loomed over them, dripping with tar.

"You're right," agreed Jack quietly. "We won't pull this off unless we split up."

He'd been neighbors with the Dark for weeks. His certainty was all the confirmation Leonardo needed.

"Then let's go to the Redwoods *now*," said Pinch. "You and Mishti jumped from the Jungle to the Cove. Why can't we do that here?"

"Me too," said Viola slowly. "I got caught in the spell, and I was only in the doorway."

Leonardo paused. *Could we…?*

"Spell?" asked Jack.

47

"We do spells now," said Bates.

"Follow me." Leonardo jumped on a bench and vaulted down to the rocks. The other Ravens dropped after him while their namesake watched them through glassy eyes up the bank.

Leonardo ran up the trail, maneuvering around the dripping blackness. His clanmates followed, quiet and focused. He couldn't recall a time when they'd been so somber.

"Everyone, pay attention," he called as he jogged into the clearing where the five clans gathered. "I have an idea, but it's incredibly risky."

"Since when have we made a plan that isn't?" asked Moth. He straightened, brushing grass off his knees. "Let's hear it."

The other kids didn't look so certain.

"Remember the gap we used to jump from Snake Clan's camp to the clifftops?" asked Leonardo, moving into the center of the circle. "Why can't we do the same from here to the Redwoods?"

Blank expressions met his words. Leonardo's heart sank as he watched kids leaning close and whispering, shaking their heads and nodding gravely.

"Three people is very different from a hundred." Leonardo ran a hand along his jaw. "I'm aware of that."

But that doesn't mean it's impossible.

"It's ninety-seven more than we've ever done." Concern wavered in Viola's eyes.

Leonardo dug his nails into his palms. She was right, but he was running short on ideas.

"Plus," added Caliban, "and this is just a tiny detail…but we don't have anything to make the spell out of. We can't just jump through gaps on our own."

"A hundred?" asked Demetrius. "We're splitting up?" He stood in front of a tightly bunched pack of Dragons. They had been the least willing to assimilate into the group. Leonardo turned to face him.

"It makes sense," said Mishti, across the circle. "I was thinking about that too."

Thank you. For all of Mishti's faults, she came through when Leonardo needed her.

"Is the Hawk Clan passage still clear?" Moth stood with some Ravens to Leonardo's left. "The Highland party can travel on the river if the Redwoods party jumps with a spell."

Everyone looked at the Hawks, tied to a tree on the edge of the clearing. They were all listening intently, but none contributed a word.

"What the hell is everyone talking about?" demanded Jack.

"I'll summon another lion." Juliet brushed back her ringlets and stepped into the middle of the circle with Leonardo.

"You'll do no such thing." Mishti moved forward, intercepting her. "You've summoned enough things that could kill us."

"We need to take a risk if we want to pull this off," argued Moth. He moved up behind Juliet. "It might be the only way to get to the Redwoods."

Jack whipped his head from one speaker to the next. "What. The. Hell—"

"The Lostwoods are full of gaps, *Jack*," snapped Mishti. "The lions use them to jump around. Evidently, we can, too, with lion hair. Juliet wants to call one, and her boyfriend supports her because, evidently, he's an idiot too."

Jack's eyes widened. He was typically the most unflappable

member of Raven Clan, but Leonardo had yet to meet anyone who could take Mishti without a mild dose of shock.

"Moth has a girlfriend?" asked Cato.

"Surprise to us all," replied Pinch.

Focus. Leonardo wanted to strangle his clan sometimes.

"We'll put everyone in the boats," he said loudly. "Only Juliet, Moth, Caliban, and I will stay onshore. We just need a tuft of the lion's hair. If it works like last time, the lion will use another gap and leave again immediately."

"Are we going to discuss this?" asked Mishti. "Who made you supreme leader?"

You and Jack, he wanted to retort.

"Leo," said Viola. "We can't gamble with half our numbers."

Leonardo opened his mouth to reply, but she had a point.

"We have to try," he said weakly. "I'm out of ideas."

"I have an idea," said Puck.

Leonardo closed his eyes. *If this has something to do with battle training—*

"It doesn't need to be a fifty-fifty split. We could send less through the gap."

Leonardo blinked open his eyes. *That's true.* He'd put all his stock in keeping the numbers together, but if it meant they could get to the Redwoods faster *and* ensure they weren't gambling half their imaginations for the final fight...

Puck joined him in the middle of the clearing. "Let's pick a small party—maybe ten or fifteen—to jump through the gap. Everyone else can travel to the Highland in the boats. The big group will have strength in numbers, while we can sneak in undetected with a smaller group." He surveyed the gathered clan members.

50

"That makes sense," said Leonardo slowly.

Puck's eyes widened. "It does?"

Leonardo nodded once, then with more certainty. "Mishti and I will lead the Redwoods party. We need Kate since she's been there before, and we'll each take a few members of our clans."

If the Redwoods Clans were anything like those in the Darkwoods and the Cove, their small party would be vastly outnumbered. He wanted the best of the best.

"What about the rest of us?" demanded Jack. He placed his hands on his hips. "You just agreed to lead us. Now you're abandoning us?"

Leonardo forced himself to forget the word *abandoning*.

"Leading doesn't mean I have to stay beside you every second," he told Jack. "That was Aleksander's problem; he controlled everything. I need to trust others to follow the plans we set out."

Jack tightened his lips.

"I'd like you and several Ravens to join us," said Leonardo. "You know the Dark in different ways than we do. Everyone else will travel to the Highland, under the command of my se-com, Puck."

The words came out before he'd fully formed the idea. Puck's eyes went perfectly round.

"Me?"

Puck? a voice asked in Leonardo's head.

Yes, Puck, he countered. *He wanted more responsibility. He can handle it.*

He clapped Puck on the shoulder. "You've been there every step of the way. You know the plan, and I trust you to lead things until we meet up."

"How will we meet up?" Puck somehow managed to simultaneously puff his chest while balking from the weight of the responsibility.

"If the portal works once, it will work again. We'll use it to jump to the Highland." Leonardo worked a pebble out of the dirt with his shoe, processing the logistics. "Just stay put. Let us come to you."

"Ok." Puck nodded more confidently, drawing himself up. "We can do that."

"Who all is going to the Redwoods?" asked Viola. "We need to think this through."

"I don't know yet." Leonardo scanned the faces before him. "We'll figure that out. Step one is to summon a lion and get the hair we need. No hair, no portal. And we need to act fast. Everyone into the boats."

"Leo." Viola tilted her head.

He could read her mind. *This will be the biggest risk we've taken yet.* They were about to run headfirst into the magic of the woods.

"I'll get the flowers," said Moth, already moving toward the trail. "We brought a basket from the Cove."

Leonardo met Viola's brown-eyed gaze. Flames burned in the glassiness as she spun a bead in her fingertips. It snapped off her dress, and she flicked it away without looking. The colorful pattern was dotted with gaps and loose threads.

"We don't have time to hesitate," said Leonardo. "This might be the only way."

"*Might*," said Viola. "But what if—"

"If the Dark—"

"I know, I know." Viola closed her eyes. "Fine. You're right. Just promise you won't do anything stupid."

"I promise."

The word felt hollow.

She sighed, then leaned up and kissed his cheek. Leonardo squeezed her hand as she stepped away, blinking fast. Then she disappeared with the others down the trail, and he drew a breath.

There will be more casualties, he realized. He wanted to make a bold vow that he wouldn't let that happen, but he would be lying to himself.

"Let's get started."

Moth rejoined them with a basket of red flowers, and Leonardo eyed a smear of black on the basket's weave. This was hardly the best plan they had ever concocted. Hell, it wasn't even a *good* plan.

He steeled his nerves.

"Caliban, how do we do this without your snake pit?"

CHAPTER 7

"Here goes nothing." Juliet sparked a flintstone into a bed of kindling. The flames caught, and she quickly nursed it into a small fire. Around it, she and Moth had fashioned a pile of red petals into the shape of a lion.

Moth took the lead while she was preoccupied, and Leonardo was impressed with how much his friend had learned. They never got a chance to sit still in the Cove. He'd barely started training with Juliet in the ways of the woods, but he prepared the spell with surefooted confidence.

Smoke swirled into the sky, just as it had when Tokala's tribe occupied the clearing. Leonardo hoped they were making the right choice, doing the spell here.

It's a sacred spot, he told himself. *That has to count for something.*

Moth stepped back as Juliet's fire took hold, dusting flower petals off his hands. Leonardo drew his sword. Caliban procured a pair of knives from the folds of his cloak. All four kids turned in a slow circle, eyes on the shadows between the trees. Leonardo had witnessed two lions use gaps in the Cove, and both did it from behind the trees.

The eerie silence of the dead Darkwoods pressed against him again. Only the tiny fire's crackling disturbed it, adding fresh pungency to the burnt air.

The seconds dragged on. A breeze rattled some of the leafless branches. The rest were too heavy with blackness to move. Leonardo cracked his neck and changed his sword grip. Moth and Juliet studied their fire anxiously. Caliban slowly blinked his mismatched eyes.

"Does anyone know if lions come this far north?" he asked mildly.

"I saw one," said Moth.

"Simple question, simple answer." Caliban spun his knife. "So we wait."

"Unless…" Juliet chewed her lip.

"What?" asked Leonardo.

She tucked her hair behind her ear. "If the Lostwoods sent Moth's lion here for a reason, to guide you south…maybe another lion wouldn't come this far north just because we called it."

"I thought you said you faked the lion sign," said Caliban.

"That was another lion sign," replied Leonardo.

Juliet had a point. Just because the woods sent one lion to the Darkwoods didn't mean another would be willing to come.

"Why are lions the only animal that can use the gaps?" asked Moth. "Does anyone else wonder that?"

Leonardo frowned. *Were* lions the only animals to use the gaps? Could anyone definitively say that?

"How do you know nothing here does?" asked Juliet. "Maybe the foxes or the—"

"Crocs," said Leonardo and Moth in sync.

That's how the Dark sees, but... "What if the Dark is traveling in the gaps?" said Leonardo. "We know it entered through the Dark-woods. If our crocs can use the gaps, it could be using them to spread itself around the woods."

"Everywhere it goes, it leaves croc skulls," said Moth.

"Viola keeps saying it's everywhere," said Leonardo. "Of course it is, if it's jumping through the gaps."

"So we don't need a lion," said Caliban.

"We need a crocodile," finished Juliet.

"No," said Leonardo. "We need a crocodile skull. If that's all the Dark needs, then we can do it too. Put out that fire. We're going back to the boats."

CHAPTER 8

W e're capping the party at fourteen," said Leonardo.
He and Mishti stood before their alliance and a
ring of skulls they had arranged in the clearing. He
studied the skulls, heart racing as dozens upon dozens of empty
eye sockets watched him. *Why do the gaps exist?* he wondered. *Why
can lions and crocodiles jump around?*

"We've chosen Pinch, Moth, Viola, Bates, Nym, Pompey, and
Charley—" he started.

"Are you sure it's the best choice to bring them through the
gap?" Viola eyed the kids. "Wouldn't it be safer if they stayed with
the big group?"

Charley put her hands on her hips. Leonardo cut her off before she could voice a retort.

"The woods used them once already to pass us a message. I
want them close."

And beyond that, ever since he'd nearly lost them to Kate's

pirates, Leonardo had vowed to himself that he would never let the kids beyond his sight again.

Viola didn't argue. Silently, he knew she was happy to keep the kids close, even if the thought of exposing them to the magic scared her.

We're all vulnerable, thought Leonardo. Neither party faced a safe road ahead.

"And Sophie." Mishti picked up his roll call. "And Juliet and Kate."

"And Jack and Cato," finished Leonardo. If they faced any adversity in the Redwoods, he wanted Cato's size at his back.

"Fine with me," said Demetrius. "If you want to gamble with magic—"

"We don't *want* to, dimwit," said Sophie. "But someone has to take the risks."

She's still edgy, thought Leonardo. He would have to keep an eye on Sophie.

"Is she trying to talk like a Lost Boy?" asked Bates under his breath.

"It's *halfwit*," replied Will. "Not *dimwit*."

"That's embarrassing," said Jack.

"Right," said Leonardo loudly, shooting a look at them. "Everyone else will go north to the Highland."

"What about them?" asked Demetrius, nodding to the Hawks. Now he sounded sullen. "Are we supposed to drag them along?"

Leonardo swallowed his immediate retort. He didn't like Demetrius. If nothing else, he was relieved to part ways.

"It should be fairly easy to transport prisoners in a boat," he said patiently. "And hopefully," he added, for the Hawks' benefit, "they won't be prisoners by the end of this. Explain the Dark to them, show them what Gallus couldn't understand."

Demetrius rolled his eyes. "Great."

"I'll lead the trip to the Highland," said Cleopatra. Her tiger cub yawned in her arms, baring its fangs. "Puck can lead the Ravens, but I will assume command of—"

"Says who?" asked Caliban.

Puck held up a hand before she—or Leonardo or Mishti—could reply. "We can deal with this later," he declared. "Right now, it's more important to do the spell and get the crocodile skulls out of here before the Dark sees us."

Leonardo eyed him. He held no doubt that Caliban would attempt to establish his authority the second Leonardo's party left. But Puck was tenacious, and the Cove kids had plenty of experience negotiating. They would work out a compromise.

For now, the other leaders fell silent. Puck's logic was sound.

"Good luck, everyone." Puck sniffed, a tremor in his voice. "We'll see you again soon."

Leonardo embraced him. Puck hugged him harder than he expected, and Leonardo let out a small gasp of air.

"I believe in you," he said softly, so only Puck could hear. "Go get us the Highland."

He freed himself from Puck's arms and frowned as Charley and Pompey crouched near the edge of the clearing.

"Hey, you two," he called. "What are you—"

"I'm freeing Lion." Charley glanced back, her small face carefully arranged in the bravest expression she could muster. She blinked away tears. "I don't want him to get hurt if the spell goes wrong."

59

She has a good heart, thought Leonardo.

"The spell's not going to go wrong," said Juliet.

"Well, if it does, he's safe now." Charley returned to the group, hands on her hips and sharp defiance battling with the emotion swimming in her eyes. Juliet nodded gently and stepped aside so she and Pompey could rejoin. An empty basket lay abandoned in the grass behind them.

"Is everyone ready?" asked Leonardo. He stepped into the ring of skulls, followed by Mishti, Viola, Sophie, Kate, and the rest of their party. Nym watched the dark eyeholes with an unblinking concentration that sent shivers up Leonardo's spine.

"Remember the words?" asked Caliban.

"You're not the only one who can use magic, Caliban," said Juliet.

Caliban shrugged. "Suit yourself."

"Moth, take my hand," said Juliet. "Everyone, hold hands. Kate, I need you to think about the Redwoods."

"What's this?" Viola bent and fished something out of the grass.

Leonardo frowned as she revealed the scratched glass face of a brass pocket watch.

"This was my grandfather's," said Viola, wonder in her voice.

Suddenly, Leonardo had a vivid memory of Tokala pulling it from his robes while he and Aleksander sat in the chief's tent. The clock's hands had been frozen, and there was no logical reason for Tokala to pull it out. Leonardo recalled the chief studying the broken watch, then returning it to his pocket.

Why did he show it to me that day?

Leonardo took it from Viola, dangling it by its thin brass

chain. All three hands were neatly bunched just before twelve-o-clock, exactly as they had been before.

"He must have dropped it when they left," said Viola.

Leonardo's frown deepened as the second hand gave a tiny twitch, then wobbled to the next tick.

It's works?

"Leo, can we get back to the spell?" asked Moth. "I don't like being inside these skulls. What if the Dark uses them to get here...*to us?*"

"You're right." Leonardo handed the pocket watch back to Viola. She slipped the chain around her neck and took his hand as Leonardo reached for Nym's on his other side. They could examine the watch more once they got to their destination.

"Everyone shut up," said Kate. "I can't visualize anything with you all talking."

She fixed her trilby hat and closed her eyes. Leonardo slowed his breathing, watching the gently stirring branches behind her. He listened to the whisper of the woods, feeling for the shift as Juliet tapped the magic of the woods. A burning sensation distracted him, concentrated to the size of a thumbprint on his leg.

The rock key?

He reached in his pocket, then jerked his fingers back, burnt by the scalding rock.

"What the hell—"

Wind whipped around them, cold and biting, in sharp contrast to the stinging heat. Leonardo's stomach jumped to his throat. This didn't feel like the Dark's wind. This was frigid and clear as the river water, tousling their hair and chilling their skin as it circled.

61

"One last thing," called Caliban. "We don't know how powerful this spell will be compared to—"

"Ow!" shouted Viola. She let go of Leonardo's hand to grab for the pocket watch. "It's hot!"

"Don't let go of each other!" yelled Moth.

Leonardo jumped, grabbing Viola's hand before she could get to the chain on her neck.

"Leo, it hurts!" Viola gritted her teeth, and Leonardo stared at the watch. Moth's urgency kept his fingers in a vice grip on hers. The rock burned in his pocket.

"Ow! Dammit," Moth swore. "My compass!"

The wind blasted hard. Squinting, Leonardo watched Caliban and the rest of the Highland party run down the trail. Beside him, Viola bowed her head, letting the pocket watch swing away from her body. He wanted to yank it off her neck, but they kept their fingers fused together. The rock in his pocket grew hotter by the second.

And Moth's compass? Leonardo's mind reeled, trying to—

A screech split the treetops. He clenched Viola and Nym's hands harder, snapping his gaze to the sky, where a pattern of greens saturated the grey. The marbling took definition until he realized they were treetops. He was looking down on a vast forest, inexplicably suspended above him.

Are we upside-down?

He frowned at his feet, then all the blood rushed to Leonardo's head, and a wall of noise slammed his senses.

CHAPTER 9

A throbbing pain pulsed in Leonardo's skull so forcefully that he winced awake, grabbing the back of his head.

He blinked around at a place he'd never seen before. The rest of his party lay around him, cushioned on what he first thought was a strange reddish straw. A second later, he realized they were pine needles—millions of long pine needles, covering the ground in a thick mat as far as he could see. Their pungent aroma permeated everything, wafting in the utter stillness.

He caught his breath. *It worked?*

Sunlight dappled his clanmates' faces, and distant birdsong warbled down to Leonardo. He appeared to be at the base of a canyon, between giant, ruddy cliff walls.

He leaned back, pressing his palms into spongy piles of dead needles, and gazed up the cliffs. He frowned, trying to make sense of a forest that grew horizontally from the cliff face. Hundreds of pine trees swayed overhead, growing from both faces, their tops meeting in a haphazard crisscross.

Wait. Leonardo pushed himself to his feet, turning in a slow circle as the rest of the kids began to wake, grunting in pain and rubbing at their skulls.

A stone arch curved from the base of one cliff near him, then disappeared underground close to the other wall. Leonardo approached it, eyes widening as he studied the strange texture.

That's not stone.

He ran a hand along the ancient archway towering over his head. *It's wood.*

He turned to the cliffs with new eyes, realizing that they weren't cliffs at all.

"Are those…" started Moth.

"Trees," said Leonardo. He could hear the wonder in his own voice. Trees so thick, their circumference was impossible to guess. What he'd mistaken for a horizontal forest were heavy branches, weaving in a canopy a mile overhead. The archway was a root, bursting from the ground ten times Leonardo's height.

"We're here," said Kate quietly. She drew a heavy breath, gazing at the trunks.

It worked, thought Leonardo. He closed his eyes, flooded with relief. *It worked.*

"Is this the first time you've returned?" asked Moth.

"Shh." Kate nodded and straightened, dusting redwood needles off herself.

"Follow me. We should get out of sight before they spot us."

Leonardo jogged back to the group. "The other clans?"

Kate nodded. "The Blue Flags and the Red Flags are equally dangerous. We need to find them before they find—"

"The who?" asked Leonardo.

Kate blinked at him. A quizzical look came over her face. "The clans. I told you all of this on the river."

"No…" Leonardo frowned. "No, you didn't."

"*Yes*, I did." She looked to Mishti. "Come on, tell me I'm not going crazy. I know I was on the edge already, but—"

Blank stares met her seeking gaze.

"Wait…" Kate's confidence flickered. "No one remembers?"

Everyone shook their head.

"What?" Kate whipped around, her tailcoat flapping. "No one?"

The hairs stood up on Leonardo's neck. Now everyone was looking around, fingers curling around their swords.

"Then something happened to all of our memories," whispered Sophie. She paled behind her freckles.

"The woods do alter kids' memories when they travel from one corner to another," said Moth. "We know that."

"But it's never altered ours," said Bates quietly.

Why would it want us to forget details about the Redwoods? That wouldn't help the woods, that would help—

"What if the Dark is controlling it?" breathed Leonardo. "Like it does with Nym's arms. What if it forced the woods to change our memories?"

"Well, that's terrifying as hell," said Pinch.

"Guys…" said Bates. "Where is Nym?"

The dread took Leonardo's breath away. He scanned over

every face, and his panic grew with every alarmed expression. The Ravens and Lions all started talking at once.

"The croc skulls didn't come with us, either," said Jack.

"Where is the Dark?" asked Pompey.

High overhead, the canopy was a rich green, and the trunks of the trees didn't show a hint of the rot from the Darkwoods.

"It's like it's not here yet," said Sophie.

"It's everywhere," said Moth. He looked at Viola. "Right? And now it's taken Nym."

Viola tightened her lips.

"Everyone, stop!" shouted Mishti. Her voice echoed in the stillness.

Leonardo froze, twisting to look at her. Dead redwood needles hung ensnared in her black hair, and her gold robe was disheveled, but her eyes were serious.

"If we stay here," said Mishti. "The clans Kate was talking about will kill us."

Leonardo blinked at her. One half of his mind shouted that he'd just lost another friend, and the other half knew that Mishti was completely right, and it was his responsibility to look after more kids than just Nym.

"We don't know where Nym went," said Mishti. "He could still be alive. The spell might not have worked on him. But he's not here, so let's get ourselves somewhere safe."

Leonardo nodded. "Ok. Ok, let's go. Kate—"

"Follow me." Kate jogged through the fallen needles along the base of one tree.

Leonardo swore, casting one last look around the barren canyon as he ushered the rest of his alliance after her. He didn't like this at all. He glanced over his shoulder at the shadowed tunnel behind them, then followed Kate and the others.

The Redwoods were humid, almost like the Cove, minus the salt. The air here was perfumed with the tang of pine needles, and the vastness absorbed all noises, as if the entire place were muted under a blanket.

"Keep your eyes open for lions," called Kate. "They walk the forest floor."

"Lions?" said Jack. His voice sounded small, dwarfed below the ancient trees.

"I want to fight a lion," said Cato, yanking his sword from his belt.

"It would maul you, Cato," said Moth.

"Not if I mauled it first." Cato guffawed. "Stupid lion."

Leonardo glanced at them as Moth rolled his eyes.

Are there lions in the Highland, too? he wondered. According to Aleksander, they used to roam the Darkwoods, too, before they died out.

"And put your sword away, you halfwit," snapped Bates. "There's no lion right now!"

Another giant tree stood like a sentry adjacent to the first two. Roots as thick as full trees snaked from the ground, and Kate ducked under one of them, peering into a hollow as black as the Dark.

"This looks familiar…" she said slowly, running a hand along the root. She paused at a row of old scars in the wood. Then a grin split her face. "Ha!"

Kate vanished down the hole. Bates and Jack hesitated behind her, glancing back at Leonardo.

"Kate," called Leonardo softly. "Are you sure it's—"

"Safer than you are out there," she replied.

Leonardo glanced at Viola. She shook her head, helpless.

"If I die in a hole beneath a tree," said Pinch. "I'm coming back as a ghost to haunt you all."

"What if we all die?" said Moth.

Pinch didn't say anything. He straightened his hat and followed Kate down the hole. Leonardo took Viola's hand and squeezed it once, and then they ducked under the root and into the hollow. Leonardo squinted at the scars Kate had found. The wood had healed since it was first written, but the words *Red Flags forever* were still legible.

Is this their camp? A twinge of unease tugged at him. The earth changed beneath Leonardo's feet as he picked his way down the steep decline, shifting from the soft, padded floor of the forest to hard, smooth wood.

A whoosh to his right startled him as a miniature hot air balloon illuminated Pinch's face, its tiny flame flickering above the basket. It floated over their heads, throwing light across the walls of a circular wooden room carved into the trunk of the tree.

"Get rid of that," hissed Kate. "No fire in the tree."

Leonardo and Pinch had both witnessed the effects of fire in a hollowed-out tree. Leonardo wasn't interested in reliving it.

"Pinch," he said. "Put it out."

"But how are we supposed to—"

"If we can't see," hissed Kate, "then no one else can see us either."

What have we gotten ourselves into?

"Fine." Pinch procured his slingshot and fired a pebble through the balloon. It popped with another whoosh of air and clattered to a burning pile on the wooden floor. Sophie stomped it out, plunging them back into darkness, but not before Leonardo spotted a staircase leading up into the tree.

"Kate," he asked the dark room, keeping his voice hushed. "Where are we?"

"We're in a stair tree."

That means absolutely nothing to me, he wanted to snap at her.

"Why did it say, '*Red Flags forever*' outside?" he asked instead.

"We used to carve that everywhere. I did that one myself," she added proudly.

"So, this isn't a camp or something? We're alone here?"

Kate laughed quietly. "No, Leo. No one lives on the staircases."

He drew a slow breath through his teeth. *But someone else could be climbing it. Or descending right into us.*

"How dangerous are these people?" he asked.

"I don't know," she replied. "I haven't been here in a hundred years."

"But they were dangerous before?" he pressed. His nerves buzzed, and it took a lot of effort to keep his annoyance quelled.

"Correct," said Kate. "Let's keep moving."

Leonardo extended his arm in front of him, feeling shoulders and heads as they crossed to the stairs. His hand met the wall, then Viola tugged him to the right, and Leonardo's fingers slid off the corner as they started up the spiral steps.

"What if there's someone else up there?" whispered Viola.

"I don't know," replied Leonardo, leaning close to her. "But what other choice do we have? Kate knows this place; we don't."

Whispers filled the darkness as they climbed, then Kate shushed them again, and silence fell over the group.

Leonardo scowled. *What will they do if they find us?* Maybe bringing the clans of the Redwoods into their alliance might not be as simple as he'd hoped. *And where is Nym?* A rock weighted Leonardo's stomach. They had used crocodile skulls to access the gap. If there was enough Dark present in them, could it have claimed Nym?

No. Leonardo wouldn't let himself believe that Nym was gone for good. He may be a hostage of the Dark, but Leonardo vowed they would find him. Nym kept saying the only way to save him would be to defeat the Dark. Well, now he needed saving more than ever. He understood the Dark better than any of them—it lived inside of him. If he said it could be defeated, Leonardo believed him.

He knows the Dark better than any of us.

The inkling of an idea trickled into Leonardo's mind. *The woods take risks.* The woods used its children as pawns in its games. He tilted his head, surrounded by complete black and the hot breath of his clanmates.

What if the woods let *Nym get infected?* What if the woods were trying to give Leonardo a window into the Dark? Nym didn't think it could be defeated, he *knew.* He'd told Leonardo specifically that he *knew* the only way to cure him was to kill the Dark.

How many times had Leonardo used that mantra to keep fighting? *This is for Nym...I can't let Nym down...*

Without that, would Leonardo be so sure that the Dark was beatable?

What else can Nym tell us? Leonardo chewed his lip. *We need to get him back.*

If the woods had facilitated Nym's infection, then the woods knew he could gain information to save it and the rest of them. And if he truly was a hostage of the Dark now, he could be gaining new information every second.

Leonardo ran a hand over his scalp, piecing together a plan. The only problem was, he had no idea how to find Nym.

***

Three breaks later, and what felt like a lifetime of climbing, Kate stopped them. Which consisted of her stopping the people directly behind her and everyone else bumping into each other's backs. Swears and grunts echoed through the space.

"Everyone back up," she hissed.

Leonardo stepped down, one hand on the wall for support. Little tremors shook the abused muscles in his legs.

"Ow!" snapped Pinch. "Dammit, who stepped on my foot?"

"Shit," said Jack. "Guys, watch it!"

They retreated a dozen steps until Kate stopped them again.

"We're near the top," she whispered. "Stay here. I'm going up to look around."

"Hey," whispered Leonardo. "I'm coming too."

He needed out of the stairway. Even just a glimpse of something other than blackness.

"Me too," said Mishti, a few stairs below him.

"Fine," said Kate. "But be quiet."

Leonardo edged around the kids in front of him, one hand on the smooth grain of the redwood.

"Kate," he whispered. "Where are you?"

"Right here." Her fingers found his shoulder, then trailed slowly down his chest.

"Kate," he hissed. *I thought we were past this.*

"Fine." She pulled away.

Leonardo squared his jaw. He was grateful for the Darkness, so Viola couldn't see.

The scuffing of Mishti's footsteps preceded her as she climbed the steps. Then she ran into Leonardo's back.

"Damn," she swore. "Why do you keep stopping?"

"Let's go," snapped Leonardo. Claustrophobia ate at him. When they reached the spot where Kate had first stopped them, a dozen steps up, Leonardo realized why they had halted. The first hints of light inched around the curve of the wall. Leonardo blinked at the red-hued wood in relief as they continued climbing, and their surroundings became visible through the gloom.

"Well, at least that proves I didn't go blind on the climb up," said Mishti.

They rounded the wall and stopped a few feet below an opening. The sun was heavily filtered through the canopy, but Leonardo's pupils were accustomed to the dark. He squinted at the painful light. Mishti grimaced beside him, shading her eyes.

"Keep your voice down." Kate pulled the brim of her hat down to block the sun and crept to the opening.

Leonardo ascended the last few steps and caught his breath. Miles of crisscrossing branches sprawled out before them, like interwoven freeways between the behemoth walls of tree trunks.

It reminded him of a grand version of the old Raven Clan camp, except there were no rope bridges or rails here. A dizzying drop to the forest floor awaited anyone who lost their footing.

There were also no people.

"Where is everyone?" he asked.

"Hiding," whispered Kate.

"From us?" A jolt of alarm spiked in his nerves.

"Do they know we're here?" demanded Mishti.

"I hope not," retorted Kate. "But how would I know? I've been in the tree with you."

"Then what are they hiding from?" Leonardo scanned the forlorn canopy. A squirrel raced up the ancient bark of a redwood, then vanished into a cluster of oversized pinecones. A massive spiderweb spanned the gap between two boughs, alight in a square of sun. The cords of silk were as thick as the strings on Mishti's robe, spun in a dense weave at least twenty feet high. He shuddered, reaching for his sword.

"Each other," said Kate.

We need more information. Whatever Kate claimed to have told them on the river, Leonardo needed to know it now.

Why would the woods alter our memories?

If he was right—if the Dark was controlling the woods—then their situation was even more dire than he'd thought.

The less we know about this place, the harder it will be to unite the clans.

And if Kate alone possessed information that the Dark was trying to keep from them, he worried about her safety.

"If they're hiding, does that mean they're watching too?" asked Mishti.

Kate nodded. "Most likely. Which means we need to act fast if we want to find them first."

She pointed to a mess of crisscrossing boughs. "See that stand of branches? Us three could make a break for it. From there, we'll move to another hiding place until we spot someone."

"What about everyone else?" asked Leonardo.

Kate's eyes darted with intelligence under her trilby. "The clans don't visit the ground often." She peered back into the darkness. "The odds are slim that someone will enter this tree before we find the Red Flags. We'll come back for them when it's safer."

Leonardo looked at Mishti. She shook her head, and he had to agree. He wasn't abandoning his clan in a new corner of the woods. He eyed the branches again, twisting and sloping and blanketed in pine boughs. The trunks of neighboring trees loomed, pocked with dark hollows and shaded crannies.

"We all go together," he said. "It's too dangerous to split up."

Kate bit her lip. "Fine." The urgency in her jittering fingertips heightened Leonardo's own anxiety.

"But if the Blue Flags find us," continued Kate. "I'm blaming you."

It was a weak attempt to hide her nerves. She pressed her shaking hands against the salt-stained leather of her coat.

She's vulnerable now, he realized. *Maybe for the first time in her life, she knows she can be vanished.*

"Let's get everyone up here," said Leonardo. "The sooner we get moving, the sooner we—"

Something whistled past his head. Leonardo jerked back, staring wide-eyed at a wooden dart, its tip buried in the wall. A stripe of blue paint ran down its length.

"Damn!" Kate gasped, throwing herself against the other wall. "Get back!"

She yanked Leonardo and Mishti's arms, dragging them down the steps and away from the opening.

"What was that?" demanded Leonardo. He craned over his shoulder.

"A blow dart," said Kate. "Forgot about those."

"You *forgot?*" Leonardo whirled to face her.

"Don't use that tone with me." Kate stared past him, locking her unblinking gaze on the doorway. "It's been a hundred years."

"What do we do now?" demanded Mishti. "Will we need to fight our way out?"

"Possibly," said Kate. "Stop, stop, listen…" She paused, fighting to quiet her breathing. Leonardo held his breath, listening to the silence inside the tree.

"Things change fast here," said Kate slowly. She adjusted her hat and curled her fingers around her sword handle. Leonardo did the same, resisting the urge to draw it.

"What does that mean?" Mishti dropped a throwing ring into her hand, leaning to see up the stairs.

Leonardo eyed the space inside the tree. If they had to fight their way out, it would be through a bottleneck and at an incline. He didn't like their position at all.

Outside, the hammer of footsteps sprinted across the branches. Leonardo's pulse quickened, and he quietly slid his sword from his belt. Kate drew her sword so smoothly that Leonardo didn't even notice until he caught its glint.

The attackers drew closer; then, just as their steps reached the opening, three voices cried out in quick succession. Three thuds followed, like bodies hitting wood. Leonardo winced, his stomach jumping to his throat.

Branches shook, and he frowned at the sound of fabric ripping.

"There's his flag," said someone. "Bye-bye!"

"Got this one's!" said a girl. "Idiot tried to hide it in his pocket."

"And what about this one?" More fabric tore. "Bingo."

Next to Leonardo and Mishti, Kate licked her nips nervously.

"What's going on?" hissed Leonardo.

"Red Flags ambushed the Blue Flags who were after us," breathed Kate.

"Red Flags?" whispered Mishti. "We're looking for the Red Flags, right?"

Kate quieted her as the voices up top spoke again.

"Who were they shooting at?" asked the girl.

"The girl looked like Bea. Hey, Bea!" the second voice called into the tree. "Is that you? We vanished these idiots for you."

"Listen carefully," whispered Kate. "We're going to go back down where it's dark. And then we negotiate."

"Hello?" called the voice again.

"We're from the Cove," called Kate. "We want to talk."

Leonardo winced. Mishti flinched beside him.

"Let's go," hissed Kate. She grabbed their arms and ran down the stairs. Leonardo stumbled after her, glancing over his shoulder as they plunged back into darkness.

CHAPTER 10

C ome out in the light," called the Red Flag up the stairs. He spoke with a slight accent, as if he'd come from somewhere exotic before landing in the woods. Suspicion fringed his tone. "This is ridiculous."

"Really?" replied Kate. "We heard most negotiations here happen in the dark."

Silence met her statement. If Leonardo strained, he thought he could hear whispering.

Finally, the girl up top cleared her throat. "Where did you hear that?" She sounded even more on-edge than her clanmate.

"Everyone knows," replied Kate. "The paranoia of the Redwoods is famous. We've also heard you'll stab everyone in the back, first chance you get. Is it true?"

More silence.

Leonardo had never heard any of that before.

Did she tell us all of that on the river?

"What do you want?" called the male voice. His accent was barely noticeable. Wherever he came from, Leonardo guessed he'd long forgotten it. No child in any corner of the woods remembered their past. So, unless these kids were different than everyone he'd ever met, they shared the same common bond.

We need to use that.

"An audience with the general," replied Kate.

"The general?" Mishti's voice breathed in Leonardo's ear.

Leonardo shook his head, then realized she couldn't see him.

"I have no idea," he whispered back.

Both Red Flags answered in sync. "Not gonna happen."

"Are you sure about that?" something changed in Kate's voice. It was subtle, but it lifted the hairs on Leonardo's arms.

For the third time, the faintest hints of whispers carried down the stairs.

"Give us a moment," said the voice.

"What's going on up there?" someone hissed from lower down. The other ten members of Leonardo's party were still scattered on the stairs, frozen where Kate had stopped them.

A hand slid onto Leonardo's arm, and he jumped.

"I told you what my hat gives me, right?" whispered Kate.

Whatever you want. Yes, she'd told him. But since he'd met her, very few things seemed to go Kate's way. Pinch's hat was straightforward—it created things. To the best of his understanding, Kate's was supposed to manipulate situations in her favor.

But people are unpredictable. A hat that attempted to tamper with people's volition would have spotty results at best.

"They haven't agreed to anything yet," he reminded her.

"Just wait," said Kate. "They will."

Time stretched on as Leonardo's alliance waited in the darkness. After a few minutes, someone whispered his name, and he called out softly in reply. Bodies shuffled, footsteps tapped on the stairs, then Viola's fingers slipped into Leonardo's.

"What happened up there?" she breathed. Her familiar voice was an anchor that grounded him, and he pulled her against his chest.

"We were almost attacked," he whispered. "But the Red Flags stepped in."

"Is that who's up there?" she asked, speaking into his shirt.

Leonardo nodded. "According to Kate, it's the Reds. We'll be ok."

Viola reached up and brushed her fingers across his cheek.

"It's dark in here," she whispered. Her tone was gently provocative.

Leonardo's heart staggered a beat. His clanmates were feet away, but no one could see anything, and—

Viola pulled his head down and kissed him. Leonardo closed his eyes, breathing in the sweetness of her lips and the smell of her hair. He placed his hands on her back, feeling the lean muscles through the soft leather of her dress.

He rested his forehead against hers. She exhaled softly, her warm breath on his face. They barely got any time together, running from the Dark.

"Promise me we'll have more of this," whispered Viola.

Leonardo sighed. He wanted to make that promise, but the Dark didn't leave time for anything.

"If the Dark wins..." Viola trailed off, drawing a shaky breath.

If the Dark wins, we may never see each other again.

"I promise." Leonardo kissed her again. "I promise we'll always make time."

Silently, Leonardo hoped that was a promise he could keep. He was leading an alliance, and now he was leader of Raven Clan. They were a long way from ready to face the Dark, and it was up to him to guide them to survival.

You chose this, he told himself. But really, there hadn't been a choice. Some days, the weight of it all threatened to crush him. Other times, the fear was more manageable, and if he imagined hard enough, he could see a light at the end of it all.

We'll make it through.

He had no idea how they would reassemble everything the Dark had ripped apart, but first, they needed to survive.

Finally, the Red Flag girl spoke again.

"We have a bag of blindfolds." She sounded nervous. Uncertain. "Put them on, and we'll take you to the general."

"See?" whispered Kate. "We're in."

"No way," said Leonardo and Mishti in sync.

"I'm throwing it down," called the male voice.

Something smacked against the wall over their heads and fell past Leonardo.

"Ugh!" Moth grunted in surprise. "That was my face!"

"We're not blindfolding everyone," Leonardo told Kate, his voice hushed.

"It's common practice," Kate whispered back. "Stop making it a big deal."

"Would you like to be pushed off a branch?" he hissed. "I don't trust these people at all."

"Well, we're going to need to, if we want any chance of convincing them to work with us!"

"Leo," said Viola. She took his arm. "We're in a vulnerable position already. If they wanted to hurt us, they would have."

"Solid logic from a surprising source," said Kate.

"Excuse me?" said Viola.

Leonardo bristled. "Kate—"

"Listen to your girlfriend, Leo. Trust me. It's just a precaution. If they didn't keep their camp secret, the Blue Flags would ambush them faster than you can blink."

"I hate this," said Mishti.

"Are you doing it or not?" called the voices from up top. "We need to move. We've been in this tree too long."

"If we don't go with them, the Blue Flags will find us again," said Kate.

Leonardo wished he could see his clan's faces. He couldn't think in the darkness of the tree.

"Last chance," called the voice up top. "Do you want to meet the general or not?"

"Dammit." Leonardo squared his jaw. "Moth, hand out the blindfolds."

CHAPTER 11

O w," snapped Moth. "Whoever keeps stepping on my heel, will you kindly *stop it?*"

"Sorry," said Will. "My bad."

Moth grumbled something under his breath. Then Pompey stepped on Leonardo's heel for the dozenth time. Leonardo winced. He gritted his teeth and kept walking, staring into the void of his blindfold. He scrunched his brow, trying to work the fabric down enough to gain a sliver of visibility. But the Red Flags had adjusted everyone's blindfolds as they emerged from the tree, guaranteeing no one could cheat a peek at their surroundings.

All that Leonardo's efforts could generate was a thin line of sunlight near the top of his vision. Sweat rolled down his face, either from the stress or the humidity, he couldn't tell. The air was moist enough that he didn't even realize a fine mist of rain was falling until he noticed the smell of it, infused with the poignant aroma of tree bark crackling under his shoes.

"Hurry up," called the Red Flag girl. Her voice rose in pitch, electric with nerves. "We're too exposed."

Leonardo's heart thumped in his chest. *This was a terrible idea.*

The branch rounded away underfoot, reminding him of the drop that awaited a misstep to either side. Most of the branches were thick enough to support all of their weight, but Leonardo felt the boughs bend more than once. He tried to pick up his pace now, and the branch bounced ever so slightly. It felt uncomfortably narrow. He needed to place each step almost directly in front of the last.

Maybe the blindfold is a blessing. At least he could only imagine the tightrope of a crossing rather than actually witnessing it.

Thankfully, the off-shooting boughs offered a second chance if a foot was placed off-center. Leonardo's boot slipped once, and he was only spared from falling because it stopped hard against what felt like a pinecone as high as his knee.

Pain stabbed through his knee when it struck the unyielding edges of the spines, and he clutched the sappy wood, breathing heavily while memories of falling from the Cove flashed through his mind.

"Watch your step," called the Red Flag boy up ahead. "We're going down a staircase."

At least that meant they were getting off the branches. Leonardo straightened on shaky legs, feeling blindly for anyone nearby, so he didn't accidentally push them off, then started forward again, keeping his arms slightly spread for balance.

A moment later, the sliver of light vanished as Leonardo descended into the confines of another tree. The sharp smell of redwood cloaked him again, as dense as the walls that now sealed him in. They descended deeper and deeper into the tree, and the echoes grew sharper, the air stiller until the Red Flags called for them to halt.

For the next five minutes, the traveling party of thirteen stood on the stairs, their breaths shallow.

"Leo," breathed Viola. "Where are you?"

"Here," whispered Leonardo.

A rustle of fabric, and she gripped his arm as she stepped up beside him. She leaned close to his ear.

"You can take off your blindfold," she said softly. "It's pitch-black in here."

He had assumed as much from the complete darkness that pressed against his blindfold, but it made him uneasy that she'd tested it.

That was a risk. A big risk.

Hesitantly, Leonardo reached up and slid his blindfold off his eyes. He blinked around at nothing—the space was as dark without the fabric as it had been with. But it was a different sort of darkness. A bigger darkness, less claustrophobic than the closeness of the fabric over his eyes.

"I'm trying to map this place in case we need to escape," whispered Viola. "I've been watching us, with my mind."

"Good," he whispered back. "What can you see?" He felt like they'd gained a bit of control.

"Not much," she replied. "My visions cut in and out."

"Keep searching." He squeezed her hand.

"Ok," called the Red Flag boy. "This way. Left turn here."

"Put your blindfold on again," whispered Leonardo. He slid his back down and heard the rustle of fabric as Viola did the same.

Ten steps down, a pair of hands steered him to the right. Leonardo flinched, but it was only the Red Flag, ushering him off the stairs and through an opening. He struck his head and swore, ducking and straightening carefully in a new space with an uneven floor. He moved forward, hands in front of him, and bumped into a giant body.

Cato grunted, then he noisily turned, and Leonardo quickly shuffled back.

"Someone punched my ass," said Cato.

Leonardo sidestepped to the left, then quietly moved ahead of Cato. "I'm sure it was an accident," he said over his shoulder. "None of us can see."

"Hmph," said Cato.

Leonardo lifted his hands higher this time and stepped forward until his fingers brushed the back of someone's neck.

"I'd recommend you watch your hands," snapped Pinch. "Unless it's a girl, then you may continue."

"It's me, halfwit," said Leonardo.

"Just my luck," grumbled Pinch.

"You may remove your blindfolds," called the Red Flag boy.

For the second time, Leonardo pulled his blindfold off his eyes. *Dammit.* The room was as black as everything else.

"What the hell?" said Bates.

"You're kidding me," said Mishti. "Is this some kind of joke?"

"This is how we negotiate in the Redwoods," said a new kid's voice, deeper than the first. It came from somewhere ahead of them. "You'll find we're very serious about security here."

His tone carried a heavy undercurrent. *We don't like outsiders.*

"Are you the general?" asked Leonardo.

"I care more about who *you* are." He sounded more cautious than the first two Red Flags. "But yes, I'm the general."

His deep voice echoed in the blackness, making the chamber suddenly seem a lot larger. Leonardo frowned. The air was dead-still, and he wondered exactly how vast this space was.

"We're from the Darkwoods," started Leonardo.

"And the Cove," added Mishti.

They relayed their story to the room. Partway through, Leonardo caught a thin seam of light against a wall to the left. It flickered ever so faintly.

Firelight. He traced the seam with his eyes, up the wall and then horizontal, framing a doorway.

"That's quite the story," said the general, once they had finished. "The rest of your...*alliance*? You said they traveled north?"

"To the Highland, yes," said Leonardo.

"Well," said the general. He chuckled, though it sounded forced. "It seems you picked the better corner to visit. Here in the Redwoods, we're masters of the dark."

Leonardo didn't laugh. The darkness inside the tree trunks was nothing like the Dark. These heavy shadows were a soft cloak compared to the nightmare that ravaged both his old home and new one.

"Unfortunately, we can't help you," said the general, a bit louder than necessary.

He's nervous.

Leonardo hadn't expected anything less. Caliban and his Snake Clan were the only ones to join them without requiring any convincing. And that was only because Caliban had already attempted to harness the Dark and endangered his clanmates because of it.

Luckily, Leonardo and Mishti had a lot of experience negotiating clans into their alliance. Viola squeezed Leonardo's hand. *You can do it.*

"We're not asking you to help *us*," said Mishti. "You'd be helping yourselves."

Her robes rustled, and Leonardo realized she had stepped forward. He slipped his hand out of Viola's and moved up beside Mishti, curling his fingers around the rough leather of his sword grip. Their party's breaths echoed behind them.

"All of us need to help each other," said Leonardo. "If we stand alone, the Dark will destroy us all."

He stepped in a dip and nearly twisted his ankle. He stumbled to a crouch, pressing his hands against the hard wood of the floor, and was suddenly thankful for the blanket of shadows.

"You're not going to change my mind," said the general, as Leonardo pushed himself up. "I would love to chat some more about this adventure of yours; it sounds fascinating. But if you're only here to—"

"The Dark is like a disease," said Kate. "It will kill the trees. All these beautiful trees—"

"The trees can look after themselves," said the general.

Kate fell silent. The way she said it, the emphasis she used…*she expected the trees to be a trigger word.* Maybe the Redwoods kids loved the trees a hundred years ago, but the general's disregard was a stark shift in attitude.

"Oh. Ok," stammered Kate. "Well, um…it will kill your clan. It gets under people's skin and—"

"Then the woods will give me new kids."

Leonardo blinked. *If the Dark kills your clan, you won't be around to receive the new kids.*

He wasn't sure what surprised him more; the coldness in his deep voice or the utter absurdity of his argument.

"Well...then...um..." Kate trailed off, shell-shocked.

The Redwoods have changed since she left.

"If the Dak kills your clan," said Leonardo. "You won't be around to receive new kids."

Silence met his retort.

We're losing. He felt stranded, sensory-deprived, anchored only by the smooth wood under his soles.

"Are you all finished?" asked the general. "I already told you that you can't change my mind. If that's all you have to say—"

"Why can't we change your mind?" asked Leonardo.

"Excuse me?"

"There must be a reason," he pressed. "What would you lose if you joined us?"

"The game!" said Kate suddenly. Her voice echoed off the back wall.

"What?" Fresh wariness spiked the general's tone.

Leonardo's hairs stood on edge. *Be careful, Kate.*

"In the other corners of the woods," recovered Kate, "they say you play a game here. That you never stop playing."

Another slight pause before, "What else do they say about this game?"

"Not much," Leonardo jumped in. He could feel Kate's eyes on him, even in the Dark. "But if it's as..."

"Bloody," supplied Kate.

Leonardo swallowed. *What* is *this place?*

"*Bloody* as they say," he continued, "then maybe you could use some new players."

"Ones who know how to fight," added Mishti.

They were completely improvising. Viola stepped forward and gripped Leonardo's hand in a nervous grasp, her fingernails digging into his skin. Leonardo dried his other palm against his pants.

"You want to join the game?" said the general. Heavy skepticism filled his voice. "Willingly?"

"*Careful*," whispered Viola.

"Yes," said Kate.

Dammit, Kate. Leonardo wanted to revoke her offer, but he held his tongue.

The general didn't say anything for a long moment.

"You understand the game?" he asked, at last.

"No," said Leonardo, before Kate could speak. "Not entirely."

"Yet you want to join."

"How about this," said Leonardo. "You explain the game to us, then give us time to discuss it—"

"In private," added Mishti.

"And then we come back here and negotiate."

"Ok..." The general cleared his throat. "You must see how strange this all seems, from my perspective. But my curiosity is piqued. It's a simple game. Every new kid in the Redwoods earns either a red or a blue flag. If a Red's flag is captured by a Blue, the kid vanishes, and vice versa. We'll win the game when we capture every blue flag, and we're the only ones left."

No wonder they're so paranoid.

The entire object of the game ensured no prisoners were taken.

"And how does a kid earn a flag?" asked Leonardo.

"The woods give us two kids at a time. They fight to the death, and the winner gets a flag."

Leonardo's jaw slackened. *It's worse than how the Cove gets kids.*

"Have you heard enough?" he asked Leonardo. "Are you ready to decide?"

"Um…" Leonardo licked his lips. For all the humidity, his mouth felt exceptionally dry.

"Give us a second," said Mishti. Her annoyance mirrored Leonardo's building panic.

"Of course," said the general. "Take your time."

A moment passed. Nothing happened, and Leonardo realized they would be getting no privacy.

Of course not. "Everyone, gather up," he said through gritted teeth, staring in the direction of the general's voice. He could feel the kid's smugness from here.

Nothing about the Redwoods is going to be easy. He only hoped they could navigate it faster than the Dark could.

"Who is this?" Moth clutched Leonardo's arm.

"It's me," Leonardo whispered back. "Leo."

"Oh good," Moth lowered his voice even more. "See the outline of that door? The room behind it is full of fairies."

Leonardo's eyebrows shot up. *First lions, now fairies.* Just like the Cove.

Why are the Darkwoods so empty? And small? The Cove and the Redwoods were massive, sprawling corners of the woods. The

Darkwoods was nothing but a short stretch of river, with some treehouses and clearings up the bank.

"They want our help," hissed Moth. "They're in cages."

"We need to free them, Leo!" begged Charley. "Please?"

"Slow down," Leonardo held up his hands, even though no one could see. "And talk quieter," he whispered. "There will be time for that," he told Moth and Charley, keeping his voice hushed. "We need to talk about this game first."

"And thanks to the woods," whispered Mishti. "We're completely ignorant. Kate, care to tell us everything in sixty seconds?"

"I..." Kate drew a breath and released it. "They've changed. The kids in my time—"

"Of course they have," hissed Leonardo. "It's been a hundred years."

We don't have time for this.

"We have to join the game," said Kate. "Don't we?"

If we refuse, they'll kick us out.

"I agree," whispered Sophie.

"You do?" asked Mishti.

"I think so too," said Pinch. "If we don't, the Dark kills us anyway. Might as well die in a real fight."

"Or live and unite the clans," added Sophie.

"Well, obviously," said Pinch. "That's the entire point of this."

Leonardo had to agree. *If we don't take this risk, we're gambling with a much bigger danger.*

"Viola?" he asked.

"I think..." She gathered her words. "I agree with Pinch and Sophie. It might be our only chance."

That was the last bit of confirmation Leonardo needed.

"I say we join," he whispered. "Mishti?"

Mishti drew a breath, hesitated, then released it. "I don't think we have much of a choice."

"Have you come to a decision?" called the general. "I don't have all day."

"We're joining your game," called Mishti.

"Good choice. Lift the curtains."

CHAPTER 12

K ids around the hollow whisked curtains off of fairy cages, flooding the space with flickering light. Leonardo's stomach tightened. He glanced at Mishti as she swallowed hard. The hollow was even bigger than he'd guessed. The thirteen Ravens and Lions stood on a sort of ledge, overlooking a sunken space where ranks of kids peered up at them. Their numbers easily matched those of the entire alliance.

We could have fallen off. It wasn't a long drop, but a broken leg awaited any unwitting blindfolded missteps. His stomach flipped at the danger they had narrowly avoided.

The general stood on the ledge with Leonardo's party, a red cape draped across his shoulders. His dark skin gleamed in the fairy light. He spread his arms.

"Welcome to the Red Flags."

The kids behind him each sported a piece of red cloth, tied to their arms or around their heads like a bandana. The older the kids, the more faded and weathered their flags. The newer ones were vibrant and unsoiled. He could directly determine how long a kid had been around by the state of their flag. They looked like Darkwoods kids, in drab, patched clothes, with suspicious eyes and guarded faces. Their flags reminded him of something. The colour, the texture... Leonardo looked at Kate. The red scarf she typically wore was hidden from view.

Her scarf is her flag.

The general studied him, and Mishti, and the eleven kids around them. His flag cape was tattered with snags and tears, and he carried a long wooden tube on his back, slung by a leather strap across his chest.

What does he keep in there?

"You've traveled a long way." The general tilted his head. "You must be serious about this."

"Here's the deal," said Leonardo. "We'll play your game. You're trying to defeat the Blue Flags, right?"

"Destroy would be a better word." He stood as tall as Aleksander, but where Leonardo's brother had been thin and beakish, the general was solidly muscular. He balanced his weight on the balls of his feet, legs shoulder-width apart.

"Fine," said Leonardo. "*Destroy.* We'll help you. If you promise to join us afterward, to defeat the Dark."

"Sure." The general shrugged. "Deal."

Leonardo hesitated. His tone was too light. Almost mocking.

"You don't think we'll ever defeat the Blue Flags?" asked Kate.

"I've been playing this game my whole life." He absently

traced a line of stitches on his cape. "You haven't. Maybe you'll stumble across something we've missed."

But it's unlikely. So that was it. The general thought he'd just negotiated himself an entire batch of new troops for free. He thought the game would never end.

"Do you have a name?" asked Leonardo.

The general smiled and shook his head. "I used to. But I find the title suits me better."

He spoke with a slight drawl. It wasn't noticeable in all his words, but it made him just charismatic enough to guarantee Leonardo would never trust him. He let his gaze travel over the ranks of Leonardo's party, then stopped on Viola. He raised an eyebrow, and his smile changed into something Leonardo didn't like at all.

"The Dark is coming," said Leonardo curtly. "For everyone's sake, I hope we end this game. If we're not ready, it will destroy us all."

The general didn't flinch. "Then I suppose we'd better get started."

CHAPTER 13

In the Blue Flags," drawled the general, "they have very specific roles. Some of them gather food; others collect new recruits; others spend their days stalking and hunting us."

He, Leonardo, and Mishti walked along a tree branch, sheltered behind a wall of redwood boughs. Long needles brushed Leonardo's arm. He edged away and stepped directly into a spiderweb. He flinched, but this one was only large enough to catch flies. He wiped it off and grimaced at the sticky silk on his fingers.

"Here in the Red Flags," continued the general, "everyone shares responsibilities. That way, no one is essential. If the Blue Flags killed half my clan, we could still function like normal."

Leonardo glanced at Mishti.

She shrugged.

It's not a terrible system, he thought. Just *a cold one.*

Their branch ran flush along the face of a tree, like a narrow ledge halfway up a cliff. He rubbed his fingers over the cracked bark on his left, leaving the balled-up spiderweb behind.

"We move in small groups," said the general. "Harder to spot, and less detrimental if they're caught. We'll disperse the members of your clans into patrols so they can learn the game. Each patrol will rotate through different duties every day."

"What sort of duties?" Leonardo carefully stepped around a pinecone half his height, nestled in the screen of boughs to his right. White sap glistened on the spines.

"Well, the most important are stalking Blue Flags and vanishing them, gathering new recruits from the Nest, and collecting food."

"The Nest?" asked Mishti.

"I'll show you." The general pushed aside some of the boughs and stepped down onto a lower, narrower branch, sprouting directly from the cliff-tree. He glanced back as Leonardo and Mishti hesitantly followed.

Redwood needles brushed the back of Leonardo's neck, pungent with the tangy smell of the woods, and the new branch bobbed under their weight. Leonardo froze, hands splayed.

"Relax." The general laughed. "These trees are strong."

Leonardo peered between the swinging boughs to a harrowing drop. The general moved ahead confidently, further along the tapering limb, until it was actively sagging under them.

"Leo," whispered Mishti. "Are we sure this is a good—"

The general jumped and grabbed a thicker branch overhead. He swung his legs up, red cape tangling, and pulled himself between the boughs. He straightened to his knees and offered a hand to Leonardo and Mishti.

Mishti sighed. "I miss the Cove."

She ignored the general's hand and jumped, grabbing the branch and wrestling herself up onto it. Her gold robe snagged at the knee. She swore and yanked it harder, tearing a foot-long gash in the fabric. The general raised an eyebrow and grinned.

Leonardo rolled his eyes and took his offer, gripping the general's arm and jumping for the branch with his other hand. He kicked loose needles and smaller cones as he scrambled up.

Mishti and the Lions would need new clothes. The Cove and The Redwoods were similar in a lot of ways, but luxury wasn't one of them. Hundreds of stitched-up tears crisscrossed the general's cape. He doubted Mishti possessed the patience to sew up her silk robes every day.

All three straightened, and Leonardo blinked at the view.

A canyon opened up before them, making way for a mammoth of a tree, with branches thicker than any tree trunk from the Darkwoods. High in a crook, a giant ball of woven sticks and leaves sat wedged in place. It looked as if it grew from the tree itself.

"I present to you...the Nest." The general spread his arms grandly.

"That's where new kids arrive," said Leonardo, more statement than question. Something about the tangle of branches, like hundreds of thin arms, left him deeply unsettled.

"Correct. The woods drop them there to fight it out. If they try to get out on their own, more vines will block them. It moves to a new tree every day. It's our job to find it and free our new recruits."

"So, there's a Nest in Blue Flag territory too?" asked Mishti.

"Blue Flag territory?" The general laughed. "*Territory* here changes every day. There are trees, and there's the Nest. No one owns any of it."

Leonardo gazed around the canopy. "So, there could be Blue Flags anywhere."

The general nodded. "We pick a tree to be our headquarters for a time. As soon as it's discovered, we move. Once, both clans were in neighboring trees for weeks and didn't realize it."

"I see." Leonardo suddenly felt very exposed.

"You'll learn to curb the paranoia," said the general. "As soon as you accept the fact that there could always be a Blue Flag stalking you."

"That seems dangerous," said Mishti. "Strategically."

"Don't worry." The general cupped her hand between his. "We'll keep you safe."

Mishti yanked her hand away, and Leonardo resisted the urge to laugh.

The general chuckled, surprise glinting in his expression. "We have a feisty one here."

Mishti glared daggers at the general and edged away from him, incidentally moving closer to Leonardo. The general eyed the two of them.

"Are you two, then…"

"What?" Leonardo almost laughed again.

Mishti wasn't as good-humored. She dropped a throwing ring into each hand and advanced on the general. "How about you keep your assumptions to yourself. And if I see you making a single advance on one of my girls—"

The general held up a hand, silencing her. Mishti scoffed, and

Leonardo stared at him, incredulous for a split second until the general squinted up through the branches overhead.

The hairs prickled on Leonardo's neck.

"What is it?" he asked, his indignation replaced by sober focus.

The general took a step forward, shading his eyes in a patch of sunlight.

"Get back down to that other branch," he said softly. "You don't have flags yet. You're vulnerable up here."

"Are there Blue Flags above us?" asked Mishti, suddenly breathless.

The general lifted the long, wooden tube off his back. He fished a tiny dart from a pouch on his hip. "I think so." He fit the dart into the tube and raised it to his lips. He narrowed one eye, aiming the weapon up through the boughs.

"Go," he muttered. "I'll be right down."

Leonardo nodded to Mishti, and they dropped back to the flimsy branch, then quickly maneuvered through the curtain of boughs and onto the thicker, sheltered branch.

"Quickly," whispered Mishti. "Before he comes back, tell me your plan."

"What?" Leonardo was still thinking about the blow darts.

Why does not having a flag make us vulnerable?

Mishti slapped him in the face.

"Ow!" Leonardo stared at her. "What the hell was that—"

"Focus. I sincerely hope you have some sort of plan."

Why can't you make a plan? he wanted to snap at her. But she was right. They wouldn't get many chances to talk like this. And in fact, he did have an idea of how to move forward.

Leonardo parted the boughs and glanced around. There was no sign of the general.

"Ok, listen." He leaned close, breathing the words. "We can't start vanishing kids from the other clan. We need their help too. We need to take down this game from the inside. If we can figure out how it works, we can end it without bloodshed."

"And how do we do that?" asked Mishti.

"I don't know," said Leonardo. "But there has to be a way to end it. Kate's been here since the game started. Maybe she can tell us something."

"So, your plan is to make a plan?" demanded Mishti.

"My plan is to learn the workings of this game, from the inside. We won't be able to meet all together; that would look too suspicious. So, we'll exchange information when we can. Everything needs to get back to you and me as quickly as possible. As soon as we understand the game's weaknesses, we exploit them and end it."

"That will be easier said than done," Mishti whispered. She narrowed her heavy eyebrows, chewing the edge of her lip. Then she tilted her head. "Kate has been here since the game started."

"I know," whispered Leonardo. "I just said that."

"No, I mean, what if she started the game?"

What if she started the game. Mishti didn't even know the true nature of the woods. She didn't know it was a dream world, imagined by the first kids. Kids like Kate. Her reasoning was sound already but paired with Leonardo's knowledge....

"We need to talk to Kate," said Leonardo.

The boughs parted, and the general jumped to their branch. Leonardo flinched, shifting away from Mishti, but the general was looking over his shoulder. He tugged a dart from the back of his neck, the tip shiny with blood, and threw it away.

"I think we surprised them," he said softly. "They don't have poison darts, so they're not a stalking party. They're probably deciding whether or not to follow us. We need to disappear."

Leonardo glanced up through the needles as the general rushed ahead, his cape flapping behind him.

***

"What did you mean," asked Leonardo, "when you said we're vulnerable because we don't have flags?"

They stood pressed into a narrow crevasse in the trunk of an adjacent tree. The canopy architecture was so elaborate that the Blue Flags would have to be directly on top of them to spot their hiding place. Leonardo's heart thudded regardless, but the silence gnawed at him, and he wanted answers.

The general leaned forward and peeked outside the crevasse before replying.

"The flags are a curse and a blessing," he said as he pressed back into his hiding spot. "If my flag is captured, I vanish. *But* nothing else can vanish me. Any wound will heal. It'll hurt like hell, but it will heal."

"So if we take flags—" started Mishti.

"*When* you take flags," corrected the general. "If you're playing the game, you need a flag."

A centipede scurried up the wall of the crevasse, inches from Leonardo's face. He edged back, frowning. *The flags will make us invincible?*

From the Dark too?

"Whatever." Mishti rolled her eyes. "*When* we take flags, we'll be the same?"

"You should be." He scratched his chin. "Although, you didn't arrive through a Nest, so maybe that will change things. We'll have to test it."

Leonardo didn't like the sound of that. But if there was a chance the flags could protect them against the Dark…

"Those could've helped us," he told Mishti, heavy with intention. "Back in the Cove."

Mishti nodded slowly. Her nails plucked at a loose gold thread.

"You seem hesitant," the general mused. He eyed Mishti, then Leonardo. "If you're playing, you're in one-hundred percent. I hope you don't expect to play your own rules."

His tone reminded Leonardo that the Dark wasn't their only adversary.

Leonardo swallowed, refusing to let himself blink. "Of course not." He kept his gaze locked on the general's.

"Good." The general clapped a hand on his shoulder. "Let's go now then."

Leonardo resisted the urge to flinch.

He's trying to call our bluff. And rightly so. Leonardo was less sure of this plan than ever.

"Sure," said Mishti, sharp with her own challenge. "Which way?"

"Back to the camp first," said the general. "We'll gather your party, then we'll get you all some flags."

What are we getting ourselves into? Leonardo glanced at Mishti as they were led out of the tree, then darted his gaze away as the general looked back.

An hour later, he, Mishti, and their clans stood before the only non-redwood tree in the forest. A vast spread of leafy branches arched over the redwood boughs, hung with hundreds of red and blue flags, like some sort of festival awaiting its guests.

There are more than enough for the entire alliance. If the flags worked against the Dark, they could bring enough for everyone in the Highland party, along with all the kids of the Highland.

"Why do you hang the flags from the tree?" asked Charley.

"We don't hang them," said the general. "The tree grows them."

"What?" The kids stopped walking. Their mouths fell open.

Leonardo frowned at the flags over his head, stirring in a soft breeze. The news didn't even surprise him. The magic of the woods was becoming commonplace in his life.

But why wasn't the magic clear in the Darkwoods?

That was the one thing that bothered him. The Cove and the Redwoods were alive with magic. The Darkwoods were a different story.

"Everyone take a flag," said the general. His gaze darted around the surrounding trees. Other Red Flag kids crept through the branches, weapons at the ready in case of an ambush.

Leonardo couldn't help but scan the shadows as he and the twelve others walked out into the arms of the flag tree. The redwood branches crisscrossed through the flag-laden branches, the two canopies entwined in a partial embrace as Leonardo stepped onto smooth blonde bark.

"Oh, look at Butterfly, helping his girlfriend," declared Pinch. "How romantic."

"Shut up, Pinch." Moth caught Juliet around the waist as she dropped to the tree, then they quickly separated.

"Will you catch me?" asked Pinch.

"No."

"But what if I fall?" Pinch jumped recklessly off the branch and landed, arms pinwheeling, three feet from Moth. Juliet gasped and dropped to a crouch as the branch bobbed wildly. Moth jumped forward and steadied Pinch, who grinned wickedly.

"See. You do love me."

He wobbled once, then grabbed a thinner branch for support. His hat slid off, and he effortlessly caught it behind his back as Moth swore and closed his eyes. Their branch continued to swing as Moth shakily returned to Juliet.

Will Pinch ever grow up? Leonardo doubted it.

In his peripheral, he caught the general plucking a red flag from a branch and presenting it to Viola. Leonardo tensed. Viola hesitantly took the flag, then quietly thanked him and moved away. The general's gaze lingered on her, and Leonardo's mood darkened. His opinion of the kid was souring by the minute.

Then Charley and Pompey dropped down beside him and ran for a pair of flags, one red and one blue, dangling near the end of the bench. Leonardo winced, watching them shove each other as they raced for the red flag.

One wrong step…

They made it without disaster, and Charley ripped the red flag from the branch, taking a clump of leaves with it.

"That's not fair!" complained Pompey. "You had a head start!"

"Did not!"

"Did too! You were in front of me."

"Sore loser. Look," she pointed, "there's another one over there."

"Or…" Pompey eyed the blue flag still hanging from the branch. "What do you think would happen if I…"

He tugged the blue flag.

"Guys!" called Leonardo.

"What the…?" Pompey yanked harder, and Charley started laughing.

"Wow, you're weak." She rubbed her hands together and grabbed the flag as well. Both of them tugged, but it didn't budge.

"What?" Charley frowned at the flag.

"That's enough." Leonardo took a step toward them.

If he gets a blue flag, is he on the wrong team?

"On three," said Pompey. They braced their feet, their backs to a gap between the branches. "One…two…"

Leonardo's eyes widened. If that flag released, they would fall backward, straight out of the tree.

"Hey!" shouted Leonardo.

Both kids snapped to attention. They let go of the flag, hands behind their backs.

"Look behind you," said Leonardo sharply. His heart raced.

Both kids eyed the edge of the branch. Pompey gulped, and Charley shifted to a safer position.

"Right." Leonardo crossed to them, drying his palms. "If you two aren't careful, you'll fall like *that*." He snapped his fingers.

Both kids nodded, their eyes still perfectly round.

"What were you doing, anyway?" he demanded. "We need red flags."

"I know," said Pompey. "I just thought it would be funny—"

"No, it wouldn't." The general dropped to join them on the branch. "It would mean we'd have to kill you."

Leonardo regarded him coldly. "Excuse me?"

"He'd be a Blue Flag." The general's dark eyes glinted. "We wouldn't have a choice."

"Couldn't he just take another flag?"

The general shook his head. "Doesn't work like that. Lucky for you," he told Pompey, "the tree is smarter than us. It won't give you a blue flag because it can see you're with the Red Flags. You're not the first dumb kid to try that. Here, freshly picked." He handed Pompey a red flag.

Pompey took it quietly. Both he and Charley had fallen silent, although for Charley, it was a defiant sort of quiet. She glowered at the general, her own flag clenched in her small fist.

"Now," said the general, as if unaware. "Hold onto those flags, you two. That's your life now. Lose it, you're gone."

Neither kid said a word. Pompey's fingers shook.

"Go find Kate," Leonardo told the kids. "She'll show you what to do with them."

"Who is Kate?" asked the general as the kids ran off.

Dammit. "Kate is…a member of my clan." Leonardo crossed his arms. "She takes care of the kids."

"I see." The general studied Leonardo's eyes. Leonardo fought the urge to look away.

He knows I'm lying. But Leonardo had no intention of telling him a word more than he needed to. Especially that Kate was actually the oldest member of the Red Flags.

"You have an interesting clan, Leonardo," said the general finally.

Leonardo didn't blink. "Likewise."

"Mm. Come on," the general slapped his shoulder, a little harder than necessary. "Let's get you a flag."

CHAPTER 14

Y ou want to end the game," said Kate. Skepticism laced her voice.

Leonardo and Mishti stood with her in the dark stairwell. It was midnight, and the rest of their party slept in the tree hollow the Red Flags had assigned them. No one felt secure about closing their eyes in the midst of a clan they didn't trust, but the need for sleep overwhelmed even their most steadfast reservations.

"Yes," said Leonardo. "Unless you know another way to get them into our alliance."

"They've been playing this game since the woods began." Kate's hushed voice pierced the blackness. "Ending it is…impossible. Unless we kill all the Blue Flags."

"We need them," said Leonardo. "Vanishing them isn't an option."

"I know," said Kate.

Leonardo wished he could see her expression.

"I've been wondering," said Mishti. An undercurrent charged her tone. "Who started the game? You should know, you've been here since the woods began."

A rustle of fabric told Leonardo that Kate had crossed her arms. Her warm breath brushed his cheek when she replied, sharp and deliberate. "Well, it wasn't me, if that's what you're getting at. The game was ready when the first group of us arrived."

Something scraped against the trunk. Leonardo jumped, fingers closing on his sword. He held his breath, listening as the sound came again; a dry, raking impact.

"It's just a branch," said Kate. "It must be windy tonight. Another tree is whacking us."

The branch knocked against their tree again, scraping over the bark.

"If you didn't start the game, it means the woods did," Leonardo whispered into the darkness. "The woods created the war in the Darkwoods. That's over. The woods created the temptation game in the Cove. That's over—"

"The what?" asked Mishti and Kate in sync.

Leonardo frowned.

They didn't see it?

He'd spent a fraction of the time they had in the Cove, and he'd clearly seen what it did to people's minds.

"Everything in the Cove is a temptation," said Leonardo. "Even the guardians are sirens. If every corner is playing a game, then yours was about resisting temptation."

Both Mishti and Kate were quiet.

They really didn't see it?

"So, what's your point?" asked Mishti finally.

"That game ended too. Everyone left the Cove. That means the temptation wore off."

"We left because the Dark forced us to."

"Exactly. If we don't end this flag game, the Dark will end it for us."

"I get it," said Kate quietly. She sighed. "I get it. We need to end the game, or a lot of kids are going to get vanished. The problem is, I don't know the game anymore."

"Neither do we," said Leonardo. "So we'll learn, and we'll try to limit the vanishings in the process. As soon as we find the game's weakness, we attack it."

"Ok," said Kate.

Something creaked lower down in the tree. Leonardo jumped.

"That didn't sound like a branch," hissed Mishti.

It sounded like a foot on a stair.

"Let's get back to the hollow," whispered Leonardo.

Chills crept up his arms as they ascended the stairs, listening for noises behind them. When they ducked through the opening in the wall, back into the fairy-lit hollow, Leonardo caught Kate tying two red flags together.

She noticed him watching and struck a pose. Leonardo looked away.

"I've never had two flags," whispered Kate. "I was just going to pretend to take one from the tree, but then the general gave me this."

She stroked the silky fabric of her new flag. "Now I have a double flag."

"Does that change anything?" asked Mishti.

"I don't know. I can't exactly ask." She tucked it into the folds of her coat. "I guess we'll find out."

***

The next morning, they were divided into fifty different patrols.

Leonardo, Moth, and Pinch found themselves with the general again and two younger kids who'd supposedly just completed their training. The general didn't elaborate, but the two kids were nimble as they moved through the branches. The wind from last night continued into the day, sharp with the smell of impending rain. Branches dipped and swayed under a grey sky.

"Hurry up, halfwit," hissed Pinch, as Moth stumbled over a pinecone and crouched dramatically to regain his balance. "You're embarrassing me."

"Oh, sorry," snapped Moth. "Would you rather I fall from the tree?"

Pinch pretended to consider it, pursing his lips.

"Shut up," said Moth. "You'd be bored out of your mind without me."

"That's called *relaxation*," countered Pinch. "Before you showed up babbling about fairies, I was downright—"

"You're still going on about the fairy thing?" Moth rolled his eyes at Leonardo. "They're *real*, Pinch. Everyone knows it."

Leonardo grinned, climbing up a ladder of branches after the general. Being back in a forest—a living forest—put him in a good mood. It made him feel as if they might have a chance to survive everything after all. These were the biggest trees he'd ever seen. It would take more than a few tendrils of the Dark to drop them.

"Pipe down," the general whispered over his shoulder. "Voices carry in the trees."

Moth and Pinch fell silent as Leonardo pulled himself over a cluster of rigid vines coiled around the branch like so many snakes and stopped beside the Red Flag leader. His muscles burned, and tiny cuts and scrapes covered his skin, but the general's dark skin appeared unblemished. He wasn't out of breath either, while Leonardo, Moth, and Pinch, sucked in air.

They knelt on all fours at the lip of a canyon. The ruddy face of the next tree loomed across a daunting gap. Thick, braided vines draped like bridges from the arms of their current tree to their destination.

"Jesus Christ," said Pinch.

"Don't tell me we're supposed to cross that." Moth's wide eyes locked on the brown cable of a vine sagging before them. Maybe twice the circumference of his body, it didn't lend to a sense of security.

But Leonardo's concern lay beyond the bridge itself. He scrutinized hundreds of nooks and openings in the opposing trunk. Scores upon scores of hiding places.

The real danger here isn't falling.

The General's line of thought appeared to mirror his own.

"Olivia," he whispered to one of the new recruits. "You're the quickest. Go first."

Olivia didn't hesitate. She swung her legs over the ledge and gracefully scrambled down the slouch of the vine, disappearing from Leonardo's view.

"Everyone else, get low," said the general.

113

"What?" Leonardo frowned at him, crouching with the others.

Olivia came into sight, sprinting across the gently quivering bridge. Then she flinched, grabbing the side of her neck.

Leonardo caught his breath as she tugged a dart from her skin. She wavered, then she was falling. She struck the vine hard, and Leonardo jumped for the gap, but the general grabbed his wrist first.

"Hey—" Leonardo yanked his arm, but the general's strong fingers dug painfully into his skin. "Dammit, let me—"

"Wait," hissed the general.

Leonardo twisted to see Olivia. The adjacent vines hammocked her so she didn't fall off, but the greenery shook as two Blue Flags dropped out of the next tree and ran toward her.

The general whipped his blowgun off his back and jammed a dart into the tube. He raised one end to his lips and aimed through the boughs.

He fired just as the first kid reached her. The dart struck him in the chest, and the kid reeled back. The general loaded a second dart, but not before the other Blue Flag reached Olivia. Her flag was tied around her wrist, and he whipped it off of her before Leonardo could blink.

Olivia vanished.

Leonardo's heart stopped.

He made a choked noise, then cleared his throat, but no words would come. The girl had been no older than Charley.

"Fuck," said Pinch, just as the general fired his second dart. It missed the Blue Flag, and he scrambled back for the safety of the branches. Something whisked through the boughs over Leonardo's head. Leonardo ducked, every muscle in his body tense.

"They're firing back!" gasped the other young Red Flag, next to the general.

Pinch swore again and loaded his slingshot. He squinted one eye and fired at the Blue Flag on the run. A second later, the kid grabbed his head and crashed to his knees. The general hit him with a dart from his prone position.

Leonardo looked from one Blue Flag to the next, both slumped motionless on the vines.

"What the hell is on those darts?" asked Moth.

"Poison," said the other young Red Flag.

Another dart whistled over Leonardo's head. Leonardo flinched.

"Highly potent." The general jammed another dart in his blowgun and took aim at the source of the shot. He fired, and Pinch loosed a slingshot stone after it.

"It would kill anyone without a flag," continued the general. "For us, it just shuts down the body long enough to steal a flag."

He blew another dart. A crash, then branches shaking and the racket of something heavy dropping through the greenery. Leonardo's pulse thumped in his throat.

The general lowered his blowgun.

"You knew Olivia would be shot," Leonardo said quietly.

"Suspected. But better her than us."

"You're kidding." Leonardo's palms were slick with sweat. Gritty bits of bark stuck to his skin. His shock began to distill into anger.

"Toby," the general addressed the other kid. "It should be safe now. Go out there and—"

"No," Leonardo interrupted him. "I'll go."

Both Moth and Pinch drew a breath to argue, but Leonardo quieted them with a look.

"I have a flag now." He knotted it tighter in his belt. "The venom won't kill me."

The general spread his hands. "Suit yourself."

Leonardo regarded Moth and Pinch. "If I'm hit, make sure none of those halfwits reach me."

They nodded, loading their slingshots. Leonardo drew a breath and crouched lower, climbing over the ledge. Boughs scraped the back of his neck, leaving his skin sticky with sap, but he ignored it as he crawled down the vine, lodging his feet and knees in the loops of its braids. Tension sent tremors through the tendril as it strained under his weight, and Leonardo eased himself to his feet, arms spread for balance. A deathly drop awaited him to either side, his safety net the same adjacent stands which had caught Olivia.

His stomach jumped to his throat. Blood pounded in his skull. The two Blue Flags lay unconscious ahead of him. Leonardo moved forward, eyes darting from shadow to shadow. One hand gripped his sword, but he knew it would be useless against their blowguns.

Hundreds of branches bobbed and swayed in the wind, creaking and rattling. A few seconds and nothing happened. A few more, and the woods remained empty. Leonardo stopped at the feet of the closest Blue Flag and turned in a slow circle until he faced the blind of redwood boughs where the others sheltered.

He felt incredibly small; dwarfed among the giants. A wave of vertigo sent his equilibrium pitching, and with a blink, his vision plunged to black.

Leonardo gasped and blinked again. The world flared into color, but what had been a lush forest now transformed to a wasteland of rotten, blackened spires. The Dark's putrid tar dripped off of everything.

Oh my god.

With another blink, reality slammed back into place. The Dark was gone. A flock of silvery birds whisked past, warbling rapidly. A chipmunk flung itself to a new perch with a rattling crashlanding. A million shades of green and woodland red thrived in overgrown abundance.

Leonardo's breaths came ragged. He rubbed his eyes to make sure his perception was stable again.

It's coming. The woods were warning him. *Or*—he had a more ominous thought—the Dark was threatening him. Either way, Leonardo heard the sentiment loud and clear. *Time is running out.*

His companions seemed oblivious to it. Their tense expressions remained unchanged. They left him for a moment longer, then the general dropped over the edge, followed by Toby, Pinch, and Moth, who stumbled a bit and grabbed Pinch's arm for balance. Pinch rolled his eyes as Moth stepped back, dusting needles off his shirt.

"Can I go get his flag, please?" Toby asked the general, high voice piped even higher with excitement. Vivid blue eyes shone from under a mess of red hair. He didn't appear remotely bothered by Olivia's vanishing.

Cutthroat kid.

"He's all yours," said the general.

Toby sprinted past Leonardo, making him suck in a breath. But the young Red Flag somehow managed to pass without even touching him. Leonardo steadied himself again as Toby ran to where the second Blue Flag lay slumped, blood running down his forehead from Pinch's slingshot impact.

The general clapped Leonardo on the shoulder as he stepped around him. "Bold move." Then he leaned down and ripped a blue flag off of the kid. The kid vanished instantly, and the general tossed the flag into the wind. A gust grabbed it and flung it into the canopy.

"Onward," he declared jovially.

Leonardo started slowly after him, Moth and Pinch at his heels.

CHAPTER 15

W e're going to let them make the first move this time," whispered the general as they crept across a moss-covered branch to the next tree.

Leonardo caught glimpses of the Nest through gaps in the boughs.

The general glanced at Toby, then leaned closer to Leonardo.

"Context is important here. Olivia's sacrifice was necessary, but I'm not risking his life just to gain a less experienced kid."

Leonardo's mouth hung open as the general climbed ahead.

These kids mean nothing to him. Leonardo set his teeth and kept crawling.

When we return to camp tonight, Toby will be with us. He silently vowed it, watching the general navigate their route to the next tree.

The moss was dry and feathery under Leonardo's hands. This limb was narrower than most of the others they'd traversed, with very few offshoots to use for a foothold. They gripped it with their knees, moving on all fours. Leonardo tried not to look down.

Up ahead, Toby slipped with a gasp. His right arm fell into space, and he struck his chin awkwardly on the mossy branch. He cried out, clinging on in a bear-hug.

"You're ok," said the general over his shoulder. "Keep moving." His tone wasn't unkind but carried enough command that the boy shakily unwrapped his arms and legs.

"Poor kid," said Moth, directly behind Leonardo.

A few minutes later, they reached the next tree, with a tunnel hollowed through its trunk. A curtain of lichen hung over the opening, and the general carefully parted it. He slid a knife from where a leather cord bound it to his leg. Toby followed him.

Leonardo climbed to his feet and curled his fingers around the hilt of his sword. He shouldered the lichen aside, glancing back at Moth and Pinch.

Both of their faces were tight as they followed him into the tree.

"It's clear," called the general.

Leonardo studied the tunnel as he stepped into its half-lit confines. It was perfectly round, curving in an elbow of a path, without a flaw in its symmetry.

Toby ran a pale hand along the smooth wood, red hair flipping this way and that. "The Redwoods are full of tunnels like this," he informed them in his small voice.

Leonardo was willing to bet that whoever created the game imagined them.

But if Kate didn't create it, then who? She'd said the game was ready for them when the first kids arrived...

His next thought stopped him in his tracks.

Were there kids before *Kate and the pirates?*

"What is it?" said Moth. He and Pinch stopped abruptly behind Leonardo.

"Nothing." He couldn't talk with the Red Flags present. "Later," he whispered to his clanmates.

Leonardo's mind spun as he stared at the red-streaked wood, polished like stone. He started moving again, jogging to catch up with the general.

Kate might not even know there were kids before her. If those kids had vanished for some reason, the pirates and other 'first kids' never would have known they were actually the second group.

Except for how they believed they had imagined everything into existence.

Is there any way they could mistake that? Could the real first kids have imagined the woods and the pirates' generation somehow got it wrong?

Did the woods tamper with their memories?

Or could they just be lying?

Or am I missing something? He was missing a lot, he knew that. But something in the timeline didn't add up.

Leonardo's theory was interrupted as they reached the far end of the tunnel. The general pushed aside the curtain of lichen and stepped down, out of sight. The two kids followed him, vanishing from view.

Leonardo glanced at Moth and Pinch, then caught hold of the swinging tendrils and ducked under them. There was no branch at this end of the tunnel. Instead, a colony of giant mushrooms grew from the trunk, tiered like soft white steps.

The enormous, crisscrossing boughs from neighboring trees provided a screen to shelter them. The general stood two mushrooms down, gazing up at Leonardo and tapping his fingers on the bark. The filtered light tinted his face a translucent green.

"That opening is relatively exposed," he told Leonardo. "Just so you know."

Leonardo's focus snapped to the gap between trees. Hundreds more mushrooms and dozens of tunnel openings were visible from his position, along with the entire Nest.

"Let's get down," hissed Moth.

The hairs stood on Leonardo's neck as he quickly lowered himself onto the first mushroom, then dropped to join the general behind the screen of redwood boughs, landing in a half-crouch.

"You'll learn," said the general. "Here, you always have to think about who could be watching you. Because they usually are."

Leonardo believed him. And he was grateful his party had chosen to travel to the Redwoods. Cleopatra, Caliban, and Demetrius were hardly the sort of team he would trust to navigate a place like this. *Although*, he thought, the Highland most likely had its own plethora of challenges. *Puck can handle it*, he told himself. He prayed they could pull this off. It seemed more impossible every time he looked at it too closely.

He pushed aside the doubts as they climbed down to the next mushroom, their feet sinking ever so slightly in the dense caps. In the greenish light, Leonardo felt like he was underwater. The general kept a brisk pace, and when they finally stopped, it was atop a mushroom which had been hollowed out, with a narrow view of the Nest directly across from it.

This work wasn't as flawless as the tree tunnel. This one was obviously dug by hand, and it provided just enough space for the six of them to settle into the spongy trench. Leonardo hesitantly climbed in, half-expecting it to give way under his feet. When it held, he released a bit of breath and knelt alongside Moth and Pinch. The green-tinted wall came up to their chests, and he pressed his hand into the floor of the trench, testing its integrity. Dense fibers resisted his pressure.

A crisscrossing of redwood boughs partly blocked his view, and Leonardo straightened, peering over the greenery at the perfect sphere less than a hundred feet away, wedged in the fork of the next tree. Twigs and leafy vines swung in a gust of wind. He squinted. Through the tight weave of sticks, he thought he could make out a piece of grey fabric. Then something moved, and Leonardo caught a clear glimpse of a girl as she straightened.

"The other one better wake up quick," said Toby. "When I arrived, I vanished the girl in my Nest before she even woke up."

Pinch raised a sidelong eyebrow at Leonardo.

"Charming," muttered Moth.

"The interesting thing," said the general, "is that the woods plant a little thought in every new kid's head. They know that only one of them can survive."

Interesting. Another game. A gruesome one, but it bore the distinct signature of the woods' distasteful palate.

Another shape moved amid the twigs, and the two kids began to circle. The dense weave of the Nest blocked most of Leonardo's view, but he caught glimpses. His heart raced as the reality of the moment caught up with him.

"Can't we go in and help them?" asked Moth. He said it a second before Leonardo could.

The general appraised him. He looked disappointed.

"No. The Nest won't let us in, just like it won't let the survivor out until we free her."

"You think it will be the girl?" asked Toby.

"She would've gotten the weapon since she woke up first."

A heartbeat later, something hit the wall of the Nest from the inside. The sticks and vines moved from the impact.

"Man down," said the general mildly.

Leonardo eyed Moth and Pinch. He felt sick.

"She's trying to get out," said Toby.

Bits of Nest fell from the tree as the glint of a blade hacked through it. For a second, it looked like the girl was going to cut through the side, then new vines snaked over the exterior, rapidly weaving to fill any gaps. Sticks grew like fingers, clutching the Nest tighter and tighter.

The general swore. "Impatient child."

"What are we waiting for?" asked Toby. "Let's go get her."

"We'll let the Blue Flags make the first go. That gives us the upper hand."

The general turned to him, expelling more wisdom, and Leonardo quickly faced Moth and Pinch.

"No more vanishings." He almost breathed the words. They had to find a way to start sparing the kids of both clans without appearing to actively defy the game.

"We miss," replied Pinch, in just as soft of a whisper. "Warning shots."

Leonardo nodded, slipping his own slingshot from his belt.

Moth did the same.

Ten minutes later, Leonardo rolled his neck and placed his elbows on the edge of the mushroom. His slingshot lay on the sloped cap in front of him. Exactly where it had been sitting since they decided to try the warning shot idea.

Something darted through the branches near the Nest. Everyone in the mushroom trench shifted forward.

Leonardo picked up his slingshot and the pebble that had rolled from its pouch. Moth and Pinch did the same. The general raised his blowgun to his mouth.

Leonardo eyed him sidelong, then gave his clanmates the slightest of nods.

Here we go.

The tree branches across from them shook, and a Blue Flag emerged, creeping toward the Nest.

"He's walking straight for it," mused the general, taking his lips away from the blowgun for a second. "Impatient idiot."

That was the moment Leonardo needed. He squinted one eye, drew back his slingshot's pouch, and released it. Pinch and Moth's stones flew a second later.

All three shots hurtled through the air. From their position in the mushroom, the shots were straight enough to look like genuine attempts to hit the Blue Flag. But Leonardo and Moth's stones missed by a foot, thwacking off the next branch up.

Pinch's shot actually hit skin, but it was below his knee, and the kid stumbled, his head jerking up in alarm.

"Shit." The general drew a quick breath and fired a dart, but it was off target.

The kid was already running for shelter. He jumped from limb to limb, then threw himself behind a screen of boughs, just as the general fired a second dart.

A moment later, Leonardo caught a flash of movement as the kid ducked inside a tree tunnel.

"Sorry," said Leonardo, burying his surge of victory as the general punched the mushroom. His fist punctured the soft flesh, leaving a dent in the edge of the trench.

"It's fine." The general fixed his gaze on the Nest. "It's fine."

Before anyone could say another word, a dart stabbed into the mushroom directly between Leonardo and Pinch. Leonardo flinched back. They stared at it, wide-eyed, then another whistled over Leonardo's head. He, Moth, and Pinch dropped flat, just as the general reeled back. In a blur of reflex, he yanked a dart out of his shoulder.

"We have to move," gasped the general. He ducked as another dart hissed through the forest. "Now!"

The general vaulted out of the mushroom and down to the next.

"Go, go, go," Leonardo ushered Toby over the side. He scrambled down, and Leonardo threw himself after.

"If you're hit," called the general, "get it out before the venom can reach your blood."

He wavered and dropped to one knee on the next mushroom. Leonardo jumped down beside him. The general had ripped his dart out quickly, but Leonardo saw the victims at the vine bridge. It didn't take long.

"I'm fine. Keep moving." The general stumbled to his feet and jumped to the next mushroom. The whisk of darts filled the air as they descended lower and lower.

"How many shooters are there?" demanded Pinch. A grunt punctuated his words as he landed on a mushroom and shoved to his feet.

Leonardo spotted another tunnel in the tree, almost completely hidden by thick ivy.

"This way." He grabbed the general's arm and yanked him inside the passage. The others piled after them, and Leonardo steadied the curtain of ivy.

"Will we be safe h—"

"Yes," said the general, through gritted teeth. "We'll stay here until I burn off the poison."

He closed his eyelids and half-collapsed to the floor of the tunnel. Toby stared at him. Moth doubled over, hands on his knees as Pinch flexed his wrist, grimacing. Leonardo slumped against the wall, breathing hard. For a split second, a bead of dried sap turned as black as the Dark, and a shot of fresh adrenaline tensed his muscles. He shifted, and the sap was amber again, crystalized and tinged with white. Nothing but a trick of the light.

Calm down, he told himself. The vision from earlier had him spooked. He was liking the Redwoods less and less by the hour.

CHAPTER 16

The next morning, Leonardo woke with a jolt. Fingers gripped his shoulder, violently shaking his arm. He grabbed for his sword and rolled to face his assailant, blinking away the blurry haze of sleep. Charley's big green eyes gleamed down at him. Her blonde hair spilled out around her paperboy cap. Pompey hovered just behind her, his own green eyes sparking with nervous energy. Someone grunted in their sleep, and Pompey whipped around to locate the noise.

"What is it?" hissed Leonardo. His voice came out hoarse, his heart racing.

"Come see what we found." Charley tried to tug him upright. Despite her urgency, she didn't seem as panicked as her vigorous rousing led him to believe.

He sighed, squinting at her pale face. "What time is it?"

"Almost morning. Come on!" She yanked his arm again.

"Ok, ok." Leonardo straightened quietly among the ranks of his sleeping clanmates.

"What's going on?" Viola asked groggily from the next sleeping roll.

"You can come too!" whispered Charley before Leonardo could utter a word. "You have to see what we found."

Leonardo's senses oriented as his initial alarm evolved to a new unease.

He frowned. "What were you two doing out?"

Sophie yawned from her post near the opening of the hollow. "They've been exploring for my entire shift."

What? Leonardo gripped both kids' shoulders. Pompey let out a soft gasp.

"You're supposed to stay with the group. You can't be—"

"We can't go off on our own in a new, strange place," interrupted Charley. "Ok, ok, we promise. Now will you follow us? Hurry up!"

She ducked out of his grip and ran through the opening of the hollow, out into the rounded wooden passageway.

Still scowling, Leonardo slipped around Sophie, who yawned again. Viola stumbled after them into the soft glow of a fairy cage hanging from the corridor ceiling.

"This way." Pompey took the lead now, down a dizzying series of twists and turns until they came to a doorway deep inside the trunk. It radiated the light of a summer day, and Leonardo touched the glowing red wood as he stepped into the circular room. The whirring hum of energy vibrated the air.

Are we in the heart of the tree?

Viola clutched his arm. "Leo. Look up."

Leonardo tilted his head back and froze. Dozens upon dozens of cages hung from carved hooks, packed to the whittled bars with fairies. Hundreds of wings beat the air, echoing tenfold off the walls.

What the…

The conical ceiling spiraled up to a perfectly circular opening, several stories above the floor. The cages were suspended like a grand chandelier in the middle of it all.

They're prisoners.

He recalled Kate's cabin on *The Forever*. She'd told him that she dreamed the chandelier on purpose.

As a reminder of home?

"Are those stairs?" asked Viola. She crossed to a narrow zig-zagging ledge that started near the floor and spiraled up the rounded wall to the ceiling opening.

Who would climb that? It was steep and hand-carved and treach-erous enough to promise no forgiveness for a misstep.

"Yes!" said Charley. "The general sleeps up there."

Leonardo and Viola both snapped around to see her. She and Pompey stood in the exact center of the room, their faces alight with fairy glow.

"Keep your voice down," hissed Viola, her eyes on the open-ing.

"You went up there?" whispered Leonardo. The noise of the fairies masked their voices, but unease crept up his spine regard-less.

Pompey went stock-still. Charley half-nodded before stopping herself.

130

"Did he see you?" asked Viola.

Both kids shook their heads.

"He was asleep," said Pompey.

Leonardo gazed up at the hole, the wooden edge cast in sharp relief from the lights.

"Let's go." He took the kids by the shoulders again and propelled them out of the room. Charley tried to say something, and he shushed her until they had rounded the next bend, then two more. By the time he let her speak, his fear had evolved into a new realization.

The fairies could help us.

"They're crammed so tight in those cages." Pompey spoke first. "They can barely move."

"We have to save them, Leo!" Charley urged.

"I know," said Leonardo. The location of their prison made them eavesdroppers to every private conversation the general had. Freeing them could be the most important—and treacherous— step his party took.

***

At daybreak, Leonardo, Mishti, and Viola joined the general on a foraging trip. A hard rain sizzled through the treetops as he divided the patrols inside the dry warmth of the tree.

Me, Mishti, and Viola, thought Leonardo, the wheels turning in his mind. Sophie, Cato, and Moth were placed on a patrol together. Juliet, Will, and Bates on another. He watched the general split up everyone with strong ties. Except for his trio.

They were observing us yesterday. So why place me with Mishti and Viola? His co-leader and girlfriend. Also, for the second day in a row, the general had paired Leonardo with himself.

131

He's keeping me close.

"Ok," called the general. "Ranging teams, let's move out."

Grim faces met his words. All of the Raven Clan boys had worked rainy patrols in the Darkwoods. Spending hours out in the cold, in drenched clothes without a fire to warm themselves was not a prospect that appealed to anyone. Leonardo hoped the canopy would be dense enough to provide them some shelter.

"*What* are we doing again?" asked Mishti under her breath.

"Foraging," replied Leonardo and Viola.

"Collecting food," Leonardo elaborated.

"Some clans don't get food magically delivered to their doorstep," said Pinch.

"Shut up," said Mishti. "We had to collect our own food too."

"From your orchard," said Bates. "And your chicken coop."

Mishti crossed her arms.

"Ok, guys," said Leonardo.

They weren't the ones who had to spend the rest of the day with her.

Both boys rolled their eyes.

"Brace yourself," called Jack. "Here comes the rain."

A little ahead of Leonardo, he flipped up the collar of his tailcoat and ducked outside. Behind him, Cato pulled the back of his shirt up, stretching it over his head like the world's worst umbrella and exposing a broad swath of his pale back.

Beside him, Sophie and Bates frowned up at the absurdity of it. Then recoiled when Cato peered down at them, his face squished through the neck opening of his shirt.

"Jesus," said Bates. "You look like an idiot."

"Well…you look like…a head." Cato made a face at him and

continued up the stairs. Sophie frowned at him with unconcealed alarm.

Welcome to the strangest day of your life, thought Leonardo.

"A *head*?" demanded Bates, jogging after him. "My head looks like a head?"

"An *ugly* head," said Cato.

Leonardo couldn't suppress his grin. Next to him, Mishti and Viola watched with incredulity.

"Oh, I see." Bates didn't let up. "So, I look like an ugly head. Wow, Cato, you've really sharpened that wit, haven't you?"

"You two," called Leonardo. "That's enough."

"Aye-aye boss." Bates drew himself up as he approached the opening. "Into the rain!"

Cato narrowed his eyes at Leonardo.

Leonardo raised an eyebrow, then he shrugged. "Bates's head does look like a head; you're not wrong."

"An ugly head," repeated Cato.

"If you say so. Fix your shirt. It's not going to protect you from the rain."

Cato flared his nostrils, then he grunted and started back up the steps, tugging his shirt off his head. It fell loosely across his shoulders, stretched out now.

"Nicely done." Viola eyed Leonardo appraisingly.

"He seems...difficult," said Mishti mildly.

"Cato is *unique*," said Leonardo as his big clanmate ducked through the opening, out into the rain. Leonardo had missed him. The realization surprised him, and he tilted his head, studying Cato and Jack and the others.

A hard shower pierced the canopy, drumming against the side

133

of the tree. Leonardo enjoyed his last moment of warmth, then he stepped out into the gloom.

***

Redwood boughs swung in the downpour, their needles rustling as water poured off the ends of branches. The browns and greens were dark and vibrant, the smells of the forest rich and pungent and permeated by the fresh, sweet zing of ozone. The icy rain masked the treetops and distant branches in a haze.

Leonardo was soaked. Water ran down his face, and his clothes hung heavy. Viola's and Mishti's hair was plastered to their foreheads. They utilized the tunnels where they could, but the treetops offered far less shelter than the forest floor.

The general didn't speak much as he led the way from tree to tree on a path that felt entirely random. Any time Leonardo spotted a unique feature or opening, it would merge in his mind with a dozen others just like it, and within ten minutes, he had no faith left in his ability to recognize it again.

They climbed and crawled and edged along narrow ledges for over an hour. Leonardo, Mishti, and Viola exchanged tight expressions. He hadn't spotted anything edible thus far.

In their day and a half here, the Red Flags had fed them a wide variety of fruits, berries, vegetables, and strips of salty dried meat. Leonardo had no idea where they collected it all.

He studied the forest floor as they trekked high above it, but ferns and smaller trees dominated everything in sight. He couldn't spot a single fruit-bearing plant.

"Why do they live so far from their food?" whispered Viola.

"Yesterday," replied Leonardo, one eye on the general, "he said they move their camp constantly."

"Still doesn't explain why they moved it into the middle of nowhere," said Mishti.

Keeping a camp near the main resources would be a risky move. If the Blue Flags frequented the area, too, it would increase their likelihood of being discovered. He glanced over his shoulder, but only the swinging boughs followed them as he stepped into the glorious shelter of a tree tunnel. They had traversed dozens of them today, but Leonardo still enjoyed the brief quiet as the dense trunk muted the downpour. He shivered, ringing out the corner of his shirt.

Viola staggered a bit, closing her eyes as she leaned against the wall of the trunk.

"This patrol sucks," said Mishti.

"General," called Leonardo. The general glanced back, his dark skin cast darker in the shadows of the tunnel. "Can we stay here a bit?"

The general regarded them. His eyes lingered for a second on Viola and Mishti and their saturated clothes. Leonardo tightened his jaw. He had a growing desire to punch the other kid in the face.

"Of course," said the general after a beat. "I forget your muscles aren't used to this."

"Do you have to live so far from your food?" demanded Mishti. "Seems like a stupid choice to me."

The general simply grinned. "Sometimes we live closer. But those camps are easier for the Blue Flags to find. The further we travel, the harder it is to track us."

"Is that why all the foraging parties split up?" asked Viola, shivering.

Leonardo put an arm around her.

The general took notice, though he glanced away quickly. He nodded. "Harder to track small groups. Now, if you can all handle a few more steps, our destination lies at the far end of this tunnel."

"Really?" said Leonardo. *Finally.* Soured mood or not, he was very curious to see what they had traveled all this way to find.

"Let's go," said Mishti. "This had better be good."

Leonardo glanced at Viola, but she was already straightening. She placed a hand on his chest and nodded. "Let's go."

Water ran down Leonardo's back and dripped off his clothes as they traversed the tunnel. The space grew darker by the second until it was pitch black. The drumming of rain from up ahead guided Leonardo as he slid his fingertips along the smooth wall. The tunnel curved until the grey-lit opening came into view, and the forest beyond appeared no different from any other stretch of the Redwoods they'd seen today. Leonardo frowned at Viola and Mishti, then they reached the opening, and he stopped in his tracks.

"Welcome to the sky gardens," said the general.

CHAPTER 17

A second forest grew from the branches of the Redwoods. Thickets of berry bushes and dense underbrush filled the arms of the canopy, lush and vibrant in the rain. Trees grew from the thick mat of soil that rolled and sloped ahead of them, heavy with ripe fruit. Leonardo gazed up into the branches of an apple tree as they picked their way through the impossible landscape.

"The soil is created from rotting plants." The general ran a hand through a thicket of ferns as tall as his shoulder. "When they die, they keep this place alive."

"And the roots of the trees hold it all together," said Viola, wonder in her voice. "Look, Leo."

She pointed up to where another tier of the garden grew from a crook in the branches above. Thick roots snaked underneath the mass of soil, tying one redwood branch to the next and forming a sort of rigid web for the plant life atop to grow from. That phenomenon allowed for a wide, sprawling garden rather than one that clung only to the branches.

Leonardo and his foraging party no longer needed to navigate the mossy bridges of redwood boughs. They could simply walk across the massive expanse of greenery. It looked as if it had been cut from the forest floor and dropped into the arms of the redwoods.

He never would have ever imagined that trees could grow from trees, but it was far from the strangest thing he'd witnessed in this impossible dreamworld. A plum tree grew from a tangle of blackberry bushes as if it were the most ordinary thing in the world. The rain thinned to a gentle shower, and birds chirped from the shelter of the dense leaves. A silver jay landed on a twisted stump. Leonardo stepped closer and froze. Beyond the stump, a gaping hole opened to the true forest floor below. An ancient log lay in the ruddy soil, a dizzying drop from his position. He looked up, across the canyon, to where the garden continued in the next tree, and the tree beyond it, as far as he could see.

Leonardo backed up from the drop, fighting a wave of vertigo. A chipmunk raced down their host tree, paused to eye the four intruders, then tore back up the trunk.

This place is teeming with life. Even insects buzzed through the dry spaces beneath the apple and plum trees. Evergreen huckleberry bushes swayed and shifted in the more exposed reaches of the treetop forest.

"How big is it?" asked Viola.

"Miles," said the general. "We could walk for the rest of the day and still never find the far side."

Leonardo, Viola, and Mishti gazed around.

Miles. The Cove was massive, filled with beautiful coastlines and an island of turquoise caves. The Redwoods was a vast, sprawling forest of mammoth trees and gardens in the sky. It reminded him again of the disparity between the Darkwoods and everything else.

Why? Were the kids who created the Darkwoods so much less imaginative?

The Darkwoods can't be so dramatically different for no reason.

"Still have your sacks?" The general glanced to where they'd each strung a burlap sack through their belts. In Viola's case, it was looped through a leather cord in her dress.

"Good," he continued. "Let's start gathering. Anything edible goes in the sack."

"What about meat?" asked Leonardo. Anything they hunted would spoil long before they made it back to camp. "What kind of animals do you hunt here?"

"Deer and rabbits mostly. A lot of them live up here in the treetops. You won't see them," he added when Leonardo and the girls looked around. "They have incredible camouflage."

"How did they get up here?" asked Viola.

The general shrugged. "Why is anything what it is in these woods? To catch them, we have to lay in wait for an hour or more."

Leonardo shuddered. He was chilled to the bone already. Staying in motion was all that kept him warm.

"Not to worry. We can't build a cooking fire in the treetops, and it's too dangerous to visit the ground more often than we have to. So, once a month, we hunt, cook the meat, cover it in salt, and it lasts us a few weeks."

"Where do you get the salt?" asked Mishti, at the same time that Leonardo asked, "What's so dangerous on the ground?"

"From the saltspring. And I'll show you," he added to Leonardo.

He led them back to the stump where the jay had been, then pointed down to the forest floor. "See how exposed that is?"

"The Blue Flags could sit up here and shoot at you," realized Leonardo. If it was the general on the ground, Leonardo would have half a mind to join them.

"And there would be nothing we could do about it. Whenever we go down, we leave scouts in the trees above to protect us, but it's still dangerous."

Leonardo swallowed, scanning the shadowed corners of the gardens.

"Now you're getting it." The general patted his back. "Never stop checking over your shoulder."

"This place is so big," said Viola. "If we move deeper in, we would limit their chances of finding us."

"She's smart." The general grinned at Leonardo. "I like her."

His tone spiked Leonardo's nerves. But not for the reason he expected. It sounded lighthearted, but an undercurrent of intensity buzzed just below the surface.

He's still analyzing us. And in a different way than Leonardo and Mishti had sized each other up in their first few days. The general was a seasoned player in whatever twisted game the Redwoods were trapped in. A clockwork of calculations spun behind his eyes.

He's figuring out how to manipulate each of us. And how we'll each try to manipulate him.

"I think," said Mishti tightly. "That the longer we spend talking, the longer we expose ourselves to attack."

Her gaze darted to Leonardo and back to the general.

She sees it too.

The general smiled. "Astute observation. Then let's start gathering. And moving deeper into the sky gardens as we do it," he added to Viola.

Leonardo kept one eye on the general as they fanned out into the underbrush. The general glanced at him, his eye contact lingering as he pulled apples from a tree.

When they reached the Cove, Leonardo remembered thinking they'd come to a dangerous place.

Into the Lion's den, he thought now. But the Redwoods were something else entirely. *A spider's web.* And every one of the thirteen Ravens and Lions would have to stay perfectly sharp to avoid getting trapped in it.

He spotted a tangle of vicious-looking brambles lined with rows of barbed thorns. Hundreds of dark purple berries gleamed from between the wet leaves.

"Viola," he called. "Help me with these."

She jogged over, glanced to make sure Mishti and the general were busy picking fruit, then leaned up and gave him a quick kiss.

Leonardo closed his eyes and enjoyed it for a millisecond.

"What's wrong?" Viola asked under her breath. "You look panicked."

Back to reality.

"See," said Leonardo, at a regular volume. "There are tons of them."

141

He reached into the brambles and winced as a thorn stabbed him in the finger.

"We need to get into the game," he said under his breath.

"What do you mean?" whispered Viola. Then louder, "Put them in my sack. We'll put the bigger fruit in yours so it doesn't crush them."

"Yesterday," he replied softly. "I was on a patrol to find new recruits. Today, I'm gathering food. We're wasting time. We need to get into the *game* if we're going to figure out how to end it. He doesn't trust me. Ow!"

He pricked himself on another thorn.

"You need to be more careful," said Viola, laughing. It sounded forced, but the general was busy collecting plums and didn't seem to notice.

"Ask him," she whispered. "Say you want to join the fight. You're from a fighting clan. He'll believe that."

"You think?"

Leonardo couldn't risk raising the general's suspicion.

"You're right," said Viola. "We need to make a move. We can't sit back and wait for things to happen."

Leonardo nodded.

"Yesterday," whispered Viola. "I helped supervise the kids' training. They chase fairies through the trees and try to catch them. It's weird. Mishti was on 'camp patrol,' so she never even left the tree."

Leonardo frowned. "I think Bates's patrol and maybe Jack's went hunting for Blue Flags, but we need more than that."

"Ow!" said Viola. "I'm bleeding."

She most certainly was not bleeding.

"He was looking," she breathed.

"Do you want to leave those for someone else?" called the general. "Sounds like you're struggling."

"We're fine," called Leonardo. He forced a laugh. "Just clumsy."

"Suit yourself."

The general crossed to a patch of something vining, although Leonardo could tell he was watching them in his peripheral.

"Oh, look, a squirrel." Viola pointed to where a black squirrel paused, halfway around the trunk of an evergreen tree sprouting from the redwood's branch.

Leonardo sighed. *We need somewhere safe to talk.* They wouldn't solve anything with this broken conversation.

"Leonardo," called Mishti. "You're from a forest. Are these mushrooms poisonous?"

"We'll talk later," he whispered to Viola, then he crossed to where Mishti crouched in the ferns.

Over the next three hours, they filled the sacks with everything from wild carrots to fresh herbs, blueberries, lemons, and several heads of cabbage that Leonardo found. The sky gardens continued to surprise them with an endless reserve of life. The rain stopped after a time, and butterflies as big as the ones from the Darkwoods flapped past, stirring the air. Legions of strange mushrooms and colorful fungi coated entire trees, and thousands of flowers sprouted through the moss. Frogs chirped from the red bark of the trees, their slick skin vibrantly patterned in shades of yellow, red, and blue.

In their three hours of foraging, they never encountered a single kid from either clan, despite the fact that the general estimated at least a dozen parties were in this part of the woods.

We're smaller than flies here.

They spent another twenty minutes gathering before the general called a halt.

Good, thought Leonardo. He'd been lugging around his sack long enough. He was ready to get back to camp.

"But first," said the general. The warmth drained from his voice. "I assume you figured out that I picked you three for a reason."

A pit clenched in Leonardo's stomach.

"Take a seat."

CHAPTER 18

A woodpecker landed on a stump a few feet from Leonardo. Its black, red, and white feathers ruffled as a gust of wind carried droplets of moisture.

"Damn," said Mishti. "It's starting to rain again."

"Then we'll keep this short," said the general. "I just want some answers about your clans' intentions."

"I'm confused," said Viola. "Why am I here? Leo and Mishti are leaders, but I'm—"

"Influential to Leonardo."

Viola paused.

"Am I wrong?" he asked.

She glanced at Leonardo.

Don't say a word about se-coms or Kate, he silently pleaded her and Mishti.

"No. You're not wrong." Leonardo edged closer, putting

himself between the general and his clanmates. "So we're all here; what do you want to know?"

"How did you get to the Redwoods?" asked the general.

"We're going to be here awhile," said Mishti. "I can smell it."

She waved the woodpecker off the stump and sat down, unceremoniously depositing her sack of food on the moss beside her.

"We already told you everything," said Leonardo. "The Cove, and the Dark, and——"

"No." The general ran his fingers over an apple branch, then snapped the tip. "I mean, literally, how did you travel here? On foot?"

"Oh." That was a tougher question. Mostly because the truth sounded too strange to be true.

"With a magic spell," said Viola simply.

She leaned her sack of berries against her leg and crossed her arms.

"A magic spell?" The general flicked the branch tip away and eyed Leonardo skeptically. A pair of still-attached leaves spun like a parachute, slowing its descent as it floated through a hole and out of the sky gardens.

"It's true," said Leonardo. There was nothing to gain by lying. As much as he didn't like the general, he *did* need to get him on their side.

"We put a bunch of crocodile skulls in a circle," added Mishti. "Then we stood inside it and...poof."

The general raised his dark eyebrows.

"She's not lying," said Leonardo.

To the general's credit, he didn't question them.

"So you tapped into the magic of the woods. Using crocodile skulls. Interesting."

"Do you have any other questions?" asked Leonardo.

"Several. Such as, why do you think that gaining our help will allow you to defeat your '*Dark*'? You're putting yourselves in danger by playing the game, just to gain a few more kids in your army."

That was an easier answer.

"Because it's the only hope we have left."

The general nodded. "Hmm. You think you'll die anyway, so why not at least give it a shot?"

"*Everyone* will die," said Mishti. "Not just us."

"So you say. I also wonder, wouldn't it be more beneficial to gain both us *and* the Blue Flags? You're helping us vanish kids who could help you."

Leonardo glanced at Mishti and Viola.

Does he suspect we're trying to spare both sides?

"If we could do that, we would." Mishti wrung out the corner of her robe. "But we don't have time to negotiate."

Thank you. Her excuse was rock solid, and the general only studied her for a second before nodding.

"So you take what you can get. By helping us win the game, at least your army grows a bit."

"That's the idea," said Leonardo.

"Good." He worked out a stiff muscle in his side. "That puts my mind at ease."

It didn't put Leonardo's mind at ease. The general had accepted their answers far too quickly. Based on everything Leonardo knew about leaders, and this leader specifically, he highly doubted the general trusted them an inch more than he already had.

"Here in the Redwoods," continued the general, "everyone is loyal to one side or the other. There are only two options."

He definitely suspects something.

A raindrop splatted on Leonardo's head. Mishti glanced up at the sky.

"Are we good then?" asked Viola. "Can we go before this gets worse?"

"After one last question." The general looked them each in the eye. "Are you ready to die?"

"What?" said Mishti and Viola.

"Excuse me?" said Leonardo.

"If you're going to play the game, there's a good chance you'll be vanished. Or some of your clanmates will. Especially your youngest ones. Only half of our new recruits survive a month. If you act emotionally instead of rationally, you will put yourself and others in greater danger."

Leonardo balled his fists. He'd accepted earlier that there would be casualties. That didn't mean he would let Charley and Pompey be put in danger or that he would stand by as his clanmates were vanished. On the stump, Mishti drew her lips tight. Viola stared the general in the eye.

She'd gotten bold since he first met her. The girl who hid in the trees when Cato shouted from the clinker was no longer recognizable.

"You've already taken flags," said the general. "It's too late to turn back now, but I need to know I can trust you to play the game right."

148

"We accept the risk," said Viola. Her brown eyes were steeled, but he saw through to the fear underneath. Fear of the game, of the Dark, of the hopelessness of their position.

He squared his jaw. *We control our own fate. We'll survive the game; we'll survive the Dark; we'll survive everything.*

And for that brief moment, he actually believed it.

"I'm from a fighting clan," said Leonardo. "The risk of vanishing is nothing new. We accept the risk," he echoed. "Can you trust us now?"

The general smiled. "You have more spirit than I realized. Yes, I trust you."

"Good," said Leonardo. He glanced at Viola, remembering her advice. Then he faced the general. "Because tomorrow, I want to play the game."

CHAPTER 19

Darkness pressed a blindfold against Leonardo's eyes as he crept down the stairwell. But it was a mindless dark, the natural kind inside a hollowed-out tree. The malevolent Dark had still yet to show itself, which clawed at the inside of his stomach like a warning of something he didn't know how to prepare for.

He pushed that stress aside. *One thing at a time.* They just had to deal with each obstacle fast enough to beat the next one's punch.

Mishti, Kate, Viola, and Pinch's shallow breathing filled the space as they silently descended the steps.

A few minutes later, Kate stopped them. "This should be far enough."

"Guess what," whispered Pinch.

"What?" Leonardo whispered after a beat when it became obvious Pinch was awaiting a prompt.

"I imagined night vision goggles. Just now, with my hat."

"Seriously?" whispered Viola.

"Do they work?" asked Leonardo.

"Yessir," whispered Pinch. "I can see all your ugly faces crystal clear."

"Excuse me?" said Kate and Mishti in sync.

"Sorry," said Pinch. "Force of habit."

Kate hmphed.

"Can you make sure no one followed us then?" asked Viola. "I don't see anyone, but I don't completely trust my gift."

"Give me a sec," replied Pinch. "Actually, wait…" Fabric rustled, and something clunked.

"What are you doing?" asked Leonardo.

"Here," whispered Pinch.

Leonardo recoiled as something heavy thumped against his chest.

"Take them, halfwit," hissed Pinch. "They're boots, not snakes."

"You could have warned me." Leonardo took Pinch's ratty boots from him.

"That's no fun. 'K, I'll be right back."

Pinch's departure was silent on sock feet. Leonardo held the limp leather footwear at arm's-length, trying valiantly to ignore the waft of rankness.

"You know," whispered Mishti. "He could've made everyone a pair of goggles."

"It's Pinch," said Viola. "That's not how he thinks."

"And now," said Kate. "He can't make any more, because that pair's existence prevents it."

"He's an idiot," said Mishti.

Leonardo bristled. "He's…"

In truth, he wasn't sure exactly *what* Pinch was.

"It's fine," said Viola. "We have one pair. That's all we need."

"Hmph," said Kate again.

A few minutes later, someone blew air hard in Leonardo's ear.

"Ow! Dammit." Leonardo reeled back as socks scuffed on the stairs.

Pinch.

"Boo!" said Pinch, his voice now a few feet away. "The ghost is back!"

Mishti and Kate both swore.

Pinch laughed. "For the visually impaired, I am directly between their heads."

"Move," said Mishti. "And focus. It's the middle of the night. We're here for a reason."

"She's right," said Leonardo. "We need to talk about the general."

"He's a psycho," said Pinch.

"Correct," said Mishti.

Leonardo frowned.

Yeah, but he's clever too.

"If you had to make the call right now," Leonardo asked them. "What would you suggest we do?"

"You're talking to the wall," said Pinch.

"What?"

"You're facing the wall," said Pinch. "It's funny."

The girls sighed, exasperation heavy on their breath.

Focus, Pinch.

He turned toward Pinch's voice. "Well then, what would you suggest we do? You're a se-com."

"Well," Pinch didn't miss a beat, "I'd put an end to all these weird-ass patrols. I guarantee that Bates, Cato, and Sophie aren't talking strategy. Do they even know each other's names?"

Outside the thick wall of the trunk, waving branches scraped the bark. It didn't startle Leonardo this time; evidence he'd been in the Redwoods long enough to acclimatize. The ticking clock in his mind spun faster.

"That's what the general wants," Mishti replied to Pinch's question.

"Exactly," said Pinch. "Get me on a patrol with Butterfly and Bates. Stop letting him split us all up, and we'll figure shit out."

Huh. That was Leonardo's same instinct. But if the general was as good a mind reader as he seemed, he would be anticipating that request.

"The general's trying to figure out how we think," said Leonardo. "So we need to start thinking differently. If we try to arrange the patrols in our favor, we'll lose the general's trust."

"So we let him split us up?" asked Viola. She squeezed his arm in a way that said, *I don't think that's such a good idea.*

"Yes," said Leonardo. He placed a hand on top of hers. "And we use the opportunity to relay information. If he's constantly shuffling the patrols, he's giving us a chance to spread information throughout the party without looking suspicious in camp."

"Because the people who spend time together in camp," mused Mishti, "will be different from the ones who're on patrol together." The throwing rings clanked softly on her wrists.

153

"Exactly," said Leonardo. "We just need to be careful and only talk when the Red Flags on our patrols are out of earshot."

Nerves prickled his skin. The organic smell of the tree suffocated his senses. For a dizzying second, he thought he caught a whiff of the rotten taint that preceded the Dark, but it was gone as quick as he'd noticed it. Memories of his vision shot to the surface.

Not yet, he pleaded. *Please not yet.*

"We still need to gain their trust," said Kate. "Now that you have red flags, we won't be able to join the Blue Flags if this fails. Our only option is to keep the Red Flags' support. "

"Do you still have two flags?" asked Leonardo. He drew a breath of cedary air to clear the lingering memory of the Dark's rancidness burning at the back of his throat.

"Yup," said Kate. "I tied them together. I don't want half of me vanishing or something stupid."

"You really think your flag can vanish you?" asked Viola. "Surely you haven't kept it by your side every second for a hundred years."

Kate didn't reply.

John, Pip, and Cyrus vanished. Times were changing.

"Ok," said Leonardo. "Here's our plan. I'll keep the general occupied and not vanishing Blue Flags. While he's distracted with me, everyone else search for cracks in his clan. If we can convince enough of them that they'll be vanished without our help—"

"Convince them how?" interrupted Pinch. "It's not like we carry a handful of Dark in our pockets."

"Wait." An idea struck Leonardo. "Pinch, that's it!"

Pinch frowned.

"Maybe not in our pockets, but in your *hat.* You can imagine something 'infected by the Dark.'"

"That might just work." Mishti's thick hair swished. "We can stage it, so it appears right in front of them."

Wicked glee tinted Pinch's voice. "It'll have to be big. *Really* big."

"The general will be skeptical," said Leonardo. "But if it scares enough of them, we can force a mutiny."

"A mutiny?" Kate laughed. "You spent too much time on *The Forever.*"

A charged silence followed her words.

"*Meanwhile,*" said Viola frostily. "Moth should be talking to the fairies. We can't forget what Charley and Pompey showed us this morning."

Leonardo nodded in the darkness. The fairies could hold a trove of information. The location of their cages made them privy to all conversations in the general's quarters. Every leader had a weakness. The moment Leonardo knew the general's, he could exploit it.

"If Moth can get information from the fairies," agreed Leonardo, "they could give us everything else we need to overthrow the general. Then we march in force to the Blue Flag camp."

They would need to free the fairies at the exact right moment. In the meantime, they could still glean information while leaving the cages—and their ruse of cooperation—intact.

"So it's a three-pronged plan," said Mishti. "Work the general. Work his clan. Work the fairies."

Leonardo nodded again. "Pinch, I'll need you ready—"

"At the drop of a *hat?*" Pinch chuckled at his own wit.

"Jesus Christ." Moth groaned.

"…by tomorrow evening." Leonardo finished. "We'll do it as soon as all the patrols come in."

He trusted Pinch's creativity and understanding of his hat's capabilities. If anyone could dream up an idea to traumatize their hosts, it would be Pinch.

"Sounds easy enough," said Sophie dryly.

It sounds anything but easy. But it was a plan.

We'll win this. He had to believe that, otherwise his doubts would crush him. The only question was: *will it be fast enough?*

"Let's get back to the hollow," said Leonardo. "We've been gone a while."

"I'll go first," said Pinch. "All you blind mice follow me."

CHAPTER 20

The next day, Leonardo intercepted Charley and Pompey running down a passage, swords swinging at their hips.

"Woah," he called, raising his hands to halt them.

Both kids skittered to a stop, their faces flushed. A few fairies flitted around their heads. The first noncaptive ones he'd seen.

Leonardo frowned.

They wouldn't—

Free them? He countered his own thought. *Of course they would.*

He recalled making it explicitly clear that no one was to free any fairies yet. He glanced around for eavesdroppers, then looked the kids in the eye. "You remember what I told you, right?"

Charley picked up his implication immediately, which did little to ease his suspicions. Her gaze darted to the fairies, and she nodded emphatically.

"These ones were free already."

Pompey nodded in agreement, his eyes wide.

"Ok," said Leonardo slowly. "Good."

He wasn't entirely convinced. Actually, he was more convinced that he would find an abandoned cage tossed down some shadowy passage if he went searching.

Leonardo opened his mouth to question them harder.

"The general is looking for you," said Charley.

Leonardo's breath snagged. "Why?"

Both kids shrugged.

Leonardo's stomach tightened. "Where is he?"

***

Twenty minutes later, he found himself on the smallest patrol he'd joined yet; just himself and the general, picking their way through the treetops.

"Sorry to pull you out here so abruptly," said the general.

Leonardo ducked under a swinging redwood bough, bearing a cone big enough to knock him unconscious. The stiff, woody spines gleamed with sap.

He awaited a further explanation, but none appeared forthcoming.

Fine. He didn't need one. It was obvious the general intended to keep him on edge. Luckily, that was nothing new for Leonardo, who'd grown up with Aleksander for a brother and leader.

Test me all you want.

"At least it's not raining today." Leonardo gazed into the canopy, where dappled morning sunlight pierced the evergreens.

"It's a good day for hunting." The general straightened the blowgun on his back. "The last time the weather was this nice, I took down twenty Blue Flags."

Twenty.

158

Twenty kids who wouldn't be able to help them fight the Dark. And twenty more if the general had his way today. Leonardo had a feeling that warning shots wouldn't be enough this time.

"The objective is simple," said the general. "Hunt them, stalk them, vanish them."

"Stalk them?" asked Leonardo.

The general nodded. "They'll be hunting us too. If we rush out and attack a Blue Flag, we could be ambushed. Just follow my lead. We'll both survive. Plus, if we're lucky, they'll lead us back to their camp."

Leonardo tightened his lips and pulled himself up to the next branch.

We're going on a killing patrol, and I need to keep everyone alive.

It was an impossible position. Make noise to alert their victims, and his own patrol could very quickly become the hunted. Make any attempt at sabotage, and the general would see through it in an instant. And just to up the ante, if the general was lost in a skirmish, Leonardo would be on precarious ground, returning to camp without him.

The general glanced back as if sensing Leonardo's eyes on him, and Leonardo quickly shifted his focus elsewhere, studying the motionless boughs hanging dense around them. The sharp tang of the redwoods, overpowering in his first two days, was becoming familiar enough that he had to concentrate to notice it.

A chipmunk tore across a branch over Leonardo's head, its tail flicking as it paused to study something, then raced out of sight.

"Let's pick it up a bit," said the general. "I'm getting a bad feeling here."

159

Leonardo checked over his shoulder. The shadows looked more sinister than they had a moment ago. They ducked inside a tunnel through the trunk of a redwood, creeping into near blackness. The tunnel curved in the heart of the tree, and for a few seconds, both openings were hidden from view. In that pocket, Leonardo couldn't even see the general's cape, a foot in front of him.

Someone gasped. A girl cried out. Leonardo caught his breath. Something thudded hard in the darkness, then something else.

"What's happening?" Leonard rushed forward and caught the swish of fabric just in time. He recoiled as something swung past his face. The wind tousled his hair. Another grunt, a hard thump, then the distinct crack of a head striking the tunnel's wooden wall.

Leonardo clenched his fingers around his sword, but he didn't draw it for risk of injuring the general.

Why is it so dark everywhere? These pitch-black trees were infuriating.

A short struggle followed. Boots scuffed, voices grunted, a fist connected with flesh, and a heavy thud made him jump. Silence spread like an oil spill. Someone's ragged breathing echoed off the walls. Leonardo's heart pounded, and he fought to hold his breath and not reveal his location. He took a careful step backward.

"You still here?" asked the general.

"Here," said Leonardo.

"Good." The general swore. "She packed a punch. Help me drag these two out into the light. Let's see if they're ours or if we're lucky."

"You mean...they might be Red Flags?" Leonardo heard the

horror in his own voice. *They could be anyone.* The girl could be Viola, or Mishti, or Kate—

"Relax," said the general. "I can't kill them, remember? They still have their flags. If they're ours, they'll recover and be good as new."

Leonardo swallowed the bitter taste in his mouth and edged forward, trying not to panic as he crouched and felt for the unconscious kids. His fingers brushed over warm skin, and he jumped.

Calm down, he told himself. He reached out again and felt hair, then touched something slick pooling on the girl's face.

Shit. Shit, that's blood.

He shut his eyes. *Stop panicking.*

He reached out again and continued down until he found her shoulders, then angled himself behind her head and lifted her under the arms. The coarse fabric of her shirt didn't feel like anything the girls in his alliance wore, which allowed Leonardo to release a little of his breath.

"Let's go," said the general. He started down the tunnel, the second kid's heels dragging with a disturbing scrape. Leonardo shivered and straightened, struggling with the deadweight.

They reached the far end of the tunnel, where enough light filtered through the screen of evergreen needles to identify that neither the boy nor the girl belonged to any of their clans. They looked to be around thirteen or fifteen years old, with matching blue flags tied around their arms.

"Cocky," said the general. "Didn't even hide them."

He ripped the flag off the boy's arm, then leaned over and yanked off the girl's before Leonardo could react. One second, he was supporting her weight, then she was gone.

The general eyed the two flags, then crossed to the tunnel's opening and dropped them out of sight. Leonardo's hands shook a bit. He'd seen scores of kids vanish, but he'd never been holding one when it happened. He could still feel her weight on his arms, like a ghost.

"It's clear." The general leaned out the opening. "Let's move."

He shoved an evergreen bough aside and jumped out of sight. Leonardo swallowed the bile in his throat and hurried after him. A few seconds later, they were jogging along a thick branch, hunched low to keep out of sight.

"Get down!" The general threw himself against the branch.

Leonardo dropped to his stomach, blood roaring in his ears. The general whipped his blowgun off his back, using his elbows to crawl through the moss.

"Look," he mumbled around the mouthpiece.

A smaller treetop garden grew from the branches of a neighboring tree, about fifteen feet lower than Leonardo's current position. At first, he didn't spot anything except the ferns and the berry bushes. Songbirds flitted from the underbrush, and a giant butterfly flapped past.

"Where are they?" he whispered.

"Just wait," whispered the general. "They're hiding."

Dragonflies zipped through the tiny landscape cradled in the treetops. A breeze stirred the leathery leaves of the blackberry bushes. Tree branches swished and scraped, and then someone moved.

Leonardo caught a flash of fabric as a kid darted through the underbrush. He tracked their movement and glimpsed the boy again as he ran, hunched low, to a plum tree. A burlap sack hung from his hip.

"Foragers," said the general. "They won't be very well armed, but they'll have other kids protecting them."

Leonardo scanned the nearby trees. The vines that hid his position also impeded his view, but that wasn't necessarily a bad thing.

"We shouldn't shoot then," he whispered to the general. "Until we know where they all are."

The general nodded. "We need to find them. Follow me."

Leonardo swore under his breath. He needed to stall.

"Look up there!" He pointed to a branch in the next tree over, high above them and densely shrouded in greenery. "I just saw people."

"Are you sure?" asked the general.

Leonardo nodded earnestly. "Positive."

"Dammit." The general eyed the branch. It hung suspended in a canyon of space. No other branches extended near it.

"That's going to be hard to get to," said Leonardo.

"But not impossible." The general narrowed his eyes. "It's in a good strategic position. They'll have no reason to leave it until the foragers leave the garden."

"What if they have more kids in other trees?" asked Leonardo.

"Unlikely." The general raised himself to a crouch and studied the crisscrossing beams of tree branches. "Follow me. We'll climb down a bit, loop around the back of that tree, and get above them."

Leonardo swallowed, eyeing the gauntlet ahead of them.

It's ok. I'm keeping him occupied. That was his assignment, and he'd known it would be dangerous. He just needed to stay extra vigilant so they didn't stumble into the real Blue Flags.

CHAPTER 21

S o began the wild goose chase. The general, believing he knew the location of the Blue Flags, took far fewer precautions than before. He jogged across exposed branches and jumped without pausing to look for an ambush. Having no idea where the real Blue Flags were, Leonardo spent the entire climb checking over his shoulder and flinching at shadows.

Their saving grace was the general's paranoia. Even thinking the trees were empty, he took them down a long, switchbacking route away from the garden and through heavy curtains of greenery. For twenty minutes, they didn't catch a single glimpse of the foragers, which allowed Leonardo's heartrate to slow for a few moments.

The guards won't be out of sight from the foragers, he told himself.

The general led him down the dark mouth of a hollow vine, creeping ahead and barely breathing until he confirmed it was clear. Leonardo edged down the slippery surface, trying not to focus on how his feet flexed the rubbery green membrane. He'd thought the smell inside the trees was strong, but the botanical aroma within the giant vine overpowered all his senses.

"Hurry up," whispered the general.

Leonardo half-ran, his head ducked in the tight artery. The vine swung ever so slightly, and he wondered exactly how strong the fibers were.

Another thought popped into his head.

How obvious is the vine's movement?

If the Blue Flags saw the giant tunnel wobbling, they could position themselves for an ambush at the far end.

Neon luminescent moss grew in patches below his feet, bathing his arms and legs in a radioactive glow. He made sure to sidestep around it, one suspicious eye trained on the feathery spores. Then dappled sunlight poured through an opening in the side of the tendril, where it draped across the fork of a dead tree, leaning heavily against its living neighbor.

Leonardo grunted as he scrambled up the slope of the vine's interior and eased himself outside. No ambush awaited them on the graying bark. That should have eased Leonardo's anxiety, but instead, his breath quickened as he picked his way over the ridge of the fork.

Where are they?

The garden came into view again, now much further below them. The Blue Flags could be hidden anywhere. And their destination was an exposed branch with only one escape route. If the Blue Flags were stalking them, Leonardo and the general would be in trouble when they got there.

Which meant he needed the general to realize the branch was

empty before they climbed out on it. Unfortunately, the branch bristled with enough dense boughs and giant cones to obscure their view even as they angled themselves above it.

"I don't see anyone," whispered Leonardo.

"They're well hidden," replied the general. Electricity buzzed in his voice.

He loves this. The hunt, the chase.

"But they'll move," continued the general, slowly lifting his blowgun off his back. "Once the foragers leave the garden, the stalkers will leave with them."

"Stalkers?" asked Leonardo.

"Like us," said the general.

A branch snapped behind his back, and Leonardo whipped around. But it was only a squirrel. It leaped to the next tree, crashing into an evergreen bough and sending it swinging.

"You're getting jumpy," observed the general. He grinned. "You're starting to understand this place."

Leonardo scanned his surroundings, barely listening to the general. He'd been so focused on the decoy branch that he didn't realize how bare the one they'd climbed onto was. They were in a position to attack, not to evade fire.

"Where *are* you?" whispered the general. Only a few boughs screened his view of the branch below. He laid on his stomach again and pulled himself over the bark and moss to where a gap would offer him an unimpeded view.

Leonardo crouched low. A salamander edged out from underneath a mat of spongy greenery; its black skin slick with moisture.

"What the hell?" The general twisted to frown at Leonardo. "There's no one down there."

Leonardo knew that already, but he peered down out of instinct. The section of branch he could see was empty, superimposed over a bed of swinging, dipping redwood boughs. Even lower, through the gaps between them, one of the foragers crept through a stand of bright red berry bushes.

A gust of wind lifted the back of Leonardo's shirt, sending chills up his spine. He caught movement in his peripheral, through the dead sticks higher up the bole. A girl started to duck away, then realized Leonardo had already spotted her. She held eye contact with him for a frozen moment, a blue flag tied like a bandana around her head.

Shit.

Her lips moved as her gaze flicked to someone out of sight, shaping a word that Leonardo couldn't hear.

"Get down!" Leonardo shouted at the general. He dropped flat as a dart whisked over his head.

The general rolled onto his back. With a puff of air, he fired a dart up at their attackers. The girl disappeared from view.

"We need to go!" said Leonardo.

The general was already moving. He slung his blowgun over his shoulder, then rolled to his knees and shoved Leonardo off the branch. Leonardo had no time to react. For a split second, he could have been back in the Cove, plummeting over the cliffs with Mishti. His stomach jumped to his throat, then he hit the slender pine boughs, a hundred needles jabbing his face and the exposed skin of his arms. He crushed needles in his hands, clenching the painful boughs as tight as he could. The smell of evergreens flooded his senses.

He looked up, desperation pounding alongside his heartbeat.

A tiny owl watched him through a hollow, its eyes round and yellow. A millisecond later, the general slammed into the branches. His leg caught Leonardo in the back, and Leonardo gasped, all the wind driven from his lungs.

The prickly offshoots slid through Leonardo's hands as the general's weight forced their bough to bend at a steeper angle. Leonardo grunted, gasping and fighting to hold on. The pain of the needles stabbed at his palms and wrists.

The tree groaned. Leonardo's eyes widened. The branch was about to break.

Dammit. He clenched on tighter and drew a sharp breath as the wood snapped with a dry crack. The general pushed away from Leonardo as they tumbled through the air again. This time, the garden flew toward them. Leonardo shut his eyes, twisting just before he struck the ground.

A bed of moss caught him, compressing like a sponge under his weight. His breath expelled in one painful whoosh. The general crashed in a tangle of blackberry bushes, gleaming with rows of thorns. He cried out, twigs snapping and tearing his cape. The broken redwood branch hit the dirt a meter away.

Leonardo hacked out a painful cough. His brain felt like it had slammed against the inside of his skull. He rolled gingerly and stumbled to his feet. An imprint of evergreen needles covered his hands. Blood pooled from tiny punctures.

The general made a weak noise. His cape stretched tight over the brambles, and blood beaded from hundreds of cuts.

Leonardo stared in horror.

His flag will heal him, he reminded himself.

But how fast?

Three foragers stepped out of the shadows, and Leonardo drew his sword. All three kids were young and scrawny. He recalled what the general had said, how the Blue Flags assigned each kid to a specific duty. These were gatherers, not fighters. Leonardo glanced up to where the Blue Flags high above aimed their blowguns down at him.

"Get them!" snapped the general. He struggled to disentangle from the thorns. "Now!"

If downcoming blowdarts rendered the two of them unconscious, the foragers would take their flags in seconds.

The general wrestled the brambles with impressive ferocity. Leonardo charged. The kids' eyes widened, and they sprinted into the underbrush. He tore after them, hacking brush aside with his sword. Vines and tendrils of ivy flashed past. Dragonflies wove in and out of his path.

The Blue Flags glanced back, their mouths agape. They looked like rabbits fleeing a predator.

The fighters were high above, probably rushing down to intercept them now. And the general would be mobile again any second, running hard to catch up. Leonardo's shirt snagged on a prickly bush, and he stumbled, yanking it free with a rip of fabric.

Thoughts fired through his mind. His mission was *no vanishings*. On either side. He needed to let the foragers escape while simultaneously escaping their own pursuers.

Wait. He was the only one who knew where everyone was in that exact moment. Even if he couldn't see the stalkers higher up, he would bet anything the foragers were running to a rendezvous point. Maybe a branch that sloped down, or maybe this tree had a staircase inside it. Either way, if he split from the foragers, he was certain they would escape the stalkers too.

Leonardo ducked under a branch loaded with apples. Hurtling footsteps and the crash-thwack-snap of butchered underbrush announced the general's pursuit. The foragers hooked right into a clump of ferns. Leonardo slowed to a jog, heart hammering, and delayed just long enough to let the general glimpse him. Then he sprinted left, in the opposite direction of the Blue Flags. The strange, matted earth and moss compressed under his feet. Buried redwood joists supported the earth as he ran across their rounded ridges, then down into the hollow of a suspended garden. He glanced back to make sure his redirection had worked. The bushes shook. The general had taken the bait.

Leonardo looked forward, and his blood froze. A hole gaped in the ground, like a jagged mouth in the leaf-scattered earth. He barely staggered to a stop on the edge, bracing himself against a giant seed pod. His sword jarred against the rigid plant and sprang from his grip, spinning into space as it tumbled through the opening. He swore, helplessly watching it fall away.

Leonardo dug his fingernails into the plant's woody flesh, staring down at the barren forest floor. His sword struck the mat of needles and bounced once, throwing up a tiny shower of deadfall.

His heart pounded double-time. He eyed the red flag tied to his belt. If he fell, he wouldn't vanish. He would just be in incredible pain, hoping the Blue Flags found him first to end his misery.

He shook off the morbid thought and pushed away from the seed pod. Or at least, he tried to. A thick, glue-like sap kept his palms adhered to the green surface. Leonardo tugged harder, his breath quickening. The glue stretched, and he pulled harder, prying his hands away until they broke free with a snap. He staggered back, gaping at the sticky pod.

What the...

Gargantuan flowers. Bright blue, their petals splayed as long as his arm. Half-buried tendrils snaked through the dirt, connecting the pod and a dozen others to the blossoms. They bloomed from lush nests of vegetation, partly hidden and gleaming with an iridescent lure.

The general vaulted over the lip of the hollow, sweat and blood mixing on his dark skin. He'd bundled his tattered cape under one arm. He staggered to a stop at the sight of Leonardo, weaponless and stock-still on the edge of the gap.

"Where did they go?"

"They got ahead of me," said Leonardo, faking desperation. "I must have taken a wrong turn."

The general swore. Then he swore again. He pointed at the blue flowers. "Do you know what those are?"

Leonardo shook his head.

"They'll eat us."

"*What?*" A new dread jolted into his limbs.

"Slowly," the general continued, a haunted flicker in his grimace. "Never faster than our flags can heal us. It could be weeks before anyone finds us."

Leonardo's eyes widened.

He's seen it happen.

The general swallowed hard, a sickened sourness in the set of his teeth.

Leonardo edged further away from the sticky seed pod. The massive blue flowers leered at him through the ferns. Long spiked tips fringed the petals, and a clear fluid dripped from gaping circular centers. The longer he looked, the more tendrils he spotted, woven like snares in the underbrush.

"So." The general turned in a slow circle, his face grim. "We're the ones in danger now."

"We're trapped between the flowers and the stalkers," said Leonardo quietly.

Well done, he grimly congratulated himself.

The general nodded. "When you lose your enemy's position, it's usually because he knows yours."

"What's the best way out of here?" Leonardo didn't give the general time to consider turning the tables.

The general chewed his lip. He eyed the hole in the ground. "Follow me. And don't touch anything with shoots."

CHAPTER 22

I'm beginning to think you're bad luck, Leonardo," said the general.

They picked their way over a cluster of rocks on the forest floor, eating a walking lunch of dried meat and berries. Leonardo studied a strip of deer meat, then attempted to rip off a piece with his teeth.

"Yeah?" he said through the salty mouthful. He'd never had a healthy relationship with luck.

They had escaped the treetops by carefully lowering themselves into the arms of the root-filled underworld suspended beneath the gardens. Pale, slimy offshoots of the carnivorous flowers interwove around patches of luminescent fungus. Twice, the general had to grab Leonardo's arm before he could brush against a sticky tendril, barely visible in the dingy, sun-deprived burrows.

"Open your eyes," he'd snapped the second time.

Leonardo hadn't even bristled at the rebuke. He nodded tightly, watching the glistening shoot.

They'd followed a daunting path down the bole of the tree, traversing a combination of vines, heavy moss, and mushroom stalks until they could jump to the mat of dead needles, where they found themselves now.

"Since you started joining my patrols," the general continued. "We've missed more kills than I can ever remember."

Change the conversation, Leonardo's inner voice warned.

"Don't blame me." He shrugged. "I'm new to all of this."

He crouched to dip his fingers in the trickle of springwater that flowed between the rocks. A stronger gush sloshed from an opening in the earth nearby. It rushed, white and bubbling, over the jagged natural steps, before tumbling away in the form of a small stream.

"From what I hear," pressed the general, "the Darkwoods weren't exactly strangers to fighting."

The smell of salt and humidity filled the air. White mineral residue accumulated on every edge of the dark stone, crunching under their feet. The general paused to splash water over his arms, rubbing the dried blood off his dark skin. Underneath, the cuts and punctures were already half-healed.

Interesting. Leonardo studied his own hands. The tiny wounds he'd sustained from their fall were almost unnoticeable. A tinge of pink stained the stream's surface for a moment, then ran clear again as the general straightened.

"Fighting, yes." Leonardo tugged at another strip of dried meat with his teeth. "But not in the treetops. I'm not used to the ground swinging underneath me."

The general studied him a moment. Leonardo forced himself to keep chewing. Then the general clapped him on the shoulder. "You'll adjust."

An undercurrent charged his words. *Or else.*

Leonardo couldn't tell if it was a threat or a warning.

Even while washing away the blood, the general's eyes had never stopped scanning overhead. He ushered Leonardo forward, and Leonardo didn't hesitate. He panned his gaze through the shadows around them. Memories of lions weaving in and out of the woods made him shudder. He'd encountered enough predators lately. He was in no hurry to face another.

"So, the salt preserves the meat?" Leonardo swallowed another stringy bite.

"When you use a lot of it, yes." The general pointed back at the rocks. "We harvest it from the salt spring. Takes a full day of work, and we usually lose some kids in the process, but we lose kids picking fruit too." He shrugged. "Nothing is too complicated here. Just dangerous."

They ascended another tree in the same way they had escaped the garden. This time, it involved scaling a tangled ladder of ivy. Leonardo's exhausted arms would have preferred a stair tree, but at least they weren't in darkness this way.

They stopped to rest in a mushroom trench, and the general leaned forward as a squirrel darted a few steps toward them. He placed a blueberry on the edge of the mushroom and splayed his hands in a sort of *it's yours* gesture. The squirrel eyed him hesitantly.

While he was distracted, Leonardo caught movement across the canyon between trees. He frowned as a group of kids crossed a branch, dwarfed to the size of ants next to the immense trunk. His pulse quickened, and sweat pricked his palms. The entire trunk was carpeted in a wall of moss and colorful fungi, pocked with hundreds of hollows and lush overgrowth. But even from this distance, he could see the blue flag tied around one kid's head.

Leonardo drew a sharp breath. The general and the squirrel both looked at him. Leonardo faked a muscle cramp and pretended not to notice. When the general turned his attention away, Leonardo zeroed in on the Blue Flags again.

That kid with the bandana paused above a colony of red and white spotted mushrooms, even larger than the one Leonardo currently sat in. As he watched, the kid knocked on the trunk next to a patch of moss and ivy. Three knocks, two knocks, then four evenly spaced. A moment passed, then he knocked again, with the same pattern. This time, an entire patch of plants moved. Leonardo's eyes widened.

It's a door.

It was more of a movable wall, actually, cut from a chunk of bark with the thick moss still attached. And behind it was a tunnel. Two kids became visible as they dragged it back, and the kids on the outside filed in. The two from the inside immediately moved it back in place, glancing around quickly before sealing the tunnel again.

Is that their camp?

"What are you looking at?" asked the general.

Leonardo jumped, startling him.

The general mistook his alarm for fear. "What is it?" He whipped his blowgun off his back. "Blue Flags?"

"No, um…"

177

Leonardo's mouth turned dry. *Think!*

"I saw something strange," he said lamely. "I think it was just a raccoon."

"A raccoon?" asked the general.

"They come out in the day, sometimes. We had them in the Darkwoods too."

"I see."

The general narrowed his eyes, staring directly at the immense moss wall the kids had disappeared into. But their doorway was the size of a postage stamp, and the façade made it indistinguishable from the rest of the green.

I know the location of their camp. That was a development he hadn't anticipated, but he couldn't squander it. Kate had made it explicitly clear that trying to work both sides would end in disaster, but still…this wouldn't be the first time he'd stepped into a dangerous clan's camp. He recalled Mishti's hostility when his clan washed up on her shore.

She'd been ready to throw them back into the sea. Now she was his closest alliance. Although, he couldn't claim full credit for how that played out.

It was Juliet's fake sign that changed everything.

Leonardo tilted his head.

Would that work again? His thoughts turned as he stitched a fourth phase into the three-pronged strategy they had devised the night before.

If it's believable enough…

If it came from Pinch's hat, it could be as outlandish as they wanted. They could assault the Blue Flag camp with a two-story crocodile skull. If that didn't convince them, nothing would.

He burned the image of the hidden door into his memory, his mind made up. It was time to bring the clans together.

CHAPTER 23

P inch broke his leg." Charley met Leonardo at the threshold of their sleeping hollow.

"What?" Leonardo's stomach dropped.

Pinch reclined against the back wall, his left leg propped up on a tightly-bundled sleeping roll. A conspicuously foreign plaster cast hugged his shin. Moth, Juliet, and Viola crouched next to him, their faces drawn in the light of a single fairy cage centered on the floor. He grimaced at Leonardo.

"What happened?" Leonardo stepped around Charley and rushed to his side.

Moth and the girls edged back to give him room.

Pinch shrugged. Then winced. "I tried to imagine a hover-board."

Leonardo stared at him. "You did what?"

Pinch's hat lay next to him. He poked at it, then winced again. Sweaty black hair plastered his forehead.

"I thought it would make getting around the forest easier."

"And then the halfwit fell off," said Moth. Even in the golden glow of the fairy cage, the color had gone vacant from his face.

"He fell down *three* branches," Viola said sharply. "He's lucky he only broke his leg."

Leonardo closed his eyes. *Dammit, Pinch.*

"Don't be dramatic!" retorted Pinch. "I wouldn't have died. I have this flag, remember?"

Leonardo opened his eyes as Pinch waved his red flag in Viola's face. She met his indignance with an unimpressed eyebrow.

"That's not the point!" snapped Moth. "We can't have you falling out of trees!"

"Where did the hoverboard go?" asked Charley, lingering behind Leonardo.

"Lost," said Pinch bitterly. He made a dive-bomb motion with his hand.

Leonardo couldn't care less about the hoverboard. Even if the flag kept him from vanishing, the general had made it very clear that the injuries here were real.

"How fast do you think it will heal?" Leonardo asked. With Pinch out of commission, his idea of a two-story crocodile skull fell with the hoverboard. Unless the flag's magic could heal him in time—

"Well, I won't be dancing tonight." Pinch swatted his leg with the length of red fabric. "Still hurts like a bitch."

Dammit.

"But it won't change the plan," Pinch assured him. He flipped his hat and caught it on the other hand. "I have a *brilliant* idea to scare these halfwits with. Tell me when, and it's showtime!"

"Can your idea teleport you?" Scaring the Red Flags wouldn't be enough anymore.

"What?" Pinch twisted his leg awkwardly. "Shit!"

"I'll get you something for the pain." Juliet moved to her bag of supplies. She'd exchanged her gold robes for a more practical ensemble of Red Flag clothes, stitched and patched and hiked-up where she'd tied the baggy fabric with a length of twine around her waist. It fit her about as well as Leonardo's party had assimilated with the Red Flags.

"I found the Blue flag camp," said Leonardo.

Viola, Moth, and Pinch stared at him.

"We have a bigger opportunity than we realized," said Viola slowly.

"And I'm stuck in this tree." Pinch cursed at his leg. "Maybe I can imagine a hover disk! I can sit in it and—"

He tried to push himself upright and let out a sharp grunt. Moth, Viola, and Leonardo jumped to help him as he gingerly lowered himself back to the floor.

"No more hovering," said Leonardo. "We'll figure out another way."

"Do you *need* Pinch at the Blue Flag tree?" asked Juliet over her shoulder. "He's not the only one who can scare people."

Leonardo frowned. *She didn't need a magic hat when she tricked everyone at the Cove.*

The clans here lived in trees, surrounded by exposed wood, and Leonardo had the Darkwoods' best carver at his disposal. It would need to be the most flawless work Moth had ever executed. It would need to convince the most skeptical eye that only a divine

182

hand could have carved it. But if Juliet had succeeded with a pile of flowers, Moth could work his own magic with a knife.

And Pinch can still scare the Red Flags. He didn't need a functional leg to spook everyone in *this* tree. And so long as Moth retained his mobility, he could handle the Blues. *And then, once we've convinced both clans to gather, Pinch can dream up the final fireworks to seal the deal.*

"Charley," said Leonardo. "Gather the rest of the clan."

***

"That's a terrible plan," said Mishti.

"There are too many of us here," whispered Kate. "Someone will get suspicious."

They all clustered the sleeping hollow, carefully positioned to appear as inconspicuous as possible. Mishti and Leonardo faced opposite directions, Pinch lay on his back, leg propped and hat covering his face, and Moth whittled a carving of a raven. Juliet pressed close beside him, intently focused on the deft movement of his knife. If any Red Flags walked past, they would see nothing out of the ordinary.

"We need to make this decision as a group," replied Leonardo. "It's too important."

"Fine." Kate leaned against the wall a few feet from him, gazing at the corner of the room. "Then let's make it quick." Tension snapped in her voice.

She's getting paranoid, just like the general. She was slipping back into the ways of the Redwoods.

"I agree with Mishti," mumbled Moth, shaving off a sliver of wood. "I don't like this plan."

"It worked once," pressed Leonardo. "When Juliet faked the Lion sign, you believed it, Mishti. And it's a good thing you did," he added quickly to dispel any lingering bitterness. "That sign was the first step toward the alliance."

"But we don't know the Redwoods clans like I know Lion Clan," argued Juliet. She didn't look at him, and her tone was carefully conversational. If her voice carried through the walls, she could've been asking about the weather. "Who knows what type of sign would work on them? Kate, do you have any ideas?"

"'Signs' never held much weight," said Kate. "We didn't pray to the woods like you do."

Leonardo shook his head. They didn't understand.

"It doesn't need to have existing meaning. It just needs to scare them into believing something supernatural has come for them. Once they believe, they'll band together, just like we all did."

"The Blue Flags don't even know about the Dark," said Jack. He no longer styled his hair in a clay-fortified wave like the old days. Now it was pulled back into a knot, lending a sunken severity to his features. "What kind of *sign* could possibly do that?"

"A croc skull," said Leonardo. "On the wall inside the Blue Flag tree. And we'll burn a line down the center, just like the Dark does."

At the word *burn*, Kate stiffened. "With fire?"

That was the reaction he hoped for from the Redwoods kids.

"No clan here would use fire in the treetops," he explained. "It will be too shocking to justify with logic. Then we'll come back here, and Pinch will create a fake Dark attack for the Red Flags. When they panic, I'll tell the general that I spotted the Blue camp today and suggest we go to them for help. When we get

184

there, they'll be spooked from Moth's carving and willing to listen to us."

"That sounds intricate." Jack chewed his lip. He faced Leonardo, his back against the polished wall of their bowl-shaped room. His long fingers drummed the red wood grain.

"Of course it is," countered Leonardo. "But think about the reward. If we can get everyone together, and then Pinch manifests a second Dark attack in front of both clans, we could solve all of our problems in an instant."

"I don't know, Leo…" Jack quirked his mouth. "These clans hate each other."

"I agree," said Sophie. Like Pinch, she lay on her sleeping roll, eyes closed. "They don't meet like regular clans. Even if they both believe their signs, I'm not sure it will cause a truce."

Leonardo's heart sunk.

"Great," mumbled Pinch through the fabric of his hat. "Everyone has a reason why it won't work."

"I don't hear you suggesting anything," snapped Mishti.

"That's because I'm thinking, halfwit."

"What did you call me?" Mishti twisted to look at him, just as a Red Flag crossed the opening to the hollow. Mishti quickly extended her arms, faking a stretch.

"Red Flag," hissed Jack, for Pinch and Sophie's benefit. Both held silent, sustaining their sleeping act.

Leonardo closed his eyes. Kate was right; meeting like this was dangerous.

"If we don't take risks, we'll never survive the Dark," he said pointedly. "We know where their camp is. If they move, we lose that advantage. This might be the best chance we'll get to unite the clans."

Moth twisted the fairy cage in the center of the room, rotating long bars of shadow across the walls.

He'll put his doubts aside if I order him to. But Leonardo had never run his clan that way.

Is it worth it? he asked himself. *Does the end justify the means?*

"Sophie's right, though," said Pinch. "The general won't want to meet with the Blues. The second we suggest it, he'll put us under watch."

Unless we force a mutiny. But that had been a flimsy idea the first time Leonardo suggested it, and it seemed even flimsier now.

"So, everyone disagrees with the plan?" he asked. Disappointment and frustration sharpened his tone.

"Hold up," said Pinch, still muffled through his hat. "You didn't let me finish. The only way to guarantee the clans meet is to visit the Blue Flags *first.*"

And never give the general the chance to stop us. Leonardo frowned. It wasn't a terrible idea. It meant more lying and deception, but they were going to be hip-deep already. *What's one more lie, if it means we succeed?*

"You mean, go behind the general's back?" Mishti's voice was barely a whisper. "That could make a mess for us."

"So could the Dark," countered Leonardo. He wished he could look everyone in the eye, but the circumstances didn't offer him that luxury.

You're the leader, he told himself. *Make a decision.*

"We'll fake the carving," he said aloud. "Then visit the Blues immediately and make up a story about the Dark. Then we'll

186

come back here, and Pinch will fake a Dark attack right in the general's quarters. There's a big open space below where he sleeps. No one will have a chance to stop us, and by tomorrow morning, everyone in the Redwoods will believe in the Dark."

Silence met his words.

"Well, halfwits?" pressed Pinch. "Are we doing this?"

"I don't know…" started Sophie.

"We're in," said Mishti. "You're right. We need to act."

In Leonardo's peripheral, Sophie shifted to see Mishti, her eyes narrowed.

You're not calling the shots anymore, he thought. It troubled him that Sophie still couldn't accept that.

"Fine," said Kate. She plucked at her double flag. "Then I'm in too."

"I'm in," said Moth.

"I don't like it," said Viola. "But I agree, we can't sit around."

The six other members of their party nodded, positioned in their deliberately casual tableau around the circular hollow.

"Ok." Leonardo refocused his gaze forward. Bates's eyes flicked to the doorway, and Leonardo froze as another Red Flag walked past. She glanced curiously into the hollow and kept walking.

"Moth and I will go," whispered Leonardo, still watching the opening. "Pinch, I'll need your goggles. We'll bring a flintstone for fire—hopefully, the burn marks will convince them the Red Flags didn't do it. And we'll need some darts and some of that poison they dip them in."

"It's from a mushroom," said Kate. "I saw some near here. We can get it on the way."

187

We. She clearly intended on joining them.

No. She'll only make us easier to spot.

Viola frowned. "How many people are going?"

Leonardo started to answer *two*—himself and Moth. But a tiny voice in his head stopped him. He couldn't shake the sudden feeling that Kate would be vital to the mission.

Three people are a lot more conspicuous than two. But his instinct insisted that Kate be present. She watched him, head slightly tilted and a small smile on her lips.

Leonardo furrowed his brow. *What does she know?*

"Three of us," he answered slowly.

CHAPTER 24

There it is," whispered Leonardo. He breathed a sigh of relief. The tree with the fake patch of growth loomed ahead of them, cast bright in Pinch's night vision goggles. They looked like something an old pilot would wear, all leather and bug-eyed glass.

"Sensational," declared Kate. "Let's move."

Leonardo carefully lowered himself to the vine below, transferring his grip to the rigid tendril, then he eased his weight onto a slant of dead wood. He was learning how to chart a course through the trees, and he set his sights on a heavy branch that would take them three-quarters of the way to their destination while providing a dense screen of vegetation.

"I still don't like this plan," hissed Moth, climbing down after him. "Imagine walking into any clan's camp like this in the Cove or the Darkwoods. What do you think they would do?"

"Panic," whispered Leonardo. "Which is exactly what we want."

"And if they kill us?" pressed Moth.

Behind him, Kate silently slipped down from the vine. She moved through the trees with a practiced ease that Leonardo envied. He cringed as dry bark crackled under his shoes.

"That's why we're doing it in the night," he replied to Moth. "We have the advantage with Pinch's goggles. No one will know we're here until we want them to."

"That's the part I'm afraid of." Moth blinked slowly in the darkness, drawing a shaky breath.

"Trust me," whispered Leonardo.

Moth gave a small nod and tightened his lips. Leonardo crept closer to the towering wall of moss, placing each footfall with the utmost care. They moved through the canopy like a trio of phantoms. Hunched silhouettes in the moonlight.

The key was finding an entrance that suited their needs. The lush green cliff face offered countless openings. Their success—and survival—rested on picking the right one.

He held up a hand to stop the other two behind a tall, thin redwood standing directly between them and the Blue Flags' tree.

If this succeeds, he told himself, *we'll end the game tomorrow.*

Kate spotted an opening lower down the tree, flickering with the soft glow of torchlight.

Leonardo frowned. *Or, more likely, fairy light.*

The flintstone jostled in his pocket, next to Aleksander's rock key. They couldn't pick a completely dark opening, or their own firelight would draw attention. Plus, if they chose an abandoned tunnel, the sign might never be found.

They descended through the darkness and crept toward the glow, burning valuable minutes. But Leonardo refused to go any faster and jeopardize the plan. He crawled out on a branch, leaning down to see through the opening.

He swore under his breath. More vegetation blocked his view. Leonardo peered down to a bed of redwood limbs below him. A raccoon gazed back, its eyes glassy in the night.

Leonardo drew his sword, ever so slowly, and waved it at the rodent. The raccoon retreated, vanishing down the trunk, and Leonardo gestured for Kate to back up. Moth crouched in the shadows behind her. Leonardo dropped to the boughs, catching his breath as they dipped crazily under his weight. He clutched needle-covered branches, wincing at the pain in his barely healed punctures, heart racing as his perch swung heavily.

He clutched on harder to quell his shaking hands. Crushed needles poked the sensitive skin between his fingers. Leonardo set his gaze on the opening in the tree again. Now, he was low enough to see directly across into the glowing hollow. A single kid slumped against the wall next to a cage of fairies. A crescent-moon lock of blonde hair curled across his forehead.

The kid straightened, crossing to the opening and squinting out into the night. He gripped a knife in his hand. Leonardo held his breath.

Dammit. He heard me.

Something rustled lower, and Leonardo's blood froze. He leaned forward, just enough to see the raccoon on the next branch down, a thick log that angled back into denser greenery.

Shut up, he thought at the raccoon. But the disturbance benefitted him. The curly-haired kid spotted the animal and relaxed.

191

He returned the knife to his belt, spun on his heel, and returned to his spot against the wall.

Leonardo glanced up at Kate, lying flat above him.

"Did you see him?" he mouthed.

Kate nodded. "Leave this to me."

***

"Ready?" whispered Leonardo. He angled his face sideways, pressed flat against the bole. Kate and Moth clung to the dense moss next to him. Leonardo's fingers dug into a ledge of bark; bits of plant wedged under his nails. His legs burned as he fought to sustain his foothold, knees braced and hugging the tree.

Both nodded.

Here we go.

"Do it," he whispered to Kate.

Kate took one hand off the wall and removed a dart from her pocket. They weren't going to bother with a blowgun for this assault. She rolled the dart in her fingers and placed it between her teeth, the poison-covered tip centimeters from her lips. She winked at Leonardo, then climbed the last few feet and pulled herself up into the opening.

Leonardo's hairs stood on end. *Why is she so relaxed?*

Immediately, the kid's voice rose. "Hey, sto—"

"You're going to listen to me," interrupted Kate. "Very closely. I don't want you to yell for help. I only want you to whisper."

"I—" the kid's voice came out hoarse. He gasped. "What did you do?"

His voice was barely a scrape.

Kate's gift was the most enigmatic of the four pirates'; *I get whatever I want.* Leonardo realized he was seeing it in action for the first time.

"I come representing the Dark," said Kate. "The Dark, ok? Remember that."

"Hey!" the kid's voice grew hoarser by the second. "Stay back! Stay—"

Leonardo and Moth looked at each other. Leonardo dug his fingertips harder into the wood.

"When you wake up, you won't remember me," continued Kate. "Only the Dark."

A thump. Soft footsteps, then Kate's face peered over the ledge. She smiled sweetly. "Coast is clear."

A wave of nervous energy unsteadied Leonardo's focus. "Good work." He tried to hide how shaken he was.

Concentrate on the plan, he reminded himself. He climbed up and rolled onto the ledge where the kid lay slumped with the dart in his neck. A trio of fairies flocked to the bars of their cage. Their captor would survive, of course; he still had his flag. The important part would come when he opened his eyes and saw the horror scratched into the wall before him.

Please let none of us get caught. One mistake and they would all go up in flames.

"Focus on the crocodile skull," Leonardo told Moth. "I'm going to write a message beside it."

"What about me?" asked Kate.

He eyed the passage that hooked deeper into the tree. "If anyone comes down that tunnel, I need you to scare them off."

"Aye aye, cap'n." Kate winked and strode off.

Stop winking at me.

"Let's do this." Moth pulled his carving knife from his belt.

The plan. Focus on the plan. But he couldn't shake the uneasiness in his bones. He glanced at the curly-haired kid again, a dart protruding from his neck and Kate's magic swimming in his head.

It's too late to turn back.

Leonardo accepted a knife and stabbed it into the wall, dragging the tip down into the first letter. His heart pounded like a ticking clock.

Twenty minutes later, he stepped back to examine a rapidly etched crocodile skull. Moth didn't have the luxury of time he could typically spend on his carvings, but it was still one of the most convincing pieces he'd ever crafted. Beside it, giant, ragged letters spelled: *THE DARK IS COMING.*

"Perfect." Anxiousness tightened Leonardo's voice. "Now the fire."

"Leo." Kate peeked her head around the corner of the tunnel. "Come see this."

Leonardo glanced at her. She waved her hand urgently, then ducked away.

His stomach jumped to his throat. *Shit.*

"Here." He fished the flint from his pocket and tossed it to Moth. "I'll be right back."

Leonardo ran after Kate. He rounded the corner and almost bowled into her. She stood in the mouth of the tunnel, just out of sight of the main hollow.

"Kate!" he hissed, stumbling to an abrupt halt. She threw her hands up, bracing against his chest. He looked around. "What is it?"

"My talent is relatively...imprecise," whispered Kate. Her voice sounded strange. It set his teeth on edge.

"What?" Leonardo leaned closer, brow furrowed. A lock of brown hair hung from under her hat, partly covering one eye.

"*I get whatever I want.* Sometimes it's immediate, like how I took away that kid's voice. Other times...I have to be patient."

Leonardo became suddenly aware that Kate's hands were still on his chest.

"Kate—" He started to step back when she pushed him against the wall and kissed him.

Her lips were on his for less than a second. Leonardo shoved her off, heart racing.

Dammit, Kate.

She stumbled back, grinning ear to ear.

"Told-ya." Kate winked. "I get *whatever* I want."

Leonardo remembered his feeling back at the Red Flag camp. He'd been compelled to bring her. He'd felt she *needed* to come, and now he understood why.

It was her gift, manipulating me. So she could get what she wanted.

Leonardo's anger boiled over. He grabbed Kate by the shoulders and spun her around, so her back was to the wall. Her eyes widened. Then he jammed his hand in her jacket pocket, where she'd hidden her flag. He needed to be the one in control. He closed his fingers around the coarse fabric, and Kate grabbed his wrist. Her focus flicked down, then met his. He could vanish her with one motion. The amusement drained from her eyes.

There you are. Wake up, Kate.

He had a memory of her attempting to cross swords with him on *The Forever*, in the midst of the deep-sea monster attack.

She has no concept of reality. The higher the stakes, the more she seemed to misbehave. But he refused to take part.

"Listen," hissed Leonardo, leaning close to her face. "This is a game. The Cove tried to tempt me with Adriana, and now it's doing the same to you, with me. I snapped myself out of it," he said through his teeth. "I need you to do the same."

Kate slowly released his wrist.

"I'm immune to the woods' games." Her breath was warm on his face. "This is not—"

"This is a game," he repeated. "And I refuse to play. So, leave me alone, ok?"

He released her flag and pushed off from the wall, leaving her in the passage. He clenched his hands.

Damn it all.

Leonardo found Moth nursing a tiny fire. He lit a shard of wood and swept it over the carving. This was the most treacherous part. If the glow of the fire cast too much light on the trees outside, a guard at another post could get suspicious. And if the fire leaped out of control...

But Moth kept the smolder low, and the fairy light masked most of it.

Flames licked at the dry interior of the tree, blackening the wood in seconds. Leonardo unscrewed his canteen and splashed water over the burn mark before it could truly catch.

"Like clockwork," said Moth. Firelight cast his freckled face gold as he tossed the shard on his pile of kindling.

Leonardo's fingers shook as he screwed the cap back onto his canteen. They had been inside the tree a long time. Every extra second tempted fate.

Meanwhile, the unconscious kid lay slumped, facing their work.

Leonardo moved to stomp out the fire, and Moth stopped him.

"Wait." He ran to the kid's side and rapidly cut through the door of the fairy cage. Three tiny lights shot past his head and out into the night.

We don't have time for this. Leonardo wiped sweat off his brow. They would free *all* the fairies eventually, but tonight was not the time.

"Moth."

"I'm hurrying; I'm hurrying."

Moth ran back to the flickering nest of kindling and rolled the empty cage in it.

"What are you doing?" hissed Leonardo. The thin bars caught fire, and Moth scrambled to unscrew his canteen. He doused the blackened frame and toed it off the pile, then smothered the rest with his shoe.

"We can't leave them caged," whispered Moth. "Besides, another burnt thing will make it more believable."

He moved the charred cage back to its original spot while Leonardo swept the ashes and a handful of wood shavings to the ledge.

He wasn't wrong. Leonardo's entire plan hinged on the act defying explanation. The burnt cage did add to the ominous tone of their vandalism. But doing so used up any remaining time they had.

197

Leonardo dusted charcoal off his hands and hurried to scuff away any residue from the ground of the now shadowy tunnel. Kate still had yet to reappear, and he bit his lip impatiently.

Hurry up.

Moth crouched next to the kid and ran a sooty finger down his forehead, leaving a mark identical to the one on the crocodile skull. If the stakes weren't so high, Leonardo would have laughed.

They're going to be petrified.

The kid grunted.

"He's stirring!" Moth scrambled backward. His curls were littered with wood fragments and chips.

"Let's go." Leonardo regarded the crocodile skull on the wall. It certainly looked too strange to be human-carved.

Please let this work.

Kate finally emerged from the tunnel, her eyes directed any-where but on Leonardo. Moth pulled the dart from the kid's neck, and they fled the hollow, lowering themselves onto the moss wall and climbing precariously down to a waiting branch.

They'd survived step one, but the clock didn't stop yet. Their absence at camp could ruin things as easily as getting caught. *The longer we spend out here, the more likely it gets that someone notices we're missing.*

Meanwhile, Leonardo's mind replayed Kate kissing him. Guilt washed over him.

Focus on the plan.

"Good work, everyone," he whispered. The words sounded forced. His heart slammed against his chest as he charted a path to the main entrance.

"What was down the tunnel?" asked Moth.

Leonardo glanced at Kate. She still wouldn't make eye contact.

"Nothing," he replied. "A false alarm."

Moth was quiet for a second. Then he cleared his throat. "One thing I don't understand...Even if we can convince the leader of the Blues to meet with the general, how do we tell the general about the meeting without sounding suspicious?"

A white spider lowered itself from the branch above, dangling on a strand of silk. Ink blots of pure black mottled its back.

"We tell him the truth," replied Leonardo, watching the spider carefully set down on a cluster of needles.

"You're going to get us killed," whispered Kate.

I'm not the one being reckless.

"The *partial* truth," continued Leonardo, keeping his tone objective. "I'll tell him that I spotted the Blue Flags' camp yesterday and kept it a secret to bargain with him later. *But*, when I got back to camp, I had a bad feeling about the Dark coming, so I decided to act. We've been talking about the Dark since we got here. He'll believe it."

They ducked low and crouch-walked under a brace of greenery.

"But..." Moth wobbled and carefully steadied himself. "What do we say when he asks why we went to the Blue Flags before him? That's an odd move."

"The truth," repeated Leonardo. "That we were afraid he wouldn't let us go to the Blue Flags. That we believe the only way to survive the Dark is to unite."

"Plus," said Kate slowly. "Pinch's Dark attack in the middle of everything will just solidify our reasons."

"I hope you're right," said Moth quietly. "Because if you're not…"

If I'm not, we lose our best chance to unite the clans.

CHAPTER 25

The passages inside the Blue Flags' tree were as dark as those inside the Red Flags'. A pair of shrew-eyed kids led Leonardo and Moth by fairy light, a cage swinging in each of their hands. The girl was taller than the boy, but both kids bore a striking resemblance, with small, suspicious mouths and a loose scatter of freckles. Siblings without question. They exchanged silent looks, and Leonardo didn't need to be a mind-reader to know his and Moth's presence wasn't a welcome one.

They stooped through an opening, and Leonardo blinked at the vastness of the space before him. The boy and girl dropped blankets over their fairy cages.

Leonardo breathed in the earthy smell of the tree's interior. He wondered how many of the redwood trunks had such elaborate tunnels and chambers like this one and the tree the Red Flags occupied. There had to be a lot of them; the general said they changed camps often.

"You know coming here is suicide, right?" said the girl after a beat. Her voice sounded twenty feet away. He hadn't even heard her leave his side.

"We would like to meet your leader," said Leonardo.

"You're speaking to her." The girl used an overly cultured lilt as if she placed herself well above Leonardo's station.

You're the leader? Her shift took him by surprise. One second quiet and watchful, the next poised and challenging, which was, he supposed, by design. In a place like this, no smart leader would reveal their identity until they were safely in the darkness.

"That's perfect, then," said Leonardo, masking his surprise.

"We have no leader," the girl elaborated. "But the older kids make the important decisions, and I'm the oldest one here. Where are you from? I know you're not from the Redwoods, or else you would have known not to ask for our *leader*."

Leonardo carefully removed Pinch's night vision goggles from his pocket.

"We're from the Darkwoods." He worked the strap looser so he could slip it over his head without making a sound. "I'm the leader of Raven Clan."

"What's your name?" asked the girl.

"Leonardo. And this is Moth."

Kate remained outside, hidden in the trees. If her magic hadn't worked and the boy recognized her, it would ruin the entire plan.

Leonardo slowly lifted the goggles to his face, careful not to rustle the fabric of his clothes. He pulled the strap over the back of his head and slid the strap tight again. As soon he placed the goggles over his eyes, the room flared into clarity.

"I'm Iris," said the girl. She had a sharp brow and a severe slant to her features, which, pared with small eyes and pursed lips, didn't lend to a particularly hospitable expression. Her blonde hair was twisted in a tight knot. "Tell me again what you're here for. You said something about crocodiles?" She stood alone before them, her back to a curved edge of the hollow. The draped fairy cage rested at her side. Her brother was gone, and Leonardo focused on an opening in the wall.

He's getting reinforcements.

If Leonardo were actually playing their game, he could eliminate Iris before anyone made it to the chamber. But he had no interest in vanishing more kids.

"We're staying with the general and the Red Flags," said Leonardo. "They found us when we arrived in the Redwoods, so we had no choice. He wants us to fight you, but we're not here for that."

Leonardo and Moth explained their history with the Dark. Meanwhile, a steady stream of kids filed into the room, hands on weapons as they listened to the invisible intruders. Leonardo and Moth had been forced to surrender their weapons, but it didn't surprise Leonardo for a second that the Blue Flags were fully armed. He would've done the exact same.

"The Dark has begun to show itself," he lied. "We're afraid of what will happen next."

"If it's come," said Moth, "we need to work together to survive it."

Three boys silently moved around behind Leonardo to block the other exit. He'd memorized the route to the outside. It wasn't hard; this tree wasn't as twisting as the Red Flags'. If things went bad, he would have to rush the three boys in the dark. The one on the right wasn't big. Leonardo could overpower him and take his sword before Iris lifted the drape off the fairy cage.

It wouldn't take long to disarm the other two, then he and Moth could flee.

"This is a strange story," said Iris when they'd finished.

"I know," said Leonardo. "No one believes it until they see the Dark for themselves. But *seeing the Dark* means losing a lot of…" He hesitated as rapid footsteps echoed down the tunnel behind Iris. Moth looked sharply in that direction, along with all the kids in the hollow, despite the fact that none of them could see a thing.

"…losing a lot of clanmates," Leonardo continued. "If we unite before the Dark strikes, we can save a lot of vanishings."

"I see," said Iris, distracted as she listened to the footsteps. "And what were the guardians of the Darkwoods doing in the Cove?"

The guardians of the Darkwoods.

The Natives.

Leonardo realized that he didn't know anything about the guardians of the Redwoods. The Natives were in the Cove because the sirens weren't doing their job anymore. But…

"Who are the guardians of the Redwoods?" Leonardo asked instead of answering her question.

Iris glanced at the cage of fairies at her feet. She obviously couldn't see it, but that made the reflex even more telling.

The fairies?

Of course it's the fairies. They'd been helping Leonardo's clan since before they even reached the Cove. They were guardians, just like the Natives and the sirens.

"No one," said Iris.

Why is she hiding it? Leonardo tilted his head. *Because they cage them?*

A darker thought hit him: *Why do they cage their guardians?*

His mind began to spin as new questions and puzzle pieces linked together like all the spider webs in the canopy.

The Red Flag children spent their days trapping free fairies. The Blue Flags clearly locked them up, too; their camp was full of the same cages. He almost cursed. *Of course* they weren't just capturing them for light. The only logical reason to imprison their guardians would be if those guardians' interests deviated from their own.

What if the fairies tried to end the game? Or they know how to?

If he'd learned anything, it was that the Redwoods kids wanted—no, they needed—to *win* the game. Which meant total annihilation of their rivals. No guardian would support that, and maybe the fairies had attempted to peacefully dissolve the flags' magic in the past. It wasn't a stretch to imagine the kids intervening in the name of preserving their chances at victory. He couldn't picture any of them settling for a truce.

The footsteps rounded the tunnel, and a boy staggered out into the room, his face drawn. A finger's smear of soot stretched from his hairline to his brow.

Leonardo stifled any audible reaction. His insides twisted. *Here goes nothing.*

"Who's there?" asked someone in the crowd of Blue Flags.

"There's a…thing…on the wall…" Raw fear shook his voice.

"Shut up," snapped another voice. "We have visitors."

The kid looked around. He was as blind as the rest of them.

205

"Older kids, with me." Alarm glinted in Iris's eyes. "Everyone else, stay with these two. We'll be back in a moment, Leonardo."

She picked up the cloth-covered fairy cage and moved quickly for the door. A dozen other kids moved with her, arms extended as they felt for the opening. It looked a bit ridiculous, and Iris lifted an edge of the drape, casting enough light to see where she was going. Leonardo whipped off the goggles and shoved them in his pocket, but the light wasn't enough to even reveal the crowd of kids surrounding them. Leonardo slowly drew the goggles from his pocket again and slipped them back over his head.

Moth leaned close to him.

"Was that the kid?" he whispered.

"Yes," he whispered back, eyeing the Blue Flags to make sure no one could hear him.

The Blue Flags were too busy whispering to each other. They all looked worried, and understandably so. The kid's shaking voice was enough to panic anyone.

He pulled Moth close enough to whisper in his ear.

"If this goes bad, be ready to run."

***

When Iris and the older kids returned, it was with grave faces and trembling hands. The glow of their fairy cages preceded them, and Leonardo yanked off the goggles at the flare of light down the tunnel.

"You need to leave," said Iris.

The wash of light painted the faces of the other kids. They watched her with bated breath.

Leonardo bit his tongue. *Dammit. They know it's fake.*

"Come back here tomorrow with the general, and we'll talk."

He paused. *Or maybe not.*

"Deal," said Leonardo.

Iris briskly crossed the room, nodding to the boys behind Leonardo. He turned just as they stepped away from the exit.

"Let's go," he said under his breath, pushing Moth forward. They followed Iris out of the chamber and through the curved tunnel to the main entrance.

"Thank you for agreeing to a meeting," said Leonardo.

"That thing you talked about…" said Iris. "What did you call it again?"

"The Dark," said Leonardo.

"Right."

Leonardo could virtually see the phrase playing behind her eyes—*THE DARK IS COMING.* He'd made sure to drive his knife deep into the wood as he carved the message into the tree.

"We have reason to believe you're telling the truth," said Iris.

Leonardo kept his face impassive as he nodded. "We'll see you tomorrow."

CHAPTER 26

"H urry up," hissed Leonardo. They rushed along a heavy branch, ducking as bats dipped and dove around them.

"If the general buys our message as quickly as they did, it shouldn't be that hard," puffed Moth.

"Are you sure they bought the message?" asked Kate. She stepped in a rotten knot and nearly lost her footing. Leonardo and Moth faltered, but she waved them forward, staggering into motion again. The length of their absence from camp loomed like a hammer about to fall.

"They sent us away." Leonardo frowned at her as they ducked around a growth of luminescent moss, casting her and Moth's faces alien green. "If they thought it was a trap, they wouldn't have let us go."

Right?

They'd set the ball rolling. Now they needed to wait for to-morrow to see how it played out. Leonardo pulled Pinch's night vision goggles over his eyes again, enhancing his view of the moon-lit forest.

"Come on." He pushed the pace. "We need to get moving."

***

Leonardo slipped back into the sleeping hollow, breathless, followed by Moth and Kate. The rest of the clan slept on their rolls, vague lumps in the darkness. He'd given them explicit instructions to go about their night as normal. To preserve the alibi, nothing could appear out of the ordinary. And to the casual passerby, the absence of two Ravens and a pirate was barely noticeable. Moth crossed to where his sleeping roll had been stashed under a pile of random supplies.

Everything was falling into place.

Not everything. Memories of Kate kissing him burned in his mind like a bad dream.

How do I tell Viola? He raked his fingers through his hair. Guilt washed over him as he picked his way between the sleeping bodies. Kate been trying to steal a kiss since they were onboard *The Forever.*

I shouldn't have let her get me alone.

That was his fault.

"Leo." Kate tugged his arm. Dread weighted his stomach.

"What is it?" he whispered, sharp enough that she pulled back as if burnt.

"I…I'm sorry." She chewed her lip, opened her mouth, closed it again, then sighed.

Really? An apology from Kate? That was a twist Leonardo hadn't anticipated. He measured his words.

"Get a few minutes of sleep," he said finally. "It's going to be a long night."

Kate nodded tightly and peeled away from him, lowering to her spot near the wall. Leonardo shifted his gaze to Viola's sleeping form, curled up next to his own empty roll, and the stress of the night suddenly crashed over him. Getting in and out of the camps, faking the signs, learning about the fairies, dealing with Kate...

But he couldn't let it swallow him yet. The most intricate part of the plan still lay ahead, and he had new information to share.

He stepped around Pinch's hat and over Jack's sprawled arm, then crouched and shook Mishti's shoulder.

Mishti grabbed for her throwing ring before her eyes were even open. Leonardo stopped her arm, and she blinked up at him.

"Oh, it's you." Her tone wasn't particularly warmer than the first time they'd met. Dodge death together or not, Mishti was still Mishti.

"I need to talk to you," whispered Leonardo.

He hid Pinch's night vision goggles as they crept down the tunnels, in case they ran into a Red Flag. Only once they were on the stairs in the tree's core did Leonardo slip the goggles over his eyes.

"The fairies are guardians," he told her as soon as they'd descended out of earshot from anyone passing above.

"What?" Mishti's voice was still slurred with sleep. "The *fairies*?"

"Think about how many times they've helped us. And that's not all..." Leonardo relayed everything that had happened at the Blue Flag tree. Except for Kate.

Mishti rubbed her eyes. "So, what does all that mean?"

"Well," said Leonardo. "Do you remember the comment Thaisa made to Tokala? She said, 'you've always wanted to be guardian of everything.'"

Mishti crossed her arms. "Thaisa was bitter at everyone."

"I know," said Leonardo. "But maybe she was bitter for a reason. Tokala told me once that the Natives hadn't left the Darkwoods in ages because we killed each other faster than all the other corners of the woods. That may be true for the Cove, but here in the Redwoods, they vanish each other constantly."

"So he lied?" Mishti unfolded her arms.

"I think so. Why not travel here to help since their vanishings are clearly worse than the Darkwoods."

"Dammit, you're right," said Mishti. She sounded awake now. "Plus, the guardians of the Redwoods are being held captive. Tokala could have helped them escape."

"Exactly." Leonardo adjusted his goggles. "So what if Tokala did something a decade ago, like try to become the guardian of everything, which forced the woods to intervene?"

"What do you mean, intervene?"

"I think Tokala wasn't allowed to leave the Darkwoods. That would explain why he never came to help the fairies and why he lied about his reason for staying—he would never admit it was his prison. And maybe that's why the fairies avoided the Darkwoods…they certainly wouldn't help him out if his mistakes had stranded their own corner of the woods."

"So then," said Mishti, "when the Dark came in, and the Lostwoods needed him, he was finally allowed to return to the Cove?"

211

If all that was true, it meant things were a lot more complicated than he'd realized. And things were complicated already. In the silvery light of his goggles, Mishti chewed the edge of her nail.

"Why do you call it the Lostwoods?" asked Leonardo suddenly. He still didn't quite understand that.

"What?" Mishti glanced at him. Even though she couldn't see him, her eyes narrowed in the direction of his voice.

"Everyone from the Cove says 'Lostwoods.'"

Mishti furrowed her brow. "We're all lost, aren't we? We don't know where we came from, where we're going…Even the Lostwoods itself has no real sense of direction; it picks favorites, then gets bored of them, it starts games that can never end. We're all lost here."

"Do you really think that?"

It added up. But at the same time, it didn't. It was too obvious.

"I think we see it clearer in the Cove than anywhere else," said Mishti. "Because we're the end of the river. Everything eventually winds up in the Cove, and it's still lost."

The pirates, thought Leonardo. *The Natives, us, the fairies…*

There had to be a purpose. But he was running out of places to learn that purpose. *Does anyone have any idea what's going on?*

Rapid footsteps echoed down the stairwell. Leonardo whipped around. Whoever it was didn't carry a light, or else the glow would have already reached them.

"Get back against the wall," he breathed to Mishti, flattening himself to the smooth interior of the tree. He slowly drew his sword, and Mishti dropped a throwing ring into each hand. The steps grew closer and closer, descending the spiral of steps, until

Jack suddenly rounded the corner, one hand on the wall as a guide.

"Jack," whispered Leonardo.

Jack jumped, nearly losing his footing.

"What's going on?" hissed Mishti.

"Kids are going missing," gasped Jack, out of breath. "The general told us to do a headcount, then he ran off. If you're both gone when he gets back—"

"Let's go," said Mishti.

The Blue Flags.

The truth hit Leonardo like a wall. *We were followed.*

CHAPTER 27

"Y ou were followed?" demanded Mishti. "How could you be so stupid?"

"Shh," hissed Leonardo. They jogged down the hallway to their sleeping hollow, his goggles shoved in his pocket.

A thought struck him.

"Jack," he whispered. "Did he see the crocodile?"

"The general?" Jack shook his head, still running. "If he did, he didn't say anything."

The general rounded the corner ahead of them.

Dammit.

"There you are," stammered Leonardo. "We were looking for you."

For once, the general was too preoccupied to be suspicious. "Our camp has been infiltrated. Get your clan up and ready to move."

He tried to step around them, and Leonardo grabbed his shoulder. "How many are there?"

The general shook his head. "We haven't found them yet."

"What?" demanded Mishti.

A kid sprinted past them, red flag bound tight around his arm. He gripped a slingshot with white fingers.

"We're looking for them now," said the general. "Get everyone into the big hollow."

Then he pulled free of Leonardo and ran around the corner.

Leonardo looked at Mishti and Jack. Their wide eyes mirrored his own.

"Come on." Leonardo took off for their sleeping hollow, Mishti and Jack's steps pounding behind him.

They burst through the door to find everyone on their feet. The kids jumped at their sudden arrival, hands going to weapons.

"Is everyone here?" asked Leonardo. He scanned faces, stopping with relief on Viola. She stood with one hand on Pompey's shoulder and another on Charley's. Behind her, Cato and Bates helped Pinch stand with his broken leg.

Viola nodded. "We're all here."

Thank God. Leonardo swallowed, leaning back to see down the empty passage.

"Ok." He drew his sword. "We're moving to the big hollow. Let's go."

Mishti took the lead, a throwing ring in each hand, as Leonardo ushered everyone out of the room. Pinch pulled a grimace, hopping one-legged with an arm over each of Bate's and Cato's shoulders. Kate came last. And she was angry.

"What did you do?" she hissed.

"You were out there too," whispered Leonardo, walking backward as he exited the sleeping hollow and scanned the opposite end of the tunnel. "Did you see anyone?"

Kate made a derisive noise, then she glanced down a narrow, off-shooting tunnel. She grabbed Leonardo's arm.

"Come with me."

Leonardo stared at her, incredulous. "No."

"Do you want to find these Blue Flags or not?" Cold focus glinted in her eyes.

"Jack." Leonardo picked the closest Raven. "Come with us."

Jack eyed the tunnel, then Leonardo. "We need to stay—"

"With the group?" replied Kate. "Are you six years old? Follow me."

Jack still hesitated, but Leonardo clamped a reassuring hand on his shoulder. Jack met his gaze. He swallowed hard, then nodded. "You're the boss."

He jogged after Kate. Leonardo cast one last look over his shoulder, then swore and followed them, stooping as the tunnel grew smaller.

Why are you doing what she wants? he snapped at himself.

Because she gets whatever she wants, another voice reminded him. And she was their best chance at finding the Blue Flags. She had played this game longer than all of them combined and spent the decades since infiltrating clans' camps with the pirates in the Cove. Leonardo wasn't prepared to lose another clanmate. If Kate thought she could root out the Blue Flags, he was willing to give it a shot.

"The dangerous thing is," she whispered to him and Jack,

"this could have been the Blue Flags' tree last. They could know these passages better than we do."

She held her sword in front of her as the passage grew rapidly darker.

Leonardo fished Pinch's goggles from his pocket and pulled them over his eyes one-handed. His heart raced. He felt ready to throw up. He wanted to be with the group, to make sure everyone got safely to the big hollow.

And once they got there? Then what? The entire thing could be a big ambush.

If they know the tree as well as we do, they could be expecting us to gather there.

He stopped in his tracks.

"What now?" hissed Kate.

Leonardo voiced his realization, and Kate shook her head. "That's not how it works here. They'll pick off the loners, then they'll leave. Attacking a large group is no one's style here."

"Like us?" said Leonardo.

"What?"

"You said they'll pick off the loners." He gazed around the tunnel. "We're very alone."

Kate rolled her eyes. "No, not like us, because we'll pick them off first. Now *come on.*"

She yanked his arm, and Leonardo ran after her. Jack sprinted behind, his sallow cheeks and tattered tailcoat rendering a ghostly silhouette in the half-light.

A moment later, they stepped out into another main artery. Kids ran past with armfuls of weapons and baskets of food supplies. Each one jumped at the sight of Leonardo and Kate, and

Leonardo tensed in return, but all wore their red flags, and they nodded tersely to one another before rushing down the tunnels.

One girl stopped them, desperation on her face. "Have you seen Robin?"

Leonardo's breath snagged. His clan had lost their own Robin back in the Cove. To Kate's pirates.

"I don't know who that is. Kate scanned the passage behind the girl.

"He has brown hair," the Red Flag insisted. "He's about the same height as you," she told Leonardo. "He wears his flag like a headband."

Leonardo hadn't seen anyone like that.

"If we see him, we'll send him to the big hollow." Leonardo prayed that gathering everyone there was the right move.

The girl's face fell. She nodded, blinking back tears, and stepped around them.

"Where *are* they?" hissed Leonardo. His nerves pulsed like fireworks, crackling under his skin.

"There are lots of places to hide inside a tree," said Kate. "Attacks like this started back in my time."

The passages became quieter by the minute as everyone migrated to the big hollow. Leonardo realized just how temporary these camps were. Everything could be gathered in minutes as they prepared to abandon the tree. Only a handful of hunters crept through the passages now.

They encountered the general, and he acknowledged them with a nod, pointing them down one tunnel while he and another kid started in the direction Leonardo, Jack, and Kate had just come from.

"We already checked there," said Jack under his breath to Kate.

"Which is why the intruder might feel safe to come out," she replied, just as quiet.

Leonardo glanced at her. "You think we missed them?"

Kate shrugged. "I told you; there are lots of places to hide inside a tree."

They rounded a corner and came face to face with Viola. Her face flooded with relief.

"You're safe," she breathed.

Leonardo's panic pulsed to the front of his mind. *Why is she here?*

"What's wrong?" he asked.

Viola blinked. "You disappeared. That's what's wrong. I couldn't sit in that hollow and keep waiting for you."

"We're safe," said Kate brusquely. Her eyes darted from one end of the tunnel to the next.

"Then come back to the hollow," Viola told Leonardo. Her tone softened. "I can't lose you. I've been searching with my mind, but I can't see anything. I'm scared, Leo."

Kate looked from Leonardo to Viola. She smiled, and Leonardo's stomach clenched.

"Wait until you hear what happened over at the Blue Flag camp—"

"Kate, that's enough," snapped Leonardo. This was the last way he wanted Viola to learn that she'd kissed him.

Jack glanced at Leonardo, sword clenched. He looked wildly uncomfortable.

Before Kate could speak again, Viola stepped up to her, hands in fists. She stood a few inches shorter than the pirate girl, but her swiftness forced Kate back on her heels.

"Maybe at some point during the hundred years," she spat, "you would have learned to grow up."

"I. Can't." Kate grit her teeth. "Dammit, don't you get that? I'm stuck here. So I apologize if I'm hard to take, but I'm the last one to blame for that."

"Ok, ok." Leonardo held up his hands. The pressure inside the empty corridors was high enough already. They needed to de-escalate, fast.

"Kate," he continued. "None of us know what you've been through. I can't imagine any of it has been easy, but—"

Something pricked Leonardo's neck. He flinched, grabbing for the spot and finding the feathered tip of a dart.

Shit.

He yanked it out, just as Kate staggered back, a blue dart poking from her arm.

"Over there!" Viola loosed her slingshot as a shape ducked away down another passage. The pebble hit the wooden wall and ricocheted. Jack took off, sword flashing as he raced for the corner.

Leonardo and Kate threw their darts on the ground, and Leonardo fumbled for his slingshot. The intruder poked his head around the corner again, a blowgun to his lips, and Jack dove to the ground. Leonardo, Kate, and Viola threw themselves against the walls as a dart whisked between them.

The Blue Flag looked at Jack as he scrambled back to his feet. He raised his blowgun again, then Viola loosed another shot, and the intruder ducked out of sight.

"Let's go!" Leonardo was already running to join Jack. The corridor tilted, and he fell to one knee, blinking hard. The puncture on his neck pulsed red hot.

Jack almost reached the corner when the Blue Flag emerged again and shot him point-blank. Jack staggered back, his sword clanging against the floor as he scrabbled for the dart. The shooter swung to face the rest of them, and Kate threw herself aside, crashing into the wall. Leonardo stared down the barrel of the wooden weapon, no more than fifteen feet away. Then something struck the blowgun with a loud crack. The weapon jerked, and the Blue Flag kid dropped it, shock on his face. Leonardo glanced at Viola, slingshot in her hands.

He stumbled to his feet as the kid grabbed his blowgun and ran. Leonardo drew his sword and clenched his teeth against the waves of dizziness. He ran to the corner and stopped himself against the wall, watching the kid run away. Kate fell against the other wall, swearing under her breath. Jack lay slumped a few feet away, breathing heavy.

"Come on," said Viola. "Let's get you to the big hollow."

Leonardo squeezed his eyes shut. He could feel the poison mixing with his blood. He knew it wouldn't kill him—his flag would make sure of that. But he wasn't in any shape to fight. He managed a nod and straightened, forcing his eyes open. In his blurry peripheral, Jack struggled to his feet.

Leonardo made eye contact with Viola as they started down the corridor. It was a long walk back to the hollow, and they were now exceptionally vulnerable.

"Quicker," he urged, forcing his legs to move.

They navigated the tunnels in a blurred haze, staggering and

221

half-running and falling. Viola dragged him, Kate, and Jack to their feet every time they stumbled, checking anxiously over their shoulders. Leonardo couldn't muster the coordination to do the same, so he relied on Viola as lookout and guide. She closed her eyes at every corner, and he knew she was searching ahead with her mind.

Finally, they rounded the corner into the hum of voices and warm air of the big hollow. Leonardo blinked at the fairy-lit faces clustered together in the vast space. The first time he'd been here, it was pitch black. Now, all the cages had been removed from their hooks and clustered on the ground, casting enough glow to light the farthest corners of the room. Every supply and possession belonging to the clan was piled beside them, ready for evacuation.

Leonardo took two steps, then all the strength sapped from his legs, and he struck the ground.

CHAPTER 28

When he came to, it felt like only seconds had passed, but they were heavy seconds, and he guessed it had been a lot longer. His throat was exceptionally dry, and a vicious headache dug into his skull.

Leonardo tried to speak, but it came out mumbled. His mouth felt gummy. He grimaced and tried again, blinking up at Viola's blurry face.

"Water," he managed.

Viola said something to someone nearby. Moth appeared with a canteen, and Leonardo struggled into a sitting position. Pinch and Moth and Bates and all the others crouched nearby, watching him anxiously.

Leonardo accepted the water and swallowed a mouthful. It barely even touched the dryness.

"I'm ok," he told his clan. He drew a shaky breath. He could still feel the poison, but its effect was wearing off. Viola slipped her fingers into his, and Leonardo met her dark eyes. The fairy-lit cages reflected in their glassiness. Dried tear tracks traced a path on her skin.

"I'm ok," he told her, softer. A few feet away, Kate stirred. Jack grunted, eyes blinking open. Everyone's attention shifted to them, and Leonardo sat up straighter, pulling Viola's gaze back to him.

If not for her, all three of them would have been vanished. His guilt doubled.

You haven't been listening to her lately. When it boiled down, Viola had been at the root of almost all their successful plans. And since reaching the Redwoods, he'd barely given her a breath to voice her opinion.

"We're a team, ok?" he told her. "I promise."

Viola nodded. She started to say something, then closed her eyes and nodded again. Leonardo leaned forward and kissed her. Her lips parted into a small smile as he pulled away. Then he darted a glance at the other kids nearby.

"Later," whispered Viola, still smiling.

Leonardo nodded.

A clatter of footsteps drew his attention as Mishti and the general rounded the corner into the hollow. The general threw five flags on the ground. They were red.

The victims. Leonardo scanned a quick eye over his clan. Everyone appeared to be accounted for.

Then Mishti threw an additional four flags on the ground. All blue.

"We think we've eliminated the threat," said the general. "It's time to move."

Viola squeezed Leonardo's fingers. "Do you have the strength—"

Leonardo was already pushing himself up. He winced at a wave of dizziness, but he could stand with Viola's help. Kate and Jack were still semi-conscious, so Leonardo looked around.

"Cato, Bates," he called, cringing at the rasp of his voice. "Come help them."

To Cato's merit, he didn't resist. He lumbered across the room, stopping inches from where the poisoned kids sprawled on the floor. Jack gazed up at him, apprehension on his face, while Kate blinked unseeingly at the ground.

Be gentle, Cato, thought Leonardo. His own legs wobbled, and he gritted his teeth, fighting to stay upright. Viola held him close, and he leaned against her.

"I've got you," she whispered.

Then Cato grabbed Jack off the floor and tossed him over one shoulder. Jack let out an 'oomph' of air as Bates helped Kate upright.

"My life gets stranger by the day," said Pinch.

"Amen," grunted Jack, slung in a fireman's carry.

"Wait 'til you visit the Cove," said Pinch. "You haven't seen weird until an octopus tries to eat your face."

"He's not wrong," said Bates mildly, supporting Kate on his left side while helping Pinch back to his feet.

"Be careful—" Leonardo started to say, then he coughed, doubling over.

"Save your strength." Viola held him around the torso. "I have a feeling we're not out of it yet."

And she was right. They filed out of the tree in a tight pack, two-hundred strong, into the first breaths of the morning. The first steps of what would become an all-day journey to find a new tree. Watery light cut the gloom, and dew dripped from redwood boughs. Spiderwebs glittered in the sun. The morning birds were louder than the night birds, and they sang in full voice today.

Kate was right, too; the Blue Flags only targeted stragglers. Once the clans were bunched together, they didn't see even a flicker of Blue Flag stalkers. Which filled a missing piece of Leonardo's puzzle.

That's why neither side can win the game. They only inflict surface wounds on each other's clans.

Things got complex when the general finally found a tree. Leonardo, Kate, and Jack had mostly recovered from the darts, but he still insisted they join the first party to occupy the new tree, and Leonardo didn't complain. The hours of climbing had left him exhausted.

They joined a party of a dozen, who were asked to simply stay out of sight and watch for any Blue Flags who might have followed them. The rest of the clan splintered into more groups than Leonardo cared to count. They would spend the rest of the day and night moving from tree to tree as decoys, hunting any Blue Flags on their tails, and only returning to the new tree once they knew they were alone.

All of that disruption gave Leonardo the opportunity to meet with his clan out of the general's eyesight. The new tree had a sort of roost in its canopy, sheltered by boughs and isolated enough that a person could position themselves in such a way to know if anyone was approaching.

Jack took the first watch. Pinch reclined nearby, one arm draped over a branch and his casted leg propped up.

"They tricked us," said Leonardo. "They knew we created the fake message, and they followed—"

"Are you sure?" Moth plucked pine needles from his pant legs. "It seemed to me like they believed it."

"Then why attack us?"

"Why not?" Moth tossed the needles into the wind. "Maybe they believed the message but lied about wanting to meet the general. Maybe they think they can fight it on their own."

"Why lie about that?" Jack twisted to frown at him. "Why not just vanish you right there and get on with it?"

"Because I miscalculated," said Leonardo slowly. "I thought 'seeing' the Dark would be enough to make them set the game aside. You're right, Moth. We never specifically told them that uniting was the *only* way to defeat it. Maybe they think they can do it on their own. They might have believed it *and* taken the opportunity to follow us."

"Not that it makes a difference," said Kate dryly. "They clearly don't want to work together." She sat cross-legged on a narrow branch which bobbed every time the wind gusted. She jumped down and reached in her pocket. "In other news, I figured out a thing."

She procured her double flag and flicked the newer end to Leonardo. He caught it hesitantly, and Kate let go of the ancient, salt-stained half.

She backed up; arms spread in victory.

Leonardo frowned at the pair of flags hanging from his grip. Moth reached for the second one, but Kate darted forward first, closing it in her fist. "I think it only works because Leonardo never touched this one."

She tugged them both out of his grip. "It's not considered a capture if he never actually touched it."

Leonardo tilted his head.

"I don't think the new flag does anything," Kate elaborated. "My original flag is still *my flag*. The new one is just a useless piece of cloth. Since you never touched my real flag, I never vanished. Ta-da!"

That sort of made sense.

"So, only contact counts." Leonardo studied the pair of flags. "The new one acts like a handle, so I could hold your flag without touching it."

Kate nodded once. Her trilby hat shifted off-kilter. "Precisely."

"How did you figure that out?" asked Viola.

"It's a...long story." Kate swallowed hard, avoiding eye contact with Leonardo.

When I grabbed her flag in the tree.

He blanched. *If I had grabbed the wrong flag, would she have vanished?* He hadn't realized it was that tenuous.

He felt the conspicuous bulk of his own flag, tied around his arm. Then he realized something.

If we can dart both leaders...

"What if we tied the general's flag with Iris's?" Leonardo yanked back his sleeve, staring at the knotted red fabric. "If I tie them to mine, I can hold both without vanishing them."

Moth tilted his head. Bates frowned.

"Then they'll *have* to listen," said Pinch.

We can force them to unite.

"I can use the handle concept," pressed Leonardo. "Right, Kate?"

"So long as you only touch yours." She shrugged. "Sure."

"They'll have no choice." Leonardo drummed his fingers on his leg, excitement building as he pieced it together. "We need to find Iris again."

CHAPTER 29

That afternoon, the general sent Leonardo into the trees on an observational patrol. Leonardo supposed that was the consequence of muddling up every chance they'd had to eliminate Blue Flags on their past patrols. At least the general seemed to believe those muddled attacks were innocent mistakes and not sabotage. More than ever, Leonardo needed him to believe that.

His patrol partner was the general's second in command, a boy with a thin nose and flat hair, who went by the name Derby and appeared to be roughly the same age as Leonardo.

"Understanding how we operate is an important step to understanding the fight," said Derby.

It's also a good way to keep me out of the fight, thought Leonardo. On top of that, the general had taken Viola on his own patrol today, which got deeper under Leonardo's skin than he cared to admit. Viola could take care of herself; he knew that but he'd also seen the way the general watched her, and he despised the idea of him being alone with her.

And it didn't stop him from triple-checking that Viola carried her weapons or from slipping her a pouch of extra sharp-edged pebbles for her slingshot.

"Young ones!" Derby addressed the line of new kids standing on a wide branch. "Today, we will test your quickness." He tossed a burlap sack at each of them. "You'll be catching fairies."

This is pointless. Leonardo spent the first half of the afternoon watching the new kids sprint precariously through the treetops, bagging fairies and missing more. It wasn't until the sun edged west, filtering through the A-frame peak of two leaning boles, that Leonardo realized the good fortune of his assignment. Derby was too distracted managing the kids to keep an eye on him, and if his bearings were correct, he wasn't far from the Blue Flags' camp.

Or at least, their old *camp.* He doubted they would've stuck around after his party discovered it.

*But maybe...*Leonardo scratched his chin, slowly bending to pick up an abandoned burlap sack.

A good strategist would anticipate me returning.

He wasn't from the Redwoods. He was new to the game. They'd set a meeting for today, and he had good reason to keep it, if only to demand answers. Iris seemed smart. If she was anything like Aleksander, she would hide her clan but make herself findable to Leonardo, then follow him back to their new camp for a second attack.

Only, he wanted to be followed this time. And Iris would have the tables turned on her when she realized her flag was missing.

231

The bulk of Pinch's goggles pressed at Leonardo's hip, jammed in his belt behind his sword. If Iris kept their meeting, he was certain she would use the Redwoods clans' favorite trick and hold it in darkness.

Exactly what he needed.

He took one last look at Derby's back, then stepped out of sight.

Leonardo's stomach jumped to his throat. He started at a slow, silent jog, which evolved to a flat-out sprint once he'd cleared his patrol's earshot. At one point, he lost his balance while climbing over a dried-out shell of a tree, riddled with woodpecker holes. His foot punched through the splintered bark, and his knee struck the jagged edge hard.

Leonardo gasped, clinging to the wood for a terrifying moment, then carefully freed his leg and continued onward at a checked pace.

Derby has to have noticed I'm gone by now.

Leonardo wasn't sure how he would react. If he went back for the general, Leonardo's newest—and hopefully final—plan would be forced into action immediately. But if Derby chose instead to look for Leonardo himself, Leonardo might have time to steal Iris's flag and rejoin the se-com's patrol without raising any alarms. He could pretend he'd gotten lost and wandered away from the group. He gauged himself a window of twenty minutes before that story lost its credibility.

The big, mossy tree became visible out ahead, like a skyscraper looming between neighboring buildings. Leonardo redoubled his efforts, charting the straightest course he could manage through the overgrowth.

232

The exertion helped him think, and he'd almost reached the Blue Flag camp when a realization struck him.

It was Kate's behavior that triggered his cognizance. Last night, he'd thought, *the higher the stakes, the more she misbehaves.*

And she wasn't the only one.

The Dark only attacks during pressurized moments. The first time they ever experienced it was when he and Ajax fought over the leadership of Raven Clan. Next was during the spell that Caliban cast to amplify Viola's abilities. The Dark intercepted and cut her off, leaving a crocodile skull in the snake pit. Third, when they were outrunning the pirates, and the Dark trapped them in the lake on the Turquoise Isle. Tensions were running high when the storm struck *The Forever* at sea, and the fifth time was literally as they prepared to fight it, with all the clans of the Cove.

The Dark is fueled by our emotions.

Leonardo caught his breath. *Of course it is. It's a nightmare.* A nightmare they were all experiencing at once. Which meant that a collective sense of fear would feed it.

It needs us. The children of the woods are the catalyst. The volume of their emotions enabled it to manifest.

Keeping everyone calm wasn't an option—these kids were too volatile for that. But now, they could anticipate its strikes. And if Leonardo's move spiked tensions as much as he expected it to, an attack was coming soon. He dried his palms and kept climbing.

We're running out of time. We need to get together and prepare.

At last, he reached the mossy wall.

You might not escape this one, a voice warned him. He'd promised Viola he wouldn't take unnecessary risks. And he'd promised he

233

would listen closer to her advice. He expected she would have serious reservations about this idea.

It's too late to turn back. And this *risk* would poise his alliance to end the game. With the leaders' flags, they could coerce a truce. Even if it would be the most hostile initiation of a truce in history.

Leonardo crept low through the treetop greenery, pushing big, waxy leaves aside. A rustle to his right froze him, and Leonardo's mouth fell open as a slender, spotted deer stepped out between the boughs. It blinked at him, big and glassy, then slipped out of sight, stepping carefully along the branches.

How the hell did it get up here? Leonardo was still frowning in the direction it had disappeared when he placed his hand on a cold, slimy shoot.

Oh no.

He looked down, into the face of a tiny yellow flower, suspended on a delicate stem from the slick vine. Leonardo released his breath and lifted his palm off the sliminess. For a moment, he'd been afraid it was the carnivorous plant again.

Then the flower twitched, and a thin stream of liquid jetted from the heart of its petals.

Leonardo reeled back. It splashed into his left eye, and coldness spread across his face, tingling like hundreds of pins in his skin. He cried out, rubbing his eye as blackness blotted out his vision.

Oh my god. Icy coldness penetrated his skull as he scrambled away from the flower. He stared around wildly with his one good eye while ink enveloped the other, numbing half his face. He glimpsed movement in one of the tree's hundred openings.

Shit.

The Blue Flags.

They're waiting for me. Just as he'd expected. And here he was, flailing around and shouting and drawing all of their attention while a flower robbed half his vision.

Panic rose in his throat, a hot acid that set his heart racing. He wanted to run for cover; he wanted to know if his vision was permanently damaged; he wanted to go back in time and avoid that godforsaken flower. But he refused to bail out and let his clan down.

How many Blue Flags are in the tree? More likely than not, they'd scattered themselves among the openings. No good leader would leave a back door unguarded, and this camp possessed a plethora of back doors. He would need to act fast. In and out before they could assemble. He drew a steadying breath, then stepped out of his tree's shelter and crossed a suspended log to the plant-covered false door, his one good eye zeroed in on the target.

He'd blown the element of surprise a beat earlier than he'd hoped to, but if he moved swift enough, he could turn the odds back in his favor. He wanted Iris to know he was coming; he needed the chamber already in darkness.

Leonardo pushed the wooden panel, his fingers nestled among feathery green fungus. It slid back with a scrape, revealing an empty corridor. He leaned the door against the wall, leaving his exit route unimpeded, and started into the tree. A fairy cage hung every fifty feet, lighting his path. The miniature guardians flocked to the bars, flapping frantically and gripping the thin wood with tiny hands. Their prisons swung urgently as Leonardo jogged below them, sending shadows pitching crazily across the walls.

He squinted at the tumult overhead.

If this is a warning, he thought at them. *I already know I'm in danger.*

Leonardo retraced his steps to the large chamber where he and Moth had spoken with the Blue Flags. He picked up the pace as he hooked around corner after corner, ears trained for the softest rustle of clothing. The whine of wingbeats was a distraction he didn't need. At any moment, a dart in the neck could drop him.

It took Leonardo fifteen seconds to reach the rounded chamber opening. He'd been away from Derby for over ten minutes, and time was running thinner by the second.

The fairies in the last cage didn't panic like the others. These ones hovered with a quieter sort of anticipation, small eyes trained on him. Their glow bled a few feet into the chamber, but inky blackness awaited him beyond that. If any fairy cages existed inside, they were heavily draped.

Here we go.

Leonardo took a bold step off the stairs and into the shadows.

"Hello, Leonardo."

Iris's immediate acknowledgment made him jump. His mouth turned dry as he swallowed his nerves.

"Iris," he said tightly.

He moved deeper into the blackness. Soft step after soft step until he could be sure he'd become a ghost. Then he freed the goggles from his belt and pulled them over his head.

"I wondered if you would come back." Curiosity piqued the cultured tilt of her voice. The room flared into silver focus through a single goggle lens. She stood in the same spot as before, a draped cage by her ankle. Her brother vanished through a doorway, just like last time.

He'll be back with the others soon.

"The Dark is real," said Leonardo. "We need to work together."

"Whether or not that's true, surely you've been here long enough to realize we don't work together. We never have, and we never will."

Stubborn idiots. He hadn't expected much better, but it grated on his anxiety all the same. *This pigheadedness is going to kill us all.*

Leonardo quietly drew his sword, using the sound of her voice to drown out the soft rasp of metal on leather. His stress swelled. Stress of being inside their camp, of losing his vision, of the cold numbness spreading down his neck, of the Dark looming over them.

Stop. He pursed his lips and willed his hands to quit shaking. His mouth tasted bitter as he framed his next statement.

"I think you'll change your mind." He took a cautious step closer, one eye on the door. "We'll be easy to find when you do."

"What does that mean?" asked Iris.

Leonardo carefully described the location of the new camp. Then he took another step, and another, barely breathing. He identified the lump under her sleeve.

Her flag.

"I don't know what trick you're trying to play." Iris's severe features drew together. "But you realize we can't let you leave, right?"

Another step. Another. He was ten feet from her now.

237

"Leonardo?" She reached for the drape over the fairy cage. Leonardo charged the last few steps, twisting his sword and striking the dull hilt against her skull.

The thud of metal on skin echoed through the chamber as she dropped into his arms. Leonardo lowered her rapidly to the ground. She would live, of course; he'd only hit her hard enough to knock her unconscious, but she would have a painful lump when she awoke.

He flicked his gaze to the door. Distant footsteps carried through the corridor.

Dammit.

Leonardo grabbed the burlap sack he'd snatched from Derby's patrol and yanked it free of his belt. He slipped his arms inside, forming the world's most shapeless sock puppet. Awkward and cumbersome, but it was the best option he had. Using the sack as a barrier, he clumsily rolled back Iris's sleeve and started on the knot of her flag, working his nails into the burlap weave.

Don't poke a hole, he warned himself. For this to work, he needed the barrier intact.

Iris's knotted flag came loose, if only from sheer force of will. He flinched the moment it broke contact with her skin, but Iris didn't vanish. He dropped the flag beside her.

It worked.

He didn't have time to celebrate. The running footsteps drew closer.

He shook one arm out of the sack and ripped his own flag from his pocket. He'd untied it already during the climb. He dropped it on top of Iris's, then plunged his arm back inside the coarse bag and fumbled to tie them together, swearing under his breath at the lack of dexterity.

Hurry up, hurry up, hurry—

Finally, he got the fabric knotted. Leonardo flipped the sack inside-out, sealing the bundle inside. He tied it closed and looped it through his belt just as five Blue Flags flooded through the second door. They each carried a draped cage. More approaching footsteps promised the rest of the clan followed hot on their heels. Leonardo picked up his sword. They couldn't see him yet, but he'd be silhouetted when he reached the other doorway.

"Hello?" called the first. "Iris?"

Now or never.

Leonardo took off. He tugged Pinch's goggles from his face as he reached the light. Shouts exploded behind him, then a grunt and a crash. Leonardo winced. One of them must have tripped over Iris.

He didn't look back, taking the stairs three-at-a-time. He summited to the corridor above and threw himself around the corner. A scrawny Blue Flag boy froze before him. Leonardo recognized him from the treetop garden. He shouldered the boy into the wall. The kid hit the wood with a cry. Leonardo didn't break pace. Boots pounded the steps in pursuit as he wove through the abandoned corridors and burst into daylight.

A stunning vista of sprawling woodland awaited him, painted in late-afternoon golds and orange. He raced over the log bridge, barely dodging a slick of moss, and flung himself into the vegetation as a blowgun puffed behind him. A dart whisked over his head. Leonardo startled a hawk from a narrow perch, and it leaped airborne, patterned wings expanding with a whoosh as he

239

staggered past a sappy green tendril. He'd had his fill of the Red-woods' sinister plants and cut a wide berth around it.

His depth-perception was shot with only one eye. He careened through a blur of sunset-tinted greenery. Sticks snapped behind him. Fear stuck a knife in his chest.

They're gaining.

Leonardo sprinted into a cloud of tiny insects. He swatted them off his face and dove inside a hollow vine that bridged a sheer gorge. He slid the first ten feet and scrambled on all-fours until he could regain his footing in the stinking tunnel.

The ground quivered as his pursuers hurtled after him. Leonardo ran up the far side and vaulted through the opening, over the fork that supported it. He landed off-kilter in a patch of turquoise lichen and torqued around, spinning on all-fours until he faced the direction he'd come. The mouth of a tight gap yawned at him, formed by the vine's ill-fit into the fork. He hesitated for a split second, then dropped to his stomach and elbow-crawled underneath, scraping his back as he shimmied into the shadow of the vine.

Something snagged and tugged free of his belt. For a horrified moment, he thought it was the burlap sack, but it clunked as it fell loose.

Pinch's goggles.

He twisted, but the space was too narrow, and he never stood a chance of catching them. The goggles spiraled into space. The bug-eyed glass struck a gnarled knot and splintered with a distinct *crack.*

Shit. He punched the bark. Pain blossomed in his knuckles. He'd just lost their most valuable tool.

The gargantuan vine shook, and Leonardo's attention snapped back to his pursuers. He pulled his legs out of sight, compressing his body into the gap.

A brace of greenery hung next to his face. Leonardo grabbed it, ignoring the stab of needles, and bent it to obscure his position even more, wedged in the junction. He held it steady, pressing his mouth against his other sleeve to quiet his rapid breathing as all five Blue Flags flung themselves out of the vine, their feet inches from his head.

His faulty vision impeded his ability to see them without turning his head, but each impact cracked like a snare drum. They scrambled for purchase on the lichen and raced away. Seconds, and they were gone.

Leonardo closed his eyes, thanking the woods.

More crashing and thundering steps perked his ears.

The rest of the Blue Flags.

He released the umbrella bough and began to rapidly lower himself into the crisscross below his hiding place. His twenty-minutes had expired. He needed to find Derby again *now*.

CHAPTER 30

Iris's flag weighed like an anchor on Leonardo's hip. It took a dozen carefully inculpable answers to appease Derby's suspicions, but Leonardo would've been happy to lie his way through a thousand questions, so long as Derby was the one asking them and not the general.

Strangely, Derby didn't say anything thing about his eye, which had to mean it didn't look any different. That gave Leonardo a glimmer of hope, although the blackout remained unchanged. At least the numbness had begun to subside.

He played out an array of mental scenarios as they returned to camp. He couldn't steal the general's flag until Iris, and the Blue Flags were at their doorstep. He'd given her explicit directions, but he'd also left her unconscious and scattered her clan in pursuit of him. It would take more than a few moments for them to regroup and come after her flag.

But they'll come. He was certain of that. And he would use the blindside of their arrival to paralyze any retaliation from the Red Flags when he nabbed the general's flag. In the meantime, he couldn't look any of his hosts in the eye. The burlap sack felt transparent, and his nerves jumped at every sound.

They can't see the flag, he told himself. *They don't know what you're planning.*

He was like a parasite, moving among them in the close quarters of their treetop home. A strange guilt ate at him. All these kids were innocent. They played the *game* because it was all they knew. And he—an outsider—was about to give them an impossible ultimatum; stop playing or sacrifice your leader.

We're saving them. Even if they couldn't see it, banding together was the only way to survive. He pushed his reservations down.

But uprooting their world wasn't the biggest guilt on his mind. His kiss with Kate burned in the pit of his stomach.

You need to tell Viola, his conscience warned him.

He contemplated the alternative. *The kiss meant nothing. What does it hurt if she never knows?*

Beyond that, he needed everyone completely focused. Viola especially. Telling her about the kiss could hinder her concentration when they needed her most.

But if Kate said anything...

If Viola found out...

If I lie about it, she'll never trust me again.

He squared himself, accepting his fate. *She deserves to know.*

Once he pulled the pin on this final plan, all the chaos under the surface would finally erupt. He couldn't do that without confessing to Viola first.

Leonardo sought her out, desperately aware that Iris could

arrive any second and pull the pin for him. When he finally found Viola, she was sitting in a recessed nook, eyes closed in meditation.

He hesitated, sick to his stomach. Her delicate eyelashes fanned across the tan skin of her cheeks, slightly flushed in the warmth of the tree. Her lips parted ever so slightly, then sealed again in a twist of pensiveness. Her braid draped over the rawhide cloth of her dress, riddled with loose threads and missing beads.

He was equal parts enraptured by her and flooded with dread. She looked so peaceful and he was about to crash through with a sledgehammer.

Viola's deep brown eyes blinked open. Frustration glimmered at the edges.

"I can't find him," she said quietly.

"Who?" Leonardo frowned, so lost in his own troubles that he couldn't tie her words to a meaning.

"Nym." Viola rolled her shoulders. "I keep searching from him, but it's like looking through a haze."

Nym. Leonardo cursed himself. With the Redwoods set to explode, Nym had slipped almost completely from his mind. Leonardo's hope wavered. His vow to guide everyone out alive didn't seem as realistic as it once had.

Leonardo swallowed. His fingers twitched, and Viola drew her eyebrows together. "What's wrong?"

Leonardo opened his mouth. Closed it again. Opened it again.

Just say it.

"Kate kissed me."

Viola went very still. He searched her eyes, but the instant betrayal he expected wasn't there. Instead, a more complex storm clouded below the surface. Two teeth pressed into her lip.

"When?" she asked calmly. She shifted to give him a space to sit.

"Last night." Leonardo sat in the recess beside her. "I pushed her away—"

"The general kissed me too," interrupted Viola. She said it fast, the five words linked like one.

"What?" Leonardo vaulted to his feet. His blood pounded red-hot in his skull.

"Leo," Viola reached for his arm. "I pulled away. Trust me. He's a jerk."

Leonardo pressed his heels into the ground. He hoped the general would fight back when he captured his flag. Maybe Leonardo could *slip* and vanish him after all. His nails dug into the palms of his hands.

I need him to live, so I can negotiate.

Actually, that wasn't necessarily true.

Derby can be negotiated with…

"Leo. Sit down."

Leonardo took a step toward the recess, then one toward the main passage, then balled his fists and sat again.

"Neither you nor I initiated it," said Viola. She placed her hand on top of his, gentle and tender. "We did nothing wrong."

Leonardo nodded. She was right, of course, but she wasn't the subject of his anger. Someone *had* done something wrong, and that someone deserved a dart in the back and a punch in the face.

Viola turned his chin to face her. "I love you."

Leonardo stared at her.

I love you.

Her breath was warm, close beside him. The waft of jasmine that always accompanied her drifted to him. The electric rush of her energy pulsed like a snare drum, and Leonardo brushed his fingers across her cheek. When his mind got racing, she alone could steady him.

"I love you too," said Leonardo.

They kissed, and for the first time since reaching the Redwoods, Leonardo felt like everything would be ok.

Viola gasped and pulled back.

"What?" Leonardo's breath snagged. The look on her face made all of their problems slam back onto his shoulders.

Viola drew a shallow breath. "I know where Nym is."

CHAPTER 31

Viola sprinted ahead of Leonardo, rounding corners so fast that he nearly lost his footing following her. She hooked around a bend down a narrow tunnel, then stopped in the exact center of the passage.

"He's here." Viola eyed the smooth wood around them.

It struck him like a punch in the gut. Leonardo raked a hand through his hair as the horror sunk in.

The black sap. The putrid smell on the stairs. *The vision*; spires of dripping blackness in place of the lush trunks.

Viola had been telling them for weeks; *the Dark is everywhere*.

Just because they couldn't see it in the Redwoods didn't mean it wasn't there.

The Dark is inside the trees.

"Inside the…" he started.

Viola nodded, her eyes wide.

"What do we do?" he asked.

Viola swallowed hard. "Cut it open."

Leonardo looked at the wall, striped with red grain, then down at his sword, then back at Viola's face, sober with the implications. He cursed his blind eye. He couldn't think straight with tunnel vision.

"What if Nym—"

"He's not *here*, exactly," said Viola. "But this is the closest point. You won't hurt him."

Leonardo wasn't certain about anything, but he trusted Viola. He drew his sword and stabbed it into the wood. He yanked it out and peered into the jagged wound. Nothing. He stabbed the same spot, wrenched out his sword, stabbed it again.

"Leo," said Nym. Leonardo and Viola whipped around. Nym stood like a specter in the tunnel behind them, shaking. The veins across his hands and up his arms were black and thicker than ever, and they grew darker by the second.

"*Nym?*" they said in sync.

"Is that really you?" asked Leonardo.

"I think so." Nym looked down at himself. His voice quivered. "I've...I've been inside the Dark."

What the hell does that mean?

Nym flickered like a thin mirage, and Leonardo's heart sunk. He remembered Dakota, Viola's brother, visiting them in a similar fashion.

He's not actually here.

"Listen," said Nym. "The Dark is bound inside the trees. And I'm bound inside the Dark. If you keep cutting..."

"We'll set you free," gasped Viola.

"But we'll be freeing the Dark too," finished Leonardo.

248

Nym nodded gravely.

Leonardo pushed everything out of his mind. *There's only one choice.*

Viola voiced it for him. "Do it, Leo."

He stabbed his sword into the tree. It jammed, and he wrenched it free.

Nym flickered again.

"You're sure this will work?" Leonardo asked it even as he rammed his sword through the wound again.

Nym curled and uncurled his fingers. He pinched himself in the arm and winced. "It's working."

So Leonardo cut and cut, deeper and deeper until the blade suddenly went limp. It folded like molten steel as thick black blood flooded from the tree.

"Oh my god." Leonardo released the leather handle and staggered back, mouth agape as the Dark consumed the blade. The syrupy mass rolled down the wall and straight upward at the same time.

"My arms!" Nym bared his forearms, pale and pasty and devoid of a single black vein.

He's back.

"We need to go." The flowing mass of the Dark reflected in Viola's eyes, spilling from the wood like gallons of inky sap.

Leonardo nodded, his heart slamming in his chest. "Come on—"

A stream of the Dark shot from the wound in the tree, straight for Nym. Leonardo reacted out of reflex. He shouldered Nym aside and threw his arms up. The Dark slammed into his hands, and his sea-monster bite flared red-hot. Leonardo screamed, yanking his hands back. The Dark crystalized, frozen in a mid-air splash with Leonardo's handprints branded into it.

Pinpricks buzzed across his skin, and Leonardo backed up, staring wide-eyed at the Dark.

"Run!" yelled Viola.

"Leo." Nym yanked his shoulder. "This way."

Leonardo staggered after them. He glanced back. The Dark seeped from the wall, flowing over the frozen splash.

The trio burst into the main passage, and Leonardo braced himself against the wall. His hands burned ice cold.

Moth, Pinch, and Jack came running toward them. Pinch no longer wore his cast.

Leonardo's eyes widened. "Pinch, you're—"

"I guess the flags work." Pinch shook his previously broken leg. Then he froze. His mouth fell open.

Moth gasped. "Nym?"

"You found him." Shock filled Jack's voice.

"Don't sound so disappointed!" Nym grinned.

"It's here." Leonardo cut their reunion short. He nearly choked on the words. "It's been here the whole time."

He swore at himself. Once again, they'd taken too much time preparing. The clock wasn't running. It had *run out.*

"The Dark." Moth didn't ask so much as state the self-evident.

Leonardo nodded. "Where's Mishti?"

"She went with Juliet and Sophie to that lookout spot," said Pinch. "I think Juliet was going to tell her about the new plan. Tying the flags and everything."

Fresh dread settled in Leonardo's chest. Every time Juliet took things into her own hands, she set off a bomb in the process.

250

Dammit. "Viola, Nym, come with me."

"Wait." Moth stopped him. "The fairies started talking to me again."

Now? Leonardo gritted his teeth. He'd already put the flag plan in motion. He needed to get to Mishti and Juliet before they did something stupid.

Thankfully, Moth recognized his urgency. "I'll explain later, but we need to free them now."

"Ok." Leonardo nodded. Moth rarely asked for much. Leonardo trusted his judgment. "Do it. And get the rest of the clan ready."

"For the Dark?" asked Pinch.

"For the Dark."

CHAPTER 32

Leonardo, Viola, and Nym pulled themselves up into the lookout spot just as Mishti stepped back from Juliet, arms spread. A pair of knotted red flags hung from Juliet's right hand. Sophie watched intently from a few feet away. All three girls wore their gold Lion Clan robes. A stiffening breeze fluttered the tattered hems.

"What are you doing?" demanded Leonardo.

The setting sun painted everything rosy pink, glinting off the sheen of their robes. Tiny rips and snags proved that life in the treetops was taking its toll.

"Testing Kate's theory," said Juliet. She tossed her ringlets off her face, then her eyes widened. "Nym? Where did you—"

"Alone?" Leonardo's gaze darted from Mishti to her flag, dangling from Juliet's.

Bars of shade striped their faces. A leaf's oversized shadow curled across Mishti's cheek as if the woods were stroking her face.

He'd long sensed the woods' possessiveness, and the image set his bones on edge.

Sophie sighed. "We knew you would want to be careful with it. We don't have time for that."

I already took Iris's flag. Their test was unnecessary. They were a step behind, but it wasn't entirely their fault. He hadn't communicated his decision to initiate the plan.

I was out in the forest. I never had a chance to.

"Do you realize the risk you took?" he snapped. Of the three Lion girls conducting the experiment, only Juliet had been present to witness Kate attempt it.

"Someone had to try it." Mishti stepped forward into a beam of pink light. "And I'm not risking one of my girls."

Juliet and Sophie kept their chins high, positioned behind Mishti in a sort of triangle. Three Lions facing three Ravens. Leonardo was beginning to detest clan lines.

"We need to work together," he implored her. "We'll achieve nothing if—"

"We *are*—" started Sophie.

"Sophie." Mishti interrupted her. "Let me handle this."

Sophie froze, the rest of her argument half-shaped in her mouth. She tightened her lips.

Mishti faced Leonardo again. She crossed her arms. "We *are* working together. Remember when the storm hit the ship, and you insisted on being the one to go topside? Well, now it's my turn. And look; it worked!"

Another gust stirred her flag, dangling from the knot just below Juliet's grip. A flock of sparrows whipped past, flickering like sparks through bars of fiery sunlight.

Leonardo swallowed his retort. *Just tell her what she wants to hear.*

"It worked," he agreed hesitantly. "Now—"

"We're going to end this godforsaken game," declared Mishti, puffed with her distinct brand of self-inflated ego. "I did what needed to be done."

No, you didn't, he wanted to snap. As usual, Mishti had done what Mishti wanted and nearly left him without a co-leader.

"But we're with you," she assured him, glowing with self-importance. "It's Lion Clan's duty to protect the Lostwoods."

He resisted the urge to roll his eyes. *It's all of our duty.*

Before he could reply, Mishti frowned. "Why are you turning your head like that?"

"Excuse me?" Leonardo stared at her, then he realized he was overcompensating for his eye. He sighed. "A flower sprayed me in the face. I've been blind on this side ever since."

"What?" demanded Viola. She took his cheek and forcibly turned his face toward her, scrutinizing his eye. "When?"

"Out in the trees today—"

"Is it permanent?"

"I..." Leonardo met her distress with helpless uncertainty.

"I don't think so," Juliet stepped forward. "I've been talking to the Red Flag kids about the magic here. Your flag should heal you."

Leonardo released a breath he didn't know he'd been holding. *Thank god.*

"How soon?" he asked.

"A while, probably." Juliet shrugged apologetically. "Pinch's leg is still broken, after all."

"No, actually, it's not anymore."

Which meant Leonardo's wait might not be so long.

Unless that flower was an exception, and it doesn't heal. There were no guarantees in these woods.

The strongest gust of wind yet plastered Leonardo's shirt to his back. Juliet gasped as it tugged the flags from her grip. Sophie lunged for them.

"Sophie, wait!" shouted Leonardo.

Her hand closed around Mishti's half.

"No—" the word was torn from Leonardo's mouth as Mishti vanished.

CHAPTER 33

Sophie dropped the flags, yanking her hand back as if burnt. The knotted fabric sailed into a brace of dead sticks.

"No, no, no!" Leonardo's head rushed with blood, pounding like thunder in his ears.

"What happened?" Horror flooded Nym's face.

She's gone. His thoughts were the loudest part of it. It was like she'd simply slipped underwater, with less commotion than a breath of wind. The breeze that stirred the trees was now as hollow as the space where Mishti had stood.

Sophie's mouth hung open. The color drained from her face. "What did I do?" she said softly.

"Oh my god." Juliet looked ready to throw up.

Leonardo ran his hands through his hair, working his jaw. He didn't even understand his emotion. Something between anger—at Mishti and her impatience, at Sophie for grabbing the flag, at Juliet for still operating independently—and devastation to lose a friend, someone who he'd grown to trust implicitly and who trusted him in return.

"Why would you catch it?" he demanded.

For a suspicious second, he nearly accused her of doing it on purpose.

She's been resisting Mishit's authority for weeks. But the shock on her face was too real to fake.

"I…" Sophie stared at the red piece of fabric, flapping where it had jammed in the sticks. "Juliet said once they're tied together, we can—"

"Still only touch our own," interrupted Leonardo. He now knew where things went wrong. "Which you would've known if Juliet had told you."

To Juliet's credit, she didn't deny it.

"It's my fault." Her voice dragged with guilt. "I missed that part."

"That's the most important part!" Leonardo almost yelled it. "How do you miss that?"

Viola balled her fists. "If Sophie caught your half instead," she snapped at Juliet, "or even *touched* both flags, we would be going down there right now to tell Moth that you vanished."

Juliet went even paler. She began to shake, her breaths coming faster.

This is a disaster. Leonardo paced to the edge of the lookout, wishing for the second time today that he could go back in time.

"I'm sick of these flags." Viola swore. "We never should have accepted them."

Leonardo agreed wholeheartedly. But his ever-present subconscious chipped in with the stubborn argumentativeness that

Mishti would've provided. *If we didn't, we never would have stood a chance of uniting the Redwoods. The Dark would—*

The Dark.

"What are you all talking about?" demanded Nym. "What are these flags?"

"Later," snapped Leonardo. "Juliet, go get your flag." They'd been in the middle of a crisis already. Multiple, actually. He forced his grief down, blinking at the moss-covered branches while Juliet ruefully retrieved the knotted fabric. Viola squeezed his arm, watching him through troubled eyes.

"The Dark is here," said Leonardo. Mishti's last moments haunted his mind, burned like a brand on the inside of his eyelids.

"What?" Sophie and Juliet stared at him.

"The Dark is here," Leonardo repeated. "Minutes ago, it attacked Viola, Nym, and me. We need to move."

He watched the sober comprehension soak through Sophie's shell-shocked exterior. She drew a deep breath, started to say something, then gritted her teeth. She swallowed and squared her shoulders. "What's the plan?"

Leonardo could barely look at her. Mishti had taken the risk, and Juliet's mistake caused her disappearance, but Sophie was the one who'd grabbed the flag. Mishti's blood was on her hands, and a cold bitterness rose in Leonardo.

"We end the game and get the hell out of the Redwoods," he snapped. "Follow me."

"Uh, Leo..." Nym crouched, squinting through the sticks. "Who is that?"

"Who?" Leonardo dropped to his knees, peering down at an army of tiny figures creeping through the lowest level of greenery, too far below to distinguish any details. He wouldn't have even spotted them, if not for Nym's hyper-perceptiveness. He'd been night-watchman at Raven Clan for a reason.

"Blue Flags." Leonardo swore again. He still hadn't brought the clan up to speed. "Listen," he said briskly. "I have Iris's flag."

CHAPTER 34

W here's the general?" Leonardo asked a Red Flag girl in the corridor. She jumped at his intensity.

"In his chambers," she stuttered.

Leonardo breezed past the girl and marched down another tunnel. Viola, Sophie, Juliet, and Nym hurried after him. He'd learned that the architecture inside the biggest trees bore a consistent resemblance, and it didn't take long to find the cone-shaped room below the general's quarters, a mirror image of the one Charley and Pompey had shown him.

Leonardo burst in and froze. The general stood near the spiral stairs, surveying dozens of empty cages.

"Did you free the fairies?" he demanded, advancing on Leonardo.

Leonardo reached for his sword, but a puff of air stopped them both short. A dart whisked from the hole in the ceiling, piercing the general in the back of the neck. He grunted in pain and ripped it out, spinning to see the opening.

High above, Moth knelt in a golden glow, a blowgun at his lips. Viola moved from Leonardo's side, crossing the floor in three steps and stabbing a second dart inches from where Moth's had pierced.

This time, the general dropped to his knees. His fingers scrabbled to pull it loose, but his energy sapped too fast, and he careened over.

It all happened so quickly that Leonardo remained rooted where he'd stopped. Both Viola and Moth had acted without hesitation. Like true Ravens.

That's the kind of precision we need, he thought, *if we're going to survive this.*

Moth slung the weapon over his back and hurried down the precarious steps, followed by Charley, Pompey, and an entire flock of fairies.

Viola's red-feathered dart protruded from the general's skin. Blood beaded at the site of Moth's initial shot, a hand's-width from hers. Leonardo slowly approached his prone form.

"Leo!" declared Charley. "We freed the fairies!"

Hundreds of tiny lights wove around their heads.

"The Blue Flags have come," Leonardo told Moth and the kids. "It's time to end this."

"They're *here*?" said Moth.

"I stole Iris's flag." Leonardo untied the burlap sack.

"You did *what*?"

"Keep up, Moth," said Viola. "We're going to win."

She dropped to her knees and helped Leonardo rapidly search the general until they found his flag. Leonardo tied it to the loose end of his own, careful to not even brush Iris's. A few feet away, Nym, Sophie, and Juliet watched with enough breathless anticipation that he could taste it, like a singed undercurrent in the room. He dropped the chain of flags back inside the bag and straightened, then plucked Viola's dart from the general's neck and tossed it aside. "Let's go. Nothing keeps him down long."

They fled the chamber, a cloud of fairies behind them.

"Moth." Leonardo pointed at the swarm. "What did they tell you?"

Before he could speak, a rumble vibrated the tree. Everyone froze. A black drip ran down the wall, inches from Leonardo's head and his one good eye. He recoiled, then Viola and Juliet gasped, shrinking back from a bubbling crevasse.

Ahead of them, a river of black tar flooded from the mouth of an adjoining passage. Charley screamed. The tunnel vibrated again, and the Dark seeped thicker from the wood grain.

It's manifesting. The Dark was gaining strength.

Pinch, Jack, Bates, and Cato rounded the far end of the tunnel.

"There you are!" shouted Pinch. "I—"

They staggered to a halt at the sight of the oozing passage, as thick and heavy as a lava flow. A rancid smell drifted from the growing mass.

"It's going to consume the whole tree," shouted Leonardo. "We need to evacuate!"

A few Red Flags appeared behind Pinch and the Ravens. Their eyes widened at Leonardo's words and the sight of the Dark.

"What about the general?" hissed Sophie.

A bellow echoed from the general's chambers.

"He'll catch up," said Leonardo. "Go, go, go!"

They ran at the ooze and leaped for the far side. Eight pairs of feet struck dry wood, and Leonardo's party joined Pinch's and the Red Flags as they sprinted to abandon ship. A drip fell from the ceiling, splatting on the ground ahead of them, and Leonardo's mind was transported back to the hold of *The Forever*.

Another storm is coming.

Kate darted out of the next tunnel, and Leonardo had a sudden idea. He glanced at the Red Flag kids, then tugged the burlap sack from his belt and shoved it into her arms.

"What is—"

"Hide this." He would be the target of both Red and Blue anger. If they got a hold of him, he couldn't risk having the flags on his person. Kate was the most experienced at protecting flags; if she could preserve her own for a hundred years, he trusted her to guard these for a few minutes.

She untied the knots and squinted inside, still running, and let out an exclamation of surprise.

"The plan is in motion," puffed Leonardo, still watching the Reds. Their attention was fixed on the Dark dripping from their camp as they wove through the vibrating corridors. Kate nodded once and buried the bag inside her jacket.

They piled out the tree's entrance to the sight of the entire Blue Flag clan, positioned with blowguns raised in the twilit greenery.

Shouts erupted from both sides, and the whoosh-hiss of darts filled the air. Leonardo threw himself flat, cursing his blind eye for the millionth time. Around him, kids fell limp, blue-feathered darts in their skin. Pompey dropped next to Leonardo, his face slack. Half a dozen feathers pricked Cato's chest before he crashed to the branch, narrowly missing a barrel-rolling Bates.

Rage flooded Leonardo's senses. He yanked the dart out of Pompey's shoulder.

"Stop!" he yelled. "Everyone, stop shooting!"

Bodies littered the net of boughs.

None of them are getting vanished today, he vowed.

The Reds who'd managed to dodge fire shot back and the Blue offensive faltered. Moth fumbled with the weapon he'd taken from the general's quarters, puffing darts at their attackers.

"Leo!" Pinch elbow-crawled over Jack, who was still conscious and let out a grunt of pain. In Pinch's hand, he clutched a bull-horn, bright red and shiny like something from a carnival. His hat tilted cockeyed on his head.

"Try this." He threw it to Leonardo, who caught it and brought the mouthpiece to his lips.

Brilliant.

"Enough," ordered Leonardo, his voice booming through the canopy. "One more shot, and I vanish Iris."

The firefight was in its final breaths already. Half the shooters had abandoned their posts to pull darts out of clanmates' skin, and the volume of shots plummeted by the second. One last rogue dart zipped over his head as if challenging his threat, then the blowguns fell silent.

"Put down your weapons," Leonardo instructed both clans. In his peripheral, the general emerged from the tree. For the first time since they'd met, he looked uncertain.

"What did you do?" his voice shook.

"How did you take my flag without vanishing me?" Iris demanded.

It took Leonardo a second to locate her voice. She crouched behind a gnarled outgrowth. Even from here, he could see the glisten of sweat on her forehead.

She knows we hold the leverage.

The ambush had been a clever approach; a hail-Mary, but they'd failed to reach Leonardo, and they were now at his mercy.

Even if they had reached me, he thought, *they wouldn't have recovered her flag.*

Finally, a plan had worked. Kate crouched among the Reds, completely inconspicuous as she helped remove darts.

"I'll explain everything," he replied. "But only if everyone *drops the weapons*. If you attack us, I'll be forced to vanish you both."

"Ok, ok," Iris held up her hands. Her blonde ponytail hung frazzled and wide freckles stood out against the flush of her face. "We hear you."

Her brother crouched just behind her, a slingshot bruise on his cheek.

"Where did you get that?" The general pointed at Leonardo's bullhorn. It looked starkly out of place in the forest.

One of my clanmates imagined it with a hat.

A cracking, groaning noise emanated from inside the branch. Leonardo's blood turned to ice. Then Pinch caught his eye. He winked from under the slant of his hat.

The wood vibrated under Leonardo's knees. A statue erupted through the bark, as black as coal and three-times Leonardo's height. Screams filled the air as kids scrambled away from it. It

265

wore an inky suit of armor, with a little wooden sign clutched in its rigid grip. Jagged letters read: *THE DARK IS HERE.*

Leonardo remembered Pinch's words. *I have a brilliant idea to scare these halfwits with.*

He marveled at the giant looming over them. Even knowing it was fake, it struck a note of fear deep in his chest.

Good timing.

"What the hell is that?" a Red shouted. The same one who'd first guided Leonardo's party to the general, with a slight accent that now quivered. He sheltered behind a spiny, prehistoric-looking treetop plant, his pale eyes and paler skin ghostly in the rapidly dying light.

"The Dark," lied Leonardo. "Everyone, get to the forest floor!"

He glanced at the entrance to the tree. None of the real Dark had emerged yet, but he knew it wouldn't take long.

"*Now,*" he snapped through the horn.

Kids rushed into motion. The general ushered them forward, never taking his eyes off the statue. Wide-eyed terror replaced his typically cocksure smirk. Leonardo would've savored seeing him knocked down a peg, but his own fear soured the moment.

"Wait," said Pinch suddenly. "Where's Mishti?"

Leonardo's mood darkened.

They don't know yet. Pinch had been gathering the Ravens and Moth freeing the fairies when Mishti vanished.

"She's gone." Sophie stepped around a fern growing from the bark, a new rip marring her gold robes. She broke the news with a sort of dutiful stoicism that raised a new question in Leonardo's mind.

266

Who becomes leader of Lion Clan now? Himself, who still held a stake as co-leader, or Sophie, Mishti's appointed second-in-command? Sophie, Juliet, and Pompey were the only Lions left in their party, but an entire clan of girls awaited them in the Highland.

Pinch frowned, adjusting his hat. "You mean—"

"Vanished," said Sophie.

"She lost her flag," added Juliet before anyone could ask.

Interesting choice of words.

"Damn," said Bates.

"Fuck," said Pinch.

Leonardo was grateful the Lion girls had been present when it happened. Now wasn't the time for a detailed recount, and none of the Ravens, nor the Blue Flags, pressed for one.

He cleared the lump in his throat. "Let's keep moving."

They descended to the forest floor in a tense hush. Whispers permeated the pressurized atmosphere. Leonardo wondered if the Reds and Blues had ever gathered in their entirety like this. When they finally reached the bed of rust-colored needles, the two clans split apart, leaving Leonardo and his party of thirteen in the middle. It wasn't unlike the gathering they'd attended in the Cove's sacred cave.

Above them, the tower of the tree they'd been camping in loomed like a ruddy monolith. He contemplated how fast the Dark could melt through elements of the dreamworld. If it felled the tree, they would never be able to outrun its girth.

If it's infiltrated our tree, it's probably doing the same in all of them.

Running wasn't the answer anymore.

"Can I have the horn?" asked Kate sweetly.

Leonardo paused. *This isn't the plan.*

She took the bullhorn from his grip. Leonardo released it reluctantly. Pinch frowned, and Viola stepped up beside Leonardo, slingshot in hand. A few feet away, Moth whispered something to Juliet and nodded ever-so-slightly to the underbrush. A twinkle of light drew Leonardo's attention.

"We don't have time to waste here," announced Kate. "So, I'm going to cut to the chase."

"Kate—" started Leonardo.

"I have your flag too." A threat sharped her tone. She revealed the burlap sack, and Leonardo's heart stopped. She was right. In handing her the general's and Iris's flags, he'd surrendered his own.

What the hell?

"Everyone's going to listen to me," said Kate. "We will *not* merge the clans. We will *not* end the game—"

"Merge the clans?" demanded the general. "What are you talking about?"

Leonardo swore under his breath. *Why, Kate?*

"That's his plan." Kate pointed at Leonardo. "But I'm not going to forfeit the game."

She never stopped playing. All this time, he'd been focused on the general's resistance, but even after a hundred years, Kate was just as obsessed with winning as the rest of them.

She's insane.

"What about the Dark?" said Viola.

Kate faced her. "We can defeat it without ending the game."

That will never work. Leonardo hadn't been in the Redwoods for even a week, and he could see that was impossible. The Blues' disregard of their carved warning proved it as clear as anything. So long as the flags existed, the Redwoods kids would never be able to focus on anything but each other.

A boom shook the woods. A blast of air slammed into Leonardo, and he staggered back, throwing his arms over his face. Hundreds of kids ducked and scattered. Above them, through a gap in the trees, a black line raced across the sky like a crack in a sheet of glass.

Viola grabbed Leonardo's arm. A bolt of terror struck deep in his bones. Gasps and cries filled the air. Kate sprinted for an arching root and summited it in three strides, the bullhorn still in her grip.

He couldn't let her speak again. She was a loose cannon—she always had been, but he'd let himself ignore it. Now he paid the consequence, and they couldn't afford to have their first successful plan destroyed in her collateral.

He took a stride after her, but Viola's fierce hold on his arm stopped him short, her gaze locked on the broken sky. Then Moth grabbed Leonardo's other arm. "I can stop all of this."

"What?" Leonardo tore his eyes from Kate and zeroed in on Moth. "How?"

Around them, Redwoods kids straightened, glaring at both Leonardo's party and Kate atop the root. She still held both leaders' flags, as well as Leonardo's. If she was taken down…

"Trust me," implored Moth. "The fairies…" He hesitated as the Blue Flags and Red Flags closed in around them.

There's no time.

Leonardo hated going into a plan blind. But he trusted Moth more than nearly anyone in the woods.

"Ok." Leonardo nodded. "Do it."

Moth whipped his free arm into the air like a race marshal. Instantly, thousands of fairies erupted from the greenery, twinkling like confetti. They shot past Leonardo's head, weaving above the gathering to the buzz of wingbeats. A gold cloud cascaded below them, coating the skin of the Redwoods kids and sending them toppling to the earth.

What the…?

A few tried to break for the perimeter, but clusters of fairies hurtled after them, cutting them off and dropping them in clouds of gold. The general fell flat on his back, and Kate tumbled gracefully from the root. She landed in a bed of auburn needles, the burlap sack sliding from her limp fingers.

Within seconds, Leonardo's party of thirteen were the only kids left awake. Every one of them stared, agape.

"They put them to sleep," said Leonardo slowly.

"That's why they keep them in cages," said Moth. "The fairies have never liked the game. They're telling me to burn the flags."

*Burn the flags…*When Tokala—guardian of the Darkwoods— ended Aleksander's tyranny, he'd used fire.

"Then we'll burn them," said Leonardo. "We'll have to tie them all together first, so we can do it without 'capturing' anyone's flag."

He surveyed the hundreds of sleeping kids. It would be a massive job.

"Unless I can do it," said Nym. "I never took a flag, so technically I'm not part of the game."

Interesting.

He made a good point.

270

"I don't know if that's how it works." Leonardo chewed his lip. They had already lost Mishti testing a theory. He wasn't prepared to repeat that mistake.

He leaned back, shading his eyes at the canopy. The camp opening was too distant to make out, but Leonardo thought he caught a whiff of the Dark.

"When I was inside the Dark," said Nym, "the only reason it didn't consume me was because I learned to control it. It's made of imagination, just like everything else." He looked Leonardo in the eye, with a sort of steady wisdom he hadn't possessed before. "If we control the dream, then we write the rules."

"Ok." If Leonardo had learned anything from Aleksander's mistakes, it was this: a good leader didn't call all the shots. He needed to put faith in his clan.

Careful to keep clear of the gold dust, Nym crossed to the burlap sack laying near Kate's open hand. He leaned down and loosened the drawstrings.

"Nym!" Viola jumped forward. "Don't—"

"Don't worry." Nym glanced back. "I won't touch Leo's. It's the middle one, right?"

Leonardo nodded tightly. His stomach jumped into his chest and his lungs constricted with anticipation. He darted his gaze from the sleeping general, to Iris's prone form, to Nym, who slowly dipped his thin arm into the sack.

"Nym—" Leonardo flinched, but Nym never steered from his task. The burlap shifted, and he pulled all three knotted flags into the open.

Leonardo's heart stopped. But both leaders remained unaffected, deep asleep beneath a layer of fairy dust.

He's right. Leonardo's head spun. He grappled with the implications.

A second boom threw Leonardo off his feet. He crashed and rolled hips-over-shoulder into a pile of gold dust.

Dammit. Leonardo scrambled on all-fours and staggered to his feet, frantically brushing off the dust. The others did the same, and the fairies split formation, sparing them from the glittering shower.

Leonardo's nostrils constricted. In the wake of the second impact, the Dark's rotten taint seeped from every direction.

"Nym," Leonardo ordered. "Gather every flag. Everyone else, help him, but only Nym touches the flags."

His clan sprang into action.

"Moth, Pinch, Viola," he continued. "Start gathering wood. We're building a fire."

***

Moments later, Leonardo stood over a roaring blaze, the heat baking his face.

"Ready?" Nym watched him from across the fire, clutching the burlap sack, now stuffed with a garland of red and blue flags. For the first time in ages, he looked confident and in control.

Leonardo regarded the twelve remaining members of his party, their firelit shadows stretching long and distorted over hundreds of sleeping Reds and Blues. The Redwoods kids glittered under a net of gold dust, carefully tended by legions of fairies. The crackle of the fire and the whir of tiny wings beat an urgent rhythm. A somber truth pulsed in time with it; if Leonardo sacrificed his flag, his eye may never heal.

But we'll succeed. We can go north and find the others. His friends would stand a chance to survive.

272

Leonardo drew himself up. "Burn it."

CHAPTER 35

Nym tossed the flags into the heart of the blaze. Sparks flew skyward. The flames danced high, crackling in breathless anticipation. The fairies wove faster; a blur of carnival lights.

Leonardo remembered watching flames race along the rope bridges at Raven Clan. A guardian was involved in that fire too. And a corner of the woods was unraveled.

Am I making the right choice?

He couldn't help but see the resemblance.

Nym stepped back as the flags burned, shriveling rapidly as they charred, the colors unrecognizable. Meanwhile, dozens of kids slept, oblivious.

"Nothing's happening," said Sophie.

"Nothing's happening," agreed Leonardo.

He squeezed Viola's hand. "It works."

"Our turn," said Sophie. The Ravens and Lions solemnly

untied their own flags and dropped them into the flames. Leonardo's had gone down with the general's and Iris's, but he winced as each of his friends surrendered their safety nets.

We're vulnerable again.

Last of all, Nym lifted Kate's ancient flag and ceremoniously cast it, along with its newer counterpart, into the fire. All thirteen kids watched the final two flags burn. When the Redwoods kids awoke, they would be untethered from the game.

Moth tipped his gaze upward, the electric dance of fairy-lights reflecting in his eyes. An unspoken message passed between him and the fairies, and they lifted away from the clearing. Their dust evaporated, and the magical glow faded to the mundane flicker of firelight. Near Leonardo, the general coughed, rolling as he and everyone else began to wake.

Here we go.

"What the hell…?" The general blinked up at Leonardo. He shoved himself to his feet, gazing around wildly. Not a single kid wore a flag.

"What the…" His eyes flicked to the fire, burning in a tidy circle of soot-covered rocks. He lunged at Leonardo, grabbing him by the collar.

"Woah!" Leonardo staggered back a step. The general came with him.

"Hey!" Every member of Raven Clan jumped to Leonardo's aid.

"It's ok." Leonardo held up his hands. He didn't blink, his good eye locked inches from the general's. He didn't need his clan creating a fight.

"Who do you think you are?" hissed the general.

Around them, the rest of the Redwoods kids climbed to their feet, searching feverishly for their flags. Steel hissed as swords and knives were drawn.

This kind of tension was exactly what they *didn't* need.

We're feeding the Dark, thought Leonardo.

"Listen," he told the general, trying to keep his voice steady. "We're—"

"What did you do with our flags?" the general demanded, jerking Leonardo by the collar.

Leonardo squared himself, still locked in the kid's grip. "We burned them."

The general released Leonardo and punched him in the stomach faster than Leonardo could flinch. He gasped, folding in half.

Chaos erupted. Pinch and Bates tackled the general before he could strike Leonardo again. The general twisted, elbowing Bates hard and throwing a vicious right hook that Pinch barely dodged, his hat flying off. Then Cato hit the general, like a bull to a matador that didn't see him coming. Cato didn't even bother with his fists; he just dropped his shoulder and ran his victim over. The general's feet left the ground as he flew backward, then he slammed into a twisted root with an unforgiving crack. A breathless gasp tore from his lips.

Leonardo yanked his sword from his belt as hundreds of kids crashed together, screaming and swearing at each other. The whisk of blow-darts punctuated the first few moments, but close combat didn't lend a kind hand to shooting-style weapons, and charging kids sacked the gunners to the earth. The tragedy of it slammed into Leonardo harder than any blow; without the flags, everyone was vulnerable to the hundreds of blades swinging beneath the cracked sky. They could decimate their own numbers in minutes if this wasn't stopped.

Two kids ran at him. He couldn't tell if they were Red Flags or Blue Flags, but he didn't care. Their tenuous alliance was broken. Leonardo slashed hard as the first boy reached him. His sword rang out, vibrating the blade of his attacker, and the kid stumbled back, surprise on his face.

Never had a real fight? thought Leonardo. He hacked and cut at the other kid, disarming him in seconds, then he reversed a swing hard enough to knock the sword from the first boy's weak grip. He was desperate to spare their lives and slow the damage.

The rest of his clan wasn't as careful. This was a Darkwoods fight, and outnumbered as they were, Raven Clan had a distinct advantage. Bates, Pinch, Jack, Moth, and Nym fought through the thick of their assailants while Cato threw aside Redwoods kids.

Meanwhile, more Red Flag and Blue Flag kids tore into each other. Even without their colors, rivalries died hard. Leonardo could barely breathe as the nightmare unfolded in front of him.

"Hey!" he yelled. "Stop fighting!"

A girl ran at him, a knife in each hand, and Leonardo slashed her backward, reversing just as fast, so she dropped her knives as she fell to the ground, eyes wide. Near the middle of the clearing, Sophie leaped onto the root Kate had used before.

"The game is over!" she yelled. "Drop your weapons!"

No one even glanced at either of them. Near Leonardo, a girl ducked around a sapling and ran from the fight. She sprinted hard into the trees before a slingshot twanged, and she grabbed the back of her head, tripping into a pile of deadfall. A second later, a boy broke away on the exact same path as her. He dodged around the girl and vanished into the trees as another slingshot stone missed him and deflected off a trunk.

"The flag tree!" yelled Sophie.

Leonardo glanced at her.

"What?" he shouted back.

"He's going for the flag tree!" yelled Sophie.

Another pair of kids tore through the trees in the same direction.

To restart the game. If they brought everyone new flags, all of this would be for nothing.

Shit. Leonardo took off after them as Sophie dropped from the root into the middle of a throng of fighting kids. A hundred swords and bodies blocked her path to the trees, and Leonardo didn't wait for her. He sprinted around the edge of the battle, then spotted the fire.

What if…

Leonardo changed course. A long stick lay next to the flames; he grabbed it and shoved the tip into the fire. Ten feet away, Pinch punched a Red Flag and dropped him to his knees. He ran to Leonardo's side.

"What are you doing?"

"I need to burn the flag tree," puffed Leonardo, watching as the pair of kids disappeared into the underbrush.

Pinch frowned at Leonardo's stick as he lifted it, flames licking halfway down its length.

"You'll burn your hands, idiot." Pinch snapped his fingers and procured a gold pole with a grotesque tiki face near the top. Wild eyes and a toothy grimace leered at Leonardo, and a dense wick frayed from between twisted brows.

Oversized and cumbersome, it caught fire instantly when Pinch swept it through the blaze.

"*Voila.*" Pinch shoved it at him. "Magic fire stick."

"Brilliant." Leonardo threw his original blackening branch into the fire and closed his hands around the cold shaft. In typical Pinch fashion, the flames raged a foot high from the tiki torch's head, wildly overkill and startlingly macabre. But Leonardo didn't have time to be choosy.

"Just don't set the forest on fire." Pinch frowned at his crackling creation.

Leonardo angled it away from the branches as he raced into the twilit forest, sparks trailing behind him.

The crash of battle grew quieter, drowned by the blood thumping in his ears, and an opening in the base of a tree loomed nearby, the edge of a staircase just visible. He glanced from it to the bushes ahead. He'd already lost the kids he was chasing. From the treetops, he stood a better chance of spotting them.

You'll lose more time climbing, he warned himself. The opening in the tree drew closer.

But they'll have to climb too, eventually. All the flags grew from the canopy. And he couldn't afford to get lost on the forest floor. Leonardo eyed the bushes one more time, then ducked into the tree.

An infinity of steps awaited him, but he took them two at a time, torchlight illuminating his way. Every strain and pulled muscle from traversing the trees revealed itself now. Halfway up, his legs weighed a hundred pounds each, and his lungs burned for oxygen. He staggered, and the massive tiki head clunked against the wall.

Leonardo yanked it away.

Dammit. The wood was dry, and the fire took instantly. Images of Raven Clan's burning camp flickered through his mind's-eye.

Leonardo backed up the steps as the flames spread along the wall. Smoke clouded the passage, and Leonardo ran. His torch brushed the wall again fifty steps higher. He jerked it away and kept climbing, hunching low and coughing until his torso ached as smoke choked out the oxygen inside the tree.

It scraped at his throat, clouding and thickening and stinging his eyes. Leonardo kept climbing, teeth gritted as he staggered around the endless curve of the stairs until he finally spotted an opening and staggered through it, out onto a wide branch.

He glanced back. Smoke poured out of the smooth hole in the trunk. His muscles threatened to collapse from the climb and near-suffocation, but he couldn't stop yet. The treetops were more familiar to Leonardo than the forest floor, and he set out east. The flag tree wasn't far.

Five minutes later, Leonardo caught sight of the kids. All three boys ran along a branch forty feet lower than Leonardo's position. Seeing them gave him a boost of adrenaline, and Leonardo ran harder, ignoring his body's protests as he stumbled from one mammoth branch to the next. His thoughts shifted back to the fight, and a cold dose of dread flooded his nerves. If all the Redwoods kids vanished each other, this entire week would've been for nothing. And if more members of his clan were vanished... Leonardo shoved down the thought.

This isn't their first fight, he assured himself. *They'll survive it.*

It was a desperate hope, but he couldn't help them now. All he could do was burn the flag tree to the ground and end the game for good.

He barreled on. He'd very nearly closed the gap between himself and the kids below when one of them spotted him. Leonardo recognized Iris's brother. He shouted something at the others, and all three slowed, shading their eyes from their branch. Leonardo didn't break pace.

That hesitation was all it took for him to close the remaining distance, and a surge of victory coursed through Leonardo as he passed above them. All three started running, and Leonardo sucked in breaths as they came into view again through the redwood boughs. They were faster than him, and branch by branch, they pulled ahead again.

Dammit. Leonardo pushed harder. His chest ached, and his legs burned, but he refused to lose in the eleventh hour.

He entered a tunnel through the heart of a particularly massive tree, careful to keep his torch away from the walls this time. Leonardo hooked around the corner and through a series of twists before he burst out onto a branch on the far side.

Three things happened at once.

First, he spotted the flag tree, standing in all its grand festival colors as a breeze stirred the rows of red and blue. Second, the Redwoods kids raced across a branch toward it, and he swore, realizing they would have enough time to pick flags for half a clan before he reached them. Third, an ocean crashed over the forest floor.

CHAPTER 36

Leonardo and the Redwoods kids froze.

What the hell? Leonardo gaped as a tidal wave hurtled toward them, swallowing ferns, bushes, and smaller trees and spraying halfway up every redwood in its path. It pulled miles of water behind it, flooding the woods.

The sound was horrific; deafening, and all-consuming as the water ripped underbrush from the earth. Saplings and weaker trees rolled in the froth, slamming and splitting against the trunks of the redwoods.

A boom shook the woods, and Leonardo jumped, staggering into hard plates of bark. He leaned back, swallowing with grim certainty as another crack spiderwebbed across the moonlit sky. Then the wave struck Leonardo's tree, throwing spray toward the canopy. He stumbled back into the tunnel, lifting the torch higher as droplets spattered him.

He licked his lips. It was salty.

Saltwater.

The Cove was a week's travel away.

The woods are collapsing.

The kids below started running again. They threw themselves at the flag-covered branches, ripping armfuls of colored cloth from between the leaves. Twenty feet lower than Leonardo, they were still high enough to avoid getting caught in the rush, though spray drenched their clothes.

Meanwhile, the tidal wave continued its warpath through the trees, directly toward—

The battle. The horror hit Leonardo harder than the wave.

They're all on the forest floor.

He dropped the torch and sprinted back into the tree tunnel. He made it a dozen steps before logic caught up. Leonardo stopped himself hard against the corner, panting as he stared down the endless tunnel to the far side of the tree. He'd never make it in time.

The wave would flatten them all before he even got out of this tree. He closed his eyes and pressed his head against the wall.

They might survive, he told himself. If the wave didn't crush their lungs, if they retained consciousness, they might be able to swim to the surface. But without flags to keep them alive, anyone who struck a tree or a root under that much force would be vanished instantly.

Leonardo swore and punched the wall. Pain quaked his knuckles. He was nearing his breaking point. He punched it again and again until he staggered back, gasping for breath. He could hear music. Singing, to be exact, and it was so distinctly haunting that he would recognize it anywhere.

283

Adriana. He ran back outside in a haze, pain throbbing from his hand. His torch lay where he'd dropped it, golden eyes and flared nostrils facing the night sky as tendrils of flame licked across the flakey bark of the tree branch. Leonardo grabbed it and wove around the fire that was quickly taking hold as residual saltwater hissed into steam.

He ran out onto the end of the branch and squinted to where a shape bobbed in the new ocean, fifty feet below the branch where the three Redwoods boys stood, their arms loaded with flags.

Adriana sang in full voice, her notes curling and weaving into a tapestry of sound as ensnaring as a spider's web. Blonde locks framed a porcelain face, captured in full glory under a beam of moonlight. Turquoise scales glimmered below the surface.

The flags fell from the boys' arms, cascading like a shower of confetti. Then, one by one, the three boys fell from the branch. Immediately, Adriana stopped singing, and Leonardo shook his head, blinking back into focus.

He eyed the flag tree. Nothing made sense anymore. He was afraid and angry and desperate to know if anyone had survived. All of that culminated in a fierce need to finish what he'd started. If this was the end, if everything had failed, he wasn't letting it happen without first achieving what they had all sacrificed themselves for.

Leonardo jumped down to the next branch, then the next, then the next, until the redwood bark turned to the light golden wood of the flag tree. He glanced down at Adriana. She trod water with the three boys, all of their gazes fixed on him as Leonardo touched his torch to the branch.

Salty droplets sizzled in the heat of Pinch's oversized flame. Leonardo set the old wood alight, igniting flags and leaves on either side of himself. A few of the wetter flags didn't take immediately, but they dried fast as the fire grew, and moments later, they too were consumed. He gazed back at the destruction behind him. Interweaving branches caught, spreading the fire and burning more flags. When he reached the trunk, the inferno behind him burned so hot that sweat ran down his back.

Leonardo wound up and threw the torch like a lance with every bit of strength he had left. It sailed into the leafy heart of the tree, and he jumped off the branch.

For a moment, he was airborne. Then he plunged into the sea.

CHAPTER 37

Bubbles streamed past Leonardo's face. He held his breath, descending deeper as the water grew rapidly darker. Leonardo held his eyes open, staring into the blue. The vague shapes of tree trunks wavered in the distance. He let himself drift, suspended, for a moment. The cold stabbed sharply against his skin, a desperate contrast from the heat of the fire and the pulse of his emotions.

Down here, everything was simple. Everything was quiet. He was weightless and surrounded by ancient trees half-submerged in a spontaneous ocean. The absurdity of it brought everything into pinpoint focus.

They were dreaming. All of them. And if Nym could master his dreams, so could the rest of them and fix everything by imagining new, stronger walls.

Leonardo needed to surface. It was time to find out if anyone survived.

A blur of blonde hair and teal fins flashed past as Adriana circled him.

Leonardo kicked, driving for the surface. His lungs constricted, suddenly desperate for oxygen. And the fear came crashing back as he kicked through meters of water, realizing exactly how much weight must have come crashing down on top of his friends.

He burst through the waves, gasping for air as the world roared to life around him. Overhead, the flag tree burned out of control. Every leaf, every branch, and every inch of bark was aflame, hissing and crackling for the sky.

Adriana surfaced next to him, quiet as she watched the tree burn. Then she glanced at Leonardo, her delicate features carefully arranged in a small frown.

"Your timing is impeccable," she commented, eyeing the three boys still treading water nearby. "I was about to ask them where I could find you, and then you suddenly appeared. Although, I'm now dying to know why you burned that tree."

"What are you doing here?" he demanded. The lack of logic made his skull hurt.

"Hell if I know."

Of course not. He'd been stupid to expect answers. Nothing added up, and that was the only constant. Leonardo wiped the water out of his eyes. He wanted to go back under, where everything was simple. But reality didn't allow such luxuries.

"I need you to take me somewhere," he said instead, fighting the tightness in his throat.

"Aye-aye, captain." Adriana glanced at the boys again. "And these three?"

287

Leonardo looked around. With the water so high on the trees, dozens of branches crossed, half-submerged but offering easy rescue from the sea.

"They know these woods," he said. "They'll be fine,"

Adriana nodded, turning so he could take hold of her shoulders. "Where to?"

Somewhere Leonardo didn't want to go. He was terrified to see what awaited him—or didn't await him. But he had to.

"I'll direct you."

The three boys watched as Leonardo and Adriana streamed away. The water reflected orange from the inferno consuming the tree.

"All this water…" Leonardo swore as Adriana wove around trees and dams of redwood boughs. "Everyone was on the ground when it—"

"Ow! Lighten up!"

Leonardo loosened his grip on her shoulders. He didn't realize how hard he'd been digging in.

"Better. What are you talking about?"

"Everyone was on the ground," said Leonardo. "There was a fight. When the wave came—"

"You think it killed them." Horror filled her voice. She looked back at him, her eyes wide.

Leonardo wanted to say something bitter. Something about how she'd tried to get them killed on several occasions in the Cove, but he simply nodded. She'd seen the truth just like the rest of them, and she'd pledged herself to their cause. He couldn't turn her back into an enemy when his allies were running low.

Adriana put her head down and swam harder, picking up speed as she wove through the strange treetop ocean. It wasn't far to the site of the battle, and they covered more ground in the water. When they passed the old Red Flag tree camp, Leonardo held his breath, preparing himself for the worst. Nothing. Then they streaked out into the space where the battle had been, and Leonardo's heart stopped. No one treaded water. No one bobbed in the waves.

"No," he breathed. Waves slapped the hollow boles with a sickening *slurch* that turned his stomach.

"They can't be gone." His voice rose in panic. "They can't be!"

Viola. His friends. All the Redwoods kids.

If you hadn't forced them to give up the flags…

The bitter irony pierced his heart. The one thing he'd finally succeeded in abolishing would've saved everyone. Sure, their bodies would've been battered, but the flags could heal any wound.

I sealed their fate.

"Leo!"

Voices snapped his attention to the canopy overhead, where rows of kids filled the treetops, silhouetted in the glow of fairy light. Relief surged through him. Hundreds of kids sheltered among the swinging boughs, safe from the crush of the sea.

Thank you. Thank you, thank you, thank you.

Kids began to climb down the tree. He slid off Adriana's back and swam for the nearest branches. They hung low, the waves sloshing over them, and he swam past the needles to where he could grab the mossy branch itself.

"Where did *she* come from?" demanded Pinch. He jumped onto a giant pinecone, frowning down at Adriana.

"Beats me," said Adriana. "I came with the sea."

"Wait. Is this *our* sea?" Sophie picked her way down to the surface and crouched, running a hand through the ripples.

"I think so." Kate followed her. "The Cove is the only place with this much water."

The woods are collapsing, Leonardo thought for the second time. He grunted and swore, dragging himself out of the debris. Water ran off his saturated clothes, hanging like a dead weight from his body as he rolled onto the branch and struggled to crawl to a thicker point where he could stand.

Viola was the first to reach him. She threw her arms around him, and Leonardo held her tight, trying to stop his own hands from shaking.

"I didn't know if you'd gotten to safety," she said into his shirt.

"I didn't think you would," he replied. Then, after a beat, "How *did* you all get to safety?"

Over her shoulder, he frowned up at the hundreds of silhouettes in the treetops.

"I saw it coming," said Viola. She pulled back so she could look at him. Moth and Jack and a handful of Ravens dropped down behind her. "My gift showed me the wave a few miles away. I wanted to run after you, but..."

It happened too fast.

"I started coming back for you all too," said Leonardo.

But it would have beaten us both. Somehow, miraculously, they had survived it. The woods were a dreamworld, but it wasn't a place of miracles. There were always casualties.

"Wait. Did everyone make it?" he asked suddenly. He scanned the shapes moving through the trees overhead.

"Everyone who survived the fight," said Viola. "We all got up here before the water reached us."

"And who *didn't* survive the fight?" His breath came quickly again.

"A lot of Redwoods kids." Viola slipped her fingers into his. "But I don't think *we* lost anyone."

"Ok." Leonardo squeezed her hand tight. He didn't think he could handle another lost clanmate. "How did you get the fight to stop?"

"That was me." Kate smiled sweetly, spinning the bullhorn on her finger. "Viola's not the only one with a gift. I jumped back on that root and gave everyone *very* specific instructions. I'm stubborn, but I'm not stupid."

Viola and Kate worked together? The end times *were* coming.

"The wave changed everything." Moth climbed down from the greenery. "I think they're ready to listen."

Leonardo didn't like it. It was too easy. A bad feeling settled in his stomach as he eyed the sea. Adriana drifted twenty feet from the branch.

"Where are the other sirens?" Sophie straightened, flicking water off her fingers.

"Gone." Adriana's tone was grave. Leonardo stiffened.

"What do you mean, gone—"

She swam closer. "After you all left, the Dark came back. It wasn't as strong as before, but it attacked us. I had already split from the pod, so I only saw it happen from a distance. I've been hiding in the caves until I showed up here."

"Are you sure it killed them?" asked Sophie. "If you only saw it from a distance…"

"It was like lightning, hitting the surface over and over again." She paused. "I could hear their screams."

No one said a word.

Adriana looked from Sophie to the other kids climbing down the tree. "Where is Mishti?"

"She's gone too," said Leonardo quietly. He drew a breath. "The Dark is building strength. We need to find the rest of the alliance before—"

The current suddenly picked up. Water sprayed up trees as a wind whistled over the surface.

Shit.

"Here we go." Sophie swore.

"Everyone up," yelled Leonardo. "Get back to the canopy!"

Something rounded a tree across the water. Leonardo squinted as a panel of burnt, blackened boards spun in the current. Water frothed through a square window.

"That looks like…" started Jack.

"A treehouse wall," finished Leonardo slowly. "From the Darkwoods."

Behind it came a bamboo table, rotating and bumping against a tree trunk.

"That's our table," said Sophie.

"Leo!" yelled Cato. "Look out!"

Leonardo spun and pushed Viola, scrambling up a branch as a clinker boat rounded the corner and smashed into the spot they'd been standing. Leonardo barely got his legs out of the way in time. Wood shattered, pelting his ankles with bits of bark. Viola helped him regain his balance, and Leonardo frowned, studying Cato, looming on a perch above them.

"Thanks," he said slowly. *He's not just Aleksander's henchman anymore.*

"That's my hoverboard!" shouted Pinch.

"Your *what?*" came Nym's voice.

Oblong and jet-black with painted flames, it preceded an entire logjam of palm trees. A flock of seabirds rode the palms as they raced past.

"What's happening?" asked Jack.

Pinch's giant rusted fan floated, suspended between two logs.

"The woods are collapsing," said Leonardo.

Adriana swam under the shelter of the branch Leonardo stood on as the parade of objects whisked through the boughs. A pod of tiny sea monsters swept past, jumping and twisting so their tentacles flared in the current. One streaked away from the group, zigzagging toward them and leaping over a branch.

Leather cord snapped, and a slingshot pebble struck the creature's globe of a head. It splashed into the water and didn't resurface.

"Not today, asshole," said Pinch.

Leonardo glanced at him and froze. Beyond Pinch, the wall of trees and water shimmered, becoming a vista of the cove and its tan cliffs for a moment. Above it, a crack split the cloudless sky and blackness poured out of it, swirling and gathering. He blinked, and he was looking at the Redwoods again.

Leonardo shook his head.

"Come on." He ushered everyone up the tree, then he glanced at Adriana.

"I'm fine," she said. "Go."

Before Leonardo could say another word, Adriana plunged underwater. A length of a rope bridge caught on a branch, and the collapsed poles of a tipi carried a patchwork of animal skins. A shark fin wove through the debris, and Leonardo started climbing, heart racing. Then he realized something.

He could identify every object flowing past.

It's only things from the Cove, the Darkwoods, and here. Nothing from the Highland.

Why?

Was the Highland still intact? If the Dark hadn't reached it yet, they needed to get there *now*.

Leonardo grabbed the next branch up, and his hand went straight through it. His breath snagged as he fell forward, then slammed on hands and knees into hard-packed dirt. Leonardo gazed around wildly at the Darkwoods.

"What the hell?" Bates climbed to his feet beside Leonardo. The rest of Raven Clan, Lion Clan, and the Redwoods kids lay scattered among the trees. The Dark surrounded them on all sides, rolling like black fog through the underbrush.

Leonardo looked up and gasped. Instead of a sky, he was looking down into the Cove. The waves sparkled inside a horseshoe of sunbaked cliffs. A wave of dizziness rippled through Leonardo's mind, and he tore his eyes from the upside-down sky, pressing his hands into the soft earth. But the earth began to fall past him, and he realized that he was the upside-down one.

The kids fell one by one, tumbling from the floor of the Darkwoods and into the sky of the Cove. Viola flew past him, then Charley, her hair whipping in the wind.

Leonardo caught sight of the crack in the sky, where more and more of the Dark spilled in. A gust of wind hit him in the face, and Leonardo squeezed his eyes shut. The pressure changed and he snapped open his eyes as he plummeted through the high-ceilinged lagoon in Lion Clan's fortress.

Leonardo glimpsed the rocky edge where they'd lost Strato and Robin, then he struck the surface, plunging into a land of dark water and silence. Leonardo kicked for the surface, twisting to see hundreds of kids clawing through the water around him.

Can everyone swim?

Then a second thought struck him.

The lagoon isn't this big.

A hard current dragged him sideways. Leonardo swam harder, driving for the surface with everything he had. When he burst through, Leonardo was back in the Redwoods, in the new sea, which had become as fierce as rapids. The air was a gloomy shade of grey, and blackness completely choked out the sky.

Kids surfaced around him, bobbing and rolling in the drag of the water. A wave crashed over Leonardo's head, and he held his breath, driven under. He surfaced again, sputtering.

Adriana was swept past him, twisting and battling the current.

"Hey!" called Leonardo, struggling to keep his head above water. "You need to—"

The waves pushed him under again.

…help us.

Leonardo gasped through the waves just as someone screamed, then someone else. The water spun him around, and Leonardo wrenched himself back, just in time to see the canyon awaiting them.

The sea poured over a ledge, and the Dark poured from the sky, straight into the gap. Kids grabbed at branches and boughs, desperate for anything to cling to as the sea swept them over the cliff. Adriana grabbed for someone's sodden arm as they rolled past, then a bolt of black lightning stabbed from the mass of the Dark, striking her where she swam.

She vanished instantly. Leonardo choked on his shock. Smoke hissed from the surface.

The last of the sirens, gone.

Leonardo rolled and crawled for a tree trunk. His fingers scraped over bark, and he clawed at a crevasse, digging his nails into the wood. He held on at the very edge of the drop. Heavy white fog rose from beyond the waterfall, colliding with the Dark in a volatile explosion of steam. The fog seemed to extinguish it, but the Dark was pressing, and even as Leonardo watched, the fog began to give way.

Overhead, the whir of wingbeats preceded the arrival of thousands upon thousands of fairies. They swarmed over the water, shielding the kids as black lighting forked and stabbed, vanishing their tiny forms by the hundred.

Then someone screamed his name, and Leonardo whipped around as Viola swept past him, too far from anything to grab.

"Viola!" He lunged for her and lost his grip on the tree. Leonardo's head went underwater, then he tumbled over the edge.

CHAPTER 38

Leonardo fell into the fog. The silhouettes of a hundred kids fell alongside him. He squeezed his eyes shut, he twisted, he tried everything to shift their surroundings again.

You're dreaming. Change it. But this time, the woods held steady.

They tumbled for what could have been seconds or hours. Time didn't spin right in the woods, and it was spiraling out of control here. Then, as if he'd never been falling in the first place, Leonardo realized he was standing in a field. The burnt treehouse wall, the giant fan, the palm trees all lay scattered about like the carnage of a hurricane.

"Where are we?" asked Charley. She stood next to Leonardo, her blonde hair soaked, paperboy hat absent.

The fog rolled thick around them, turning everyone into vague shapes. Someone moved toward him, and the fog parted to reveal Puck.

"Puck!" said Leonardo. "What are you doing he—"

Puck walked right past him.

"Puck," repeated Leonardo. "Hey!"

He ran in front of Puck and grabbed him by the shoulders, shaking the pudgy boy while his head lolled.

Dammit. Leonardo shook him harder until Puck suddenly blinked. He squinted, rubbing his eyes. Leonardo's wet handprints branded his shoulders.

"Leo?" Puck gasped. "You made it! You're soaking wet."

"What's happening here?" demanded Leonardo.

"I don't..." Puck squinted around.

More shapes materialized in the whiteness. Chills ran up Leonardo's spine as an army of comatose kids passed through their ranks. His drenched companions called out to them, but not a soul replied. Sophie and Juliet shouted the names of a dozen Lion Clan girls.

"What happened in the Redwoods?" asked Puck.

Someone yelled, and both boys reached for their swords, a deeply Raven Clan instinct.

"We did it," Leonardo replied, disturbed by fog-shrouded bizarreness around him. "We united the clans. Kind of. And then—"

Puck's eyes glazed over again, and he stepped around Leonardo without a backward glance.

"Hey!" Leonardo grabbed his shoulder, but Puck shrugged him off and kept walking.

Viola stepped around Leonardo's left side. "This is bad."

Her voice struck a chord that nearly pushed his emotions over the edge. Twice in the last ten minutes, he'd thought she was lost to him.

"Are we in the Highland?" She turned in a circle, brown eyes roving.

Leonardo shook his head helplessly. He breathed in a lungful of the fog and blinked. His eyelids sagged, and he blinked hard, forcing them to stay open. The haze curled around him, muddling everyone's voices and obscuring their words. The panic rose in his chest again, hot and bubbling. He ran three steps forward and stumbled into a kid wearing a gray cloak.

Caliban turned, but his mismatched eyes looked right through Leonardo. His forehead scar poked out from under his hood as he stared into space.

What the hell is going on? Leonardo's eyelids sagged again of their own volition. A wave of fatigue flooded his system, and Leonardo's knees gave out. He staggered to the right, catching himself on Kate's shoulder. She twisted, and to his relief, recognition flashed in her eyes.

"Leo." She slurred his name a bit. Behind her, the fog broke for a moment, gauzy strands parting to reveal a cliff's edge over-looking miles of waterlogged forest. In the distance, a familiar tan-colored coastline failed to retain the sea flooding into the woods. All of it sprawled hundreds of meters below the lofty field where he stood.

Leonardo's mouth fell open. *This* is *the Highland.* But he'd never realized quite how *high* it was. From this moonlit vantage, he came to a wide-eyed understanding. The river tied the corners of the woods together, like massive twisting veins.

Of course! The water was its blood. *Which is why the Dark couldn't survive in the water.* The woods' magic would naturally be strongest there.

Water rushed through the dreamscape below, like blood gushing from broken arteries. The shock wrenched his gut—everywhere he looked, the woods were dying.

"What is…" Kate blinked hard, still facing Leonardo and oblivious to the vista as a fresh roll of fog obscured the cliff's edge behind her. "Where are we?"

Leonardo tried to answer, but his tongue was sluggish, and his body weighed a thousand pounds. He let go of Kate's shoulder and fell to the grass. His breaths came short, the fog continued to roll around him, and Leonardo toppled over.

***

The moment his head struck the ground, the world flared into brilliant clarity. His vision returned to both eyes, sharper than it had ever been. Leonardo wasn't tired anymore, and the grass beneath him had been replaced by floorboards.

Treehouse boards.

A tricorn pirate hat leaned in the corner. Leonardo would recognize it anywhere. Typically, it sat perched atop Pinch's head.

He scrambled to his feet and ran out the doorway onto a platform overlooking a rope bridge. The woods grew close around him, but it wasn't the Darkwoods. The leaves were lighter, cast in an end-of-summer glow. The air smelled sweeter, and the breeze blew warm and welcoming. And unlike the sprawling network of treehouses and bridges that made up Raven Clan's old camp, his was the only treehouse in sight.

Leonardo caught movement between the trees as a door swung open. It was a big door, made of wood with a wrought-iron edge, standing inexplicably in the middle of nowhere, on a patch of dirt between two trees. A man stepped through, far older than anyone ever grew in the woods. He kept a close-cropped beard, and he wore a carefully tucked sweater and polished shoes. He looked completely out of place in the woods, though he gazed around the trees as if it were his backyard. Leonardo edged back into the shadows of the treehouse.

Behind the man, a young boy stepped through, his eyes wide as he took in the treehouse and the lush woodland. Leonardo's heart skipped a beat.

Aleksander.

A younger Aleksander; maybe nine years old. His hair was shorter, his features softer, and he hadn't grown into the lanky height of his teen years yet, but Leonardo knew his brother's face too well to mistake it.

Aleksander gazed up at the doorway of the treehouse, his intelligent eyes glinting, and he frowned.

"Dad." He tugged the man's sleeve. "Who's up there?" His youthful voice was much less grating than the sharp drone it would grow into.

Dad? Leonardo's eyes widened. *That's our father?*

The man's focus snapped up to the treehouse, and Leonardo stumbled back inside, his heart slamming.

"Hey!" yelled the man—Leonardo's father. He sounded angry. "Who's there?"

Leonardo whirled around for an escape. Footsteps crunched the leaves below, then thudded up the rungs of a ladder. Leonardo fixed his gaze on the window. It didn't have any glass, just like the windows in the Darkwoods.

He vaulted over the ledge into the branches of the conifer outside. He'd spent the past week learning to navigate the treetops, and while these were smaller branches than those of the redwoods, Leonardo had no problem maneuvering down the tree. He dropped to the ground and sprinted into the bushes, lying flat so he could see the treehouse without being spotted.

His father crossed the rope bridge, Aleksander rushing after him. Leonardo stared at the man. He was a total stranger but bore an uncanny resemblance to Aleksander, and himself he supposed, if he looked closely.

How does Aleksander know him? Leonardo's mind reeled. *What is this?*

Their father ran into the treehouse, then his head and shoulders emerged through the window as he gazed around the forest floor.

"Is anyone there?" he called.

Leonardo held his breath. The wind shook the leaves, and his father disappeared back inside. Leonardo carefully maneuvered to a crouch and edged behind another bush, creeping to a position where he could see the rope bridge more clearly as Aleksander and their father emerged again.

"This place is unpredictable," their father was explaining. "It was probably just a trick of the woods. When I first imagined it all—"

"You imagined all this?" interrupted Aleksander.

He *imagined it?* Leonardo's breath snagged.

"I'm *imagining* it," corrected their father. "As we speak, I'm imagining life into these trees. I first dreamed about it when I was your age. Then I dreamed about it again the next night, and I saw a door in the woods. I recognized the trees around it. They were from the woods behind my house."

Aleksander watched his father with undisguised fascination. Leonardo had never seen that expression on his brother's face before.

"Guess what I did when I woke up?" asked their father.

"You went into the woods?" guessed Aleksander.

"That's right. And guess what I found?"

"The door," said Aleksander. Wonder filled his voice. Both of them looked at the door between the trees.

"The door," agreed their father. "But here's the catch; no one else could see it. To everyone else, the place where I saw the door was nothing but a blackberry bush."

"Really?" asked Aleksander. "But I saw the door."

"Yes, you did," replied their father. "Because the woods wanted you to."

"What?"

Their father drew a heavy breath. Leonardo frowned.

"That's complicated. This has been my place for a long time," he started. "I call it the Lostwoods."

Leonardo gaped. *Mishti was right?*

Aleksander looked around, his brow furrowed.

"This used to be a clearing," said their father. "But I imagine a new tree every year. See, look, that one grows flags."

Leonardo caught his breath. He'd been so fixated on Aleksander and his father that he hadn't even seen the flag tree. It was in its infancy here, with thin branches and only a few dozen flags.

How does it get to the Redwoods? wondered Leonardo. Then, a second later, *is this the Redwoods?* But no, it looked more like the Darkwoods.

Even still, it wasn't quite the Darkwoods either.

And why didn't Aleksander ever use the name, Lostwoods?

"I used to pretend I was a pirate," continued their father. "And this was my fort. Did you see my pirate hat in the corner?"

Leonardo's eyes widened. *Pinch's hat belonged to my father?*

"*You* played pretend?" Aleksander sounded skeptical. "Then how come me and Leonardo aren't allowed to?"

A shock struck Leonardo's nerves.

He knows my name. Leonardo tried to recall if Aleksander had ever expressly stated that his memories were wiped like the rest of them.

Did he remember everything the whole time?

"We have powerful imaginations, Aleksander," said their father. "It's dangerous to play with something like that. Listen to me. These woods need a dreamer at all times—someone to keep it all alive. If I leave for too long, half the trees are dead when I return."

"I don't see any dead trees," said Aleksander.

"That's because I come here so often. But I can't do that for much longer. That's why the woods is showing itself to you."

"Why not?" asked Aleksander. He sounded concerned. "Dad, are you going somewhere?"

Their father didn't reply immediately, and a sense of dread balled into a pit in Leonardo's stomach.

"I'm afraid so," he said finally. "I'm...well I..."

"What?" Anxiety pulsed in Aleksander's voice. "Dad?"

Their father took him by the shoulders. "Aleksander, I'm sick. I have been for some time now."

Aleksander tilted his head. "You don't look sick."

Leonardo couldn't see their father's expression from where he

crouched, but his silence was heavy, and Leonardo could imagine the anguish on his face.

"You'll get better, right?" asked Aleksander. Worry crept across his small features.

More silence. Leonardo's heart tore from his chest.

"No!" cried Aleksander. He grabbed his father's arm. "You can go to the doctor, he—"

Their father shook his head. "I'm afraid I've tried that already."

Aleksander looked around wildly as if he might spot bottles of medicine hanging from the trees. Even as a kid, Leonardo could see the gears turning in his mind. "Then you can imagine something to fix you!"

Their father smiled, bittersweet. "When I was younger, I thought I was invincible here. I thought that I could escape to my imagination and be a kid forever. But life has its own plans. Stop thinking, Aleksander." He straightened and placed a hand on Aleksander's shoulder. "Just listen."

"But—"

"Be careful with these woods. They're unpredictable. They'll take what you imagine and warp it into something new. You have to be smart, always. And never stay away too long."

"Dad!" Aleksander sounded desperate. "Let me try to imagine—"

"Relax, Aleksander. If you try imagining things while you're worked up like this, they won't be what you expect, I guarantee it."

Their father was tall. Not as thin as grown-up Aleksander, but his dark hair bore the same sheen.

Aleksander already possessed the wiry frame that would grow with his self-importance. Leonardo recognized the child's version of his beaked nose as Aleksander sniffed back a tear and turned away. "I don't want you to die."

"Listen closely to me." Their father turned Aleksander to face him, reaching into his coat pocket and removing a small object. "I want you to take this."

Leonardo squinted, edging forward.

It's Moth's compass, he realized, as Aleksander opened the lid.

"This is a magic compass," said their father. "It will always guide you to the door."

Then he removed another item from his pocket, dangling it before Aleksander by the gold chain.

"A pocket watch?" asked Aleksander.

"So you never lose track of how long you're away."

That's Viola's—

Then he held up a third item. A key. But it didn't look like Leonardo's key. It was broader and darker.

"This is my key to the door," their father told Aleksander. "I won't be needing it anymore."

He clapped the key between his hands, then opened his fingers, releasing a pile of sand. The air rippled a few inches from Leonardo's face, and a tiny tendril of blackness slithered out of the shimmer. Leonardo's limbs went cold. He barely suppressed his gasp as the Dark absorbed into a strand of ivy directly in front of him. Instantly, the leaves shriveled, and the stem went limp.

306

"But how will I get in?" asked Aleksander from above. He sounded on the verge of tears.

"You'll make your own key. Come." Their father led Aleksander across the rope bridge and down the ladder.

Did he cause the Dark to come in? Leonardo half-rose and edged away from the dying vine, keeping low in the bushes.

He swallowed. *But my father was way up there. The Dark came in next to me.*

Leonardo's pulse ratcheted. *Did I bring the Dark in?*

"Pick something small." Their father waved around at the bed of dead leaves and roots. "Something you can carry around with you."

A weight pummelled Leonardo's stomach and his breathing stalled. If he did bring the Dark in, what did that mean? If it destroyed everything, would the future even exist?

What would happen to me? To all of us?

Aleksander bent and pulled a smooth black pebble from the dirt. "Like this?"

Leonardo recognized that rock. He fumbled in his pocket, closing his fingers around his rock key.

"Perfect. Now take it like this." Their father closed Aleksander's fingers around the rock as Leonardo gazed at his own identical stone.

He had a sudden memory. He'd forgotten in the chaos of reaching the Redwoods, but the moment before they left, caught in the middle of the spell, Moth's compass, Viola's stopwatch, and Leonardo's key had grown hot enough to burn them.

They're still filled with magic. Old magic. Their father was a craftsman, and these were his tools.

"Here's the important part," said their father. "Close your eyes and imagine it's the key to that door."

"And that will work?" asked Aleksander.

"I promise."

"Ok." Aleksander nodded once, full of obedient focus, then he closed his eyes and wrapped his fingers tighter around the pebble. For a few seconds, nothing happened, then Aleksander gasped. Leonardo jumped, then swore at himself as their father glanced around.

"It worked!" said Aleksander, opening his palm. Leonardo leaned to see. A gold key glinted in the sunlight, identical to Leonardo's.

That's where he got the key.

"Go try it out." Pride filled their father's voice.

"I made it different than you said," Aleksander told him, running to the door.

"What do you mean?"

Aleksander glanced back. "I imagined that it can open any lock, ever."

Their father didn't reply right away. Leonardo could see him thinking as Aleksander tested the key in the lock. It worked, of course. Leonardo had used the key on numerous locks himself, years later.

Why am I here? he wondered. And more importantly, *how do I get back?*

If his fears were accurate, and the Dark had followed him here—into the past—he needed to return to the present as fast as possible. Before he caused any real damage.

"Be careful with your imagination," said their father. "I cannot tell you enough that the woods are unpredictable—"

"I don't want you to leave," said Aleksander.

"Aleksander—"

"I imagine that no one can leave," said Aleksander. Something shifted, the pressure changed, and Leonardo's skin prickled.

"Stop," said their father.

"And I imagine that no one grows up, and that no one dies, and that no one can ever be older than a kid."

"What are you doing?"

"You said you wanted to be a kid forever," said Aleksander. "You weren't sick when you were a kid."

A sharp wind whistled through the treetops, abruptly different than the soft summer breeze from before. Leonardo looked up to where branches bent over, their leaves fluttering, barely clinging on. The pirate hat blew through the open door of the treehouse, flipping and rolling across the rope bridge. Then the wind died. The hairs lifted on Leonardo's arms. Nothing good ever happened when the wind behaved like that.

Aleksander gasped, and Leonardo snapped his focus back into the clearing.

Their father was gone.

CHAPTER 39

D ad?" Aleksander's voice rose in pitch. "Dad, where are you?"

He vanished, thought Leonardo. Their father was the first to ever vanish. *From his own woods.*

The pirate hat fell from the rope bridge, hitting the dirt with a soft thud. Leonardo stared at it.

How did it get to Pinch?

Aleksander's breathing was coming fast now. He turned in a circle. His eyes glistened icy blue, piercing even in their youth. A rabbit bolted from the underbrush, and Aleksander jumped, stumbling over backward. He landed hard on his rear, hands splayed behind him. The compass and the pocket watch bounced and rolled, coming to rest in a hard-packed footprint.

I imagine that no one grows up, and that no one dies, and that no one can ever be older than a kid. It was a desperate attempt; Aleksander hadn't even asked if their father would want to return to his youth. Would

310

perpetual childhood be favorable over whatever illness consumed him? The answer seemed obvious, but Leonardo wondered if Kate would agree. He hunched lower, bathed in shadow, sheltered in a blind of thick stems and bracken.

In the end, it didn't matter. Aleksander's attempt at writing new rules had failed. Leonardo knew the future, and he could piece together easily enough how the woods' wicked sense of irony had manifested Aleksander's new rule. It was a rule that would come to define the woods and the certainty that everyone would vanish upon reaching adulthood. He wondered once more where the vanished went.

A line of ants plotted a course up a shiny flower stalk in front of Leonardo's face. He edged backward. He no longer trusted flowers.

Meanwhile, young Aleksander scrambled to his feet, swatting leaves and dirt off his pants. He looked like Pompey, all limbs and clumsy youthfulness.

"Dad!" The word came out choked. He yelled it louder, causing an echo that chased a flock of starlings from the arms of an overreaching poplar.

He's not coming back, thought Leonardo, watching the purple songbirds sweep into the sky.

Aleksander tried once more, but the cry was half-hearted, and a weight pressed at Leonardo's chest.

He knows.

Aleksander eyed the treehouse towering over him. He'd just inherited something he hadn't even known existed. Leonardo tried to place himself in Aleksander's shoes. He would be wildly overwhelmed.

Aleksander collected the compass and the pocket watch from where they'd fallen in one of their father's heavy footprints. He pursed his small lips in an expression of rapidly swelling grief, blinking back tears as he stared at the objects.

I wish I could help you. Leonardo struggled to swallow the lump in his own throat. But he dared not reveal himself to Aleksander. He had no idea what would happen if he broke the sequence of time.

Aleksander's shoulders began to shake. His chest heaved. Then he let out an anguished cry and took off, fumbling with the key as he hurtled for the door between the trees. Leonardo half-rose, preparing to follow him. Aleksander yanked the big wood and iron door open and staggered back, his eyes wide.

The door itself blocked Leonardo's view of what lay beyond it, but he recognized the white fog rolling into the clearing.

It's the same place we are. Where I am right now.

"I imagine that no one can leave," said Aleksander under his breath. "Dammit."

He's sealed himself in, thought Leonardo. Their father was the first to vanish, and Aleksander was the first to become caged.

So, what does the door do now?

Aleksander appeared to have the same question. He freed the key from the lock, squared his slight shoulders, and stepped into the fog.

Leonardo's heart thudded as he crept out from behind the bushes.

He was brave. Grown-up Aleksander was absolutely terrified of the woods. Which meant that something had to happen between now and then to instill such a deep-seated fear.

312

Leonardo's stomach jumped to his throat as he jogged to the door. He edged around it on light feet, heart pounding. He placed a hand on his sword and drew a breath, then stepped into the open.

Aleksander was nowhere to be seen. A familiar field stretched out before him, cloaked in ghostly whiteness. Leonardo glanced back at the single treehouse, then followed his brother.

CHAPTER 40

L eonardo blinked at a blade of grass inches from his face.
He lay in the clifftop field, where he'd collapsed near
Kate. Her boots sprawled a few feet away. He closed his
good eye, and he could still see.

It healed me. A jolt spiked his nerves.

If he could bring things back here—as substantial as his eyesight—it meant he needed to learn the rules of this place quickly.
The vague shapes of his companions milled about, some laying on
the ground like him, others walking aimlessly.

Is this the heart of the dreamworld?

The realization hit him hard.

*The woods are disintegrating, and we fell through the structured layers to
the heart of it.*

From here, he could dream about the past. Or step into a
dream that already happened, maybe?

Because everything that happens in the woods is a dream.

The moment that Aleksander and their father stepped through the door, out of the real world and into the clearing, they were entering their imaginations. Maybe the woods kept those dreams—it was possessive enough. And maybe it was showing him because—

These woods need a dreamer at all times. That was what his father told Aleksander. If their father was gone, and Aleksander was gone...

I'm the new dreamer.

And he had been, ever since Aleksander vanished. He was the woods' last hope at survival. He was everyone's last hope at survival.

Overhead, fists of blackness pierced through the cotton clouds of fog. It would be upon them in minutes.

Leonardo swore.

Aleksander came here. If the vision held information that could help him, Leonardo was certain it would be revealed in whatever happened next. He needed to see what Aleksander found in the Highland before it was too late.

He rolled onto his back and closed his eyes. He rested his head in the cool grass and breathed in the fog. He let it fill his lungs and swirl through him, carrying him away from the field.

A half-screech, half-roar split the air. Leonardo scrambled to his feet as hoofbeats pounded over the ground. His companions were gone, and a looming shape galloped toward him. Leonardo drew his sword and staggered back as the beast materialized through the fog. The size of a bison, but thinner, like a horse, with colored stripes down its flanks and horns on its head.

It screech-roared again, hooves thundering as it hurtled past him. Leonardo pressed his hands together to stop their shaking and squinted into the haze until he spotted a smaller, human-sized shape with a familiar tricorn hat silhouetted on its head.

Aleksander.

Leonardo started toward him, slipping his sword back into his belt. Another creature loomed in the fog, but his one didn't run. It simply watched Aleksander pass, then Leonardo a moment later, trailing well back of his brother.

At first, it resembled a zebra. Then it opened its jaws, baring a mouthful of pointed teeth.

Leonardo flinched, stumbling away. The creature didn't budge, and Leonardo checked over his shoulder every five seconds until it was out of sight.

Up ahead, Aleksander stopped as something snaked from the ground, expanding into what looked like a plant through the haze. Aleksander picked something from it, then continued walking. When Leonardo reached it, he found it to be covered in a strange blue fruit, big and round like an orange but smooth like an apple.

He sniffed it, then took a hesitant bite.

Vanilla.

He's imagining all of this, realized Leonardo. The beasts, the fruit. He moved with a restless pace as if he expected something awaited him beyond all this fog. Leonardo wasn't so sure. Their father imagined the clearing. He had a feeling Aleksander needed to imagine his way out.

Did Aleksander create the rest of the woods? Leonardo realized suddenly. *Is that what comes next?* But the woods were *old.* A hundred years or more. There were leaders of Raven Clan who came before Aleksander.

A rumble carried across the field from behind Leonardo. He tensed, turning slowly. Through the clouds of whiteness, long shadows wove in the sky. Every hair on his body stood on end.

The Dark.

Leonardo forced himself to breathe.

Did it follow me again? His heart stuttered a beat.

Leonardo couldn't even tell if this was Aleksander's sky or his own present-day sky revealing itself through the vision.

"I know you can't hurt me," called Aleksander over his shoulder.

Leonardo froze.

"I know you're following me, but you're just a figment of my imagination."

Leonardo didn't say anything. His fingernails dug into the vanilla fruit as he turned to face Aleksander's silhouette again.

"It's ok," called Aleksander. "You can stay. I've been here a week—did you know that? Probably not; you just showed up."

His hazy form twisted, glancing back at Leonardo. Leonardo knew Aleksander couldn't make out his face from this far, but regardless, he fought the urge to run.

"I'm lonely," continued Aleksander. "That's probably why I imagined you. I wonder if I can create more people."

Am I real? Viola had asked Leonardo a lifetime ago. Or a lifetime in the future.

How many people did Aleksander imagine?

"Do you speak?" asked Aleksander. "I don't think so, or you would have spoken to me by now. If I make more people, I'll need to make sure they can speak."

Aleksander started walking again.

317

Stress knifed at Leonardo's mind. *Hurry up.*

The Dark swirled in the distance behind them.

What happens to the future, he thought again, *if it catches us here?* Images of his friends vanishing hammered through his mind. Simply popping out of existence. Gone. And what about him? If he was taken by the Dark here, would his body in the present cease to exist too?

He walked faster, his chest tight.

I'll return to them. He refused to abandon his friends. He repeated the words until they echoed in his mind. He wasn't sure if it was a vow or a plea.

"I should try making someone now," said Aleksander. "Watch this."

Aleksander raised a hand and snapped his fingers. At the same time, a silhouette took shape a hundred feet from Leonardo and even further from Aleksander.

Leonardo stared, awestruck. *It worked.*

Aleksander turned in a circle, and Leonardo realized the kid was too far away for him to see.

"Hmph," said Aleksander. "I guess it's just you and me for now."

Leonardo glanced at the kid in the distance again, then back at Aleksander. He didn't want to miss a word Aleksander said, but he was desperately curious about the identity of the kid.

Leonardo made a split-second decision and bolted toward the new kid. Aleksander's back was turned. He wouldn't realize Leonardo was gone until the fog obscured him.

As Leonardo drew closer to the kid, he began to recognize features. He was younger than the version Leonardo knew, but his blonde hair and stoic features were unmistakable. John appeared to be sleeping on his feet. His eyes were shut, but his chest moved with living breaths.

Aleksander created John.

Leonardo frowned. *Did he create all the pirates? Is that why they've been here forever?* But if Aleksander created them, that meant he too was much older than Leonardo had realized. *Aleksander has been in the woods since the beginning.*

John's eyelids twitched, and Leonardo caught his breath. He sprinted back in Aleksander's direction before John could wake up.

He'll be all alone, thought Leonardo. *He'll be confused. But he'll find Kate, and Pip, and Cyrus. After Aleksander creates them too?*

John was the only pirate who claimed to be from the Highland. If Aleksander did create the others, it would have to happen later in the timeline, after he left the Highland. His silhouette came back into view, and Leonardo jogged toward him.

"Oh, good." Aleksander glanced over his shoulder. "You're back. I have a family; did you know that? My dad created all this when he was my age. I don't even think he told my mom."

Leonardo walked sideways, keeping one anxious eye on the gathering Dark.

"I'm going to find a way to bring my brother, Leonardo, here," continued Aleksander. "He's only six years old. His favorite animals are lions because his name means 'lion.'"

Suddenly, Aleksander gasped. "I have an idea! I'm going to imagine a bunch of lions for him to play with."

The lions are for me? There was love in Aleksander's voice, and the ground shifted under Leonardo's feet.

"The twins are too little," continued Aleksander. "They're just babies. But one day, I'll bring them here too!"

Twins? Leonardo stared at Aleksander's hazy silhouette. *We have two more siblings?*

"I like crocodiles," Aleksander was saying now. "I'm going to imagine a bunch of crocodiles too."

The timeline skipped ahead. Leonardo staggered through a glitch in the air, and Aleksander turned to face him. Behind them, only a thin veil of fog remained as the Dark deepened to a rolling wall. Static electricity charged the still air, crackling against Leonardo's skin. Either it didn't concern Aleksander, or he couldn't see the thunderheads, which raised a brand-new crop of questions.

"I have a plan," he called. "This time, I'm going to create a person *and* a place. Then he'll be easier to find. Ready?"

Leonardo had forgotten quite how smart his brother was. Aleksander turned to face forward again and raised both hands over his head. The snap of his fingers was loud in the empty field. And all at once, the entire horizon ahead turned dark. Fear lanced Leonardo's bones, and he froze on the spot. But this was a different sort of shadow, as an unmistakable treeline blinked into existence.

"Whoa," shouted Aleksander. "That's bigger than I meant it to be!"

Leonardo gazed from one end of the woods to the other.

"I hope we can find him in there." Aleksander started running. "Come on."

CHAPTER 41

Frogs chirped and birds sang as Leonardo followed Aleksander through the woods. Dew ran off every leaf, dripping to the wet, mossy soil. Leonardo crept through the shadows from tree to tree, enwreathed in the organic aroma. Aleksander seemed to have accepted that this particular 'figment of his imagination' was reclusive and didn't like to be seen.

Leonardo could play that part. It gave him an excuse to dart out of sight if Aleksander glanced his way and allowed him to stay close enough to his brother to get answers. Pressure strained his chest. He couldn't track the Dark from here, and it ate at his nerves. Meanwhile, he was even blinder to the present.

Is my body still lying in that field? Has the Dark reached us yet?

He prayed not. Half his mind screamed at him to get out, to try to wake up and prepare. But the more persistent half pressed that the woods had brought him here for a reason. The key to saving everyone was here, if only it would *hurry up.*

A moment later, Leonardo spotted someone in the under-brush, down a game trail. Pip was even easier to identify than John. The ancient version of him hadn't grown much from the version Leonardo spotted. And Aleksander would have spotted him too if it wasn't for a stick snapping in the opposite direction.

"Is someone there?" called Aleksander. Excitement filled his young voice as he high-stepped through the brush.

Leonardo kept to the shadows and glanced back at Pip, who opened his mouth to say something before the screech of a giant gold bird drowned him out. Aleksander continued to rush in the opposite direction, and Leonardo hurried after him, leaving Pip behind.

First, the stick snapping, then the bird... It almost seemed like the woods were intentionally guiding Aleksander away from Pip.

Aleksander and Leonardo ran through the forest too fast for Pip to catch up until Aleksander stopped in a clearing. Leonardo halted on the edge, crouching behind a giant fern. The churn of a river gurgled nearby.

Aleksander swore, walking in a circle.

Why would the woods hide Pip from him?

Because it's possessive, Leonardo answered himself. He'd known that since he first set foot in the Darkwoods. He remembered something Kate said. She'd talked a lot about how much the woods loved her and the other pirate captains.

Because they're made from the fabric of the woods itself?

Pure imagination.

Did the woods steal Aleksander's creations? Leonardo frowned at the mulchy earth.

"I lost him too," said Aleksander. "But I have a new plan."

Aleksander snapped his fingers, and a treehouse appeared, identical to his father's. It was in a much taller tree, but the ladder rungs extended all the way down the trunk.

"I'm going to wait up there until he shows up. The woods aren't *that* big. He'll come find me."

Leonardo closed his eyes, realizing what he had to do. He was watching the infancy of a war between his brother and the woods. A war that would drive Aleksander to insanity and eventually claim him. He had a chance to save Aleksander now.

Leonardo drew a breath and stepped out of the bushes.

Aleksander whipped around. His small mouth fell open as he looked up at Leonardo.

"You're…" His eyes darted to Leonardo's sword. "I—"

"It's me," said Leonardo. He spread his hands placatingly.

"But…You're older than me! That's impossible. You're—"

"I'm from the future, Aleksander."

Aleksander shook his head. "I'm imagining you. You're not real."

Leonardo smiled, trying to hide how anxious he was. He had no idea how the woods would react to this.

"I'm very real," he told young Aleksander. "I promise you that."

"Why…What are you doing here?" Aleksander stammered. His blue eyes pierced into Leonardo's. It reminded Leonardo of the moment Aleksander vanished.

He shivered.

Over Aleksander's shoulder, a tree branch began to rot. A second branch shriveled even faster.

It's back.

Three times now; and each perfectly aligned with Leonardo's arrivals. His mouth turned dry. The heavy proof was undeniable. The blame was his.

I need to get out before it takes hold.

"I'm here to warn you." Leonardo's voice shook, and he struggled not to jumble the words. "You can't fight the woods."

"Why would I—"

"The woods are dangerous," he continued. "It will try to manipulate you. If you fight back, you're going to start a war that you can't win."

Aleksander shook his head. "This is my world. I promised Dad I would rule it."

That wasn't what Leonardo recalled their father asking him.

"Aleksander—"

"Why are you trying to stop me?" asked Aleksander. He frowned, and a flicker of familiar mistrust glinted in his eyes. "You're my brother. You should be helping me."

"I *am* helping you," insisted Leonardo. "I'm telling you to stand down. You can't—"

"And let it win?" Aleksander put his tiny hands on his hips, and Leonardo was startled to realize how intimidated he was by his brother. Old emotions died hard.

"Don't you remember what Dad always told us?" demanded Aleksander.

No, Leonardo didn't remember. Down the trail, a willow tree began to rot, hanging tendrils blackening at an alarming pace.

"He said to never back down," supplied Aleksander. "If the woods want to fight me, I'll just imagine more things. Bigger things. Leo, I'm going to build an army, and I'm going to win."

He narrowed his eyes, and Leonardo staggered back a step. The hostility radiating from him was all too familiar.

"And you can't stop me," finished Aleksander.

My god, thought Leonardo. *This is why he hates me.*

When young Leonardo arrived in the woods, some time from now, Aleksander would remember this moment.

He knew he would lose because I just told him. His only hope was to change the course of history and turn me into an ally. If we fought the woods together, the outcome might have changed.

The dream skipped again. Leonardo stood on the forest floor of the Redwoods, gazing at the mammoth trees he'd grown accustomed to. The blood rushed to his head, and he wavered, bracing himself against the rough bark for support. A girl with brown hair walked away from him. Then he was in the Cove, atop the cliffs. He crouched to keep his balance, pressing his palms into the tufty grass and blinking through the dizziness. A stiff wind whipped off the sea, tossing his hair. Below him, a lanky kid paced in the sand.

He didn't need to see either of their faces to know it was Kate and Cyrus.

A blink, and he was standing by the river while canoes filled with Natives rowed past. Leonardo's stomach flipped with every jump. He retched, doubling over on his knees. Then he slammed underwater, surrounded by sirens. Half a second later, he stood in the branches of a redwood while thousands of fairies streamed past him. Water ran down his face. Acid burned the back of this throat as he staggered sideways, struggling to keep conscious.

I'm witnessing the creation of the woods, thought Leonardo. *Aleksander's imagination was out of control.* He shut his eyes at the headache pushing harder against his skull and felt his surroundings shift again.

Leonardo blinked at a house. His nerves all fired at once.

Houses didn't exist in the woods. Anywhere. Treehouses maybe, but this structure was firmly planted in the ground. White plastic siding and glass windows hunkered before a picket-fence and a scatter of dandelions.

Leonardo hadn't noticed the dreamy veneer that coated the woods until now—in its absence. The oversaturated, ultra-vibrant wash of colors that painted his world faded to the cold light of reality beside this house. And the fear pierced his chest like an arrow.

I'm outside the woods.

A little girl swung on a tire suspended from the branch of an oak tree. Then she vanished.

What the—

The house morphed into a creek, glittering in the same cold, hard sunlight. The leaves of the bushes stirred like faded green paper. Two boys sprinted through the water, shouting and laughing.

They vanished, the echo of their voices lost in the creek. Leonardo's heart snagged.

Were they the twins?

But no, one had been noticeably taller. Those boys were close in age but not close enough.

The creek morphed, and Leonardo stepped through the doorway of a clay house, somewhere humid. A girl played on the packed-dirt street outside. She vanished.

Time fishtailed, skipping sideways and dragging Leonardo through folds of dizzying visions. A hundred or more kids vanished from their backyards, gardens, streets, neighborhoods until he slammed back into the spot where he'd started, beneath Aleksander's treehouse. The rosy, warm glow of the woods' embrace washed over him. Only now, dozens more treehouses were materializing, with rope bridges strung between them.

Kids' voices echoed from the riverbank nearby as Leonardo hunched on all-fours, heaving for breath and fighting the headrush. The voices multiplied as he watched the Raven Clan camp bloom into existence.

A burst of silver butterflies manifested like confetti. A silky white horse bolted through the underbrush with a thunder of hooves. Flowers pushed through the earth, multi-colored petals unfurling in the dappled sunlight.

The kids' imaginations are converging.

Aleksander's silhouette moved into the doorway of the original structure, his trench coat stirring around his ankles. Then a boom shook the air, and Leonardo's gaze snapped to the sky as a crack spiderwebbed over the cloudless blue. Dread filled his chest.

I stayed too long.

He knew what was coming a moment before the Dark poured out of it.

CHAPTER 42

There's no way to destroy it," said Tokala. A younger
Tokala.

Time had skipped again. Stars rushed in Leonardo's
eyes, and he blinked through the light-headedness. The chief stood
on the riverbank, Aleksander beside him. His hair, pebble grey in
the time Leonardo knew him, was mostly black now, interwoven
with only a handful of chalky strands.

Leonardo crouched in the ferns. *I caused the first Dark attack.* He
felt sick. *It's all my fault.*

"But we just did," argued Aleksander. He gripped a sword in
his right hand.

"We suppressed it," corrected Tokala, "but it is not gone. Did
you see the way it went into the river? I'm afraid it has entered
whatever lives there, the same way it tried to enter all of us during
the fight."

"The crocs," said Aleksander. "I'll fix it."

He lifted one hand, fingers poised to snap.

"Aleksander," said Tokala. "Stop."

"I can change the rules," said Aleksander.

"The woods don't like when you rewrite its rules." The first signs of wrinkles creased Tokala's dark skin.

"So?" Aleksander let his arm drop, fingers un-snapped. "How do you know that, anyway?"

"Because I am the guardian of the woods." Tokala's eyes were nearly black, charged with a pulsing energy that would grow deeper and steadier with age. But even now, he was much older than Aleksander, and he carried himself with sober importance.

"You're *a* guardian," corrected Aleksander in return. "Not *the*—" he broke off as Tokala pulled the pocket watch from his rawhide robes.

"Where did you get that?"

"The woods gave it to me. This is bigger than you now, Aleksander. It's time you stopped trying to control it."

"Give me back my watch." Aleksander grabbed for it, and Tokala whisked it away.

"This is not *yours*; it belonged to your father."

"How do you know my father?"

"I am made from the fabric of the woods," said Tokala. "This watch, the compass, your key, and your father's hat contain immense power. They are all that remains from the original woods— before it was corrupted."

If that last statement was meant to trigger a reaction, Aleksander failed to oblige.

"What kind of power?" Hunger radiated from Aleksander's voice. He leaned forward, blue eyes searching.

Stop trying to win, snapped Leonardo silently. He hunched lower, placing a hand in the moist soil. He wasn't going to reveal himself again. He felt like a pawn being moved through a game he was blind to.

"The kind which you cannot be allowed to possess. Your… *expansions* to this world have caused irreversible damage in this corner."

"Irreversible? Tokala, you're forgetting, I can imagine whatever I—"

Tokala sighed. "You still haven't learned. You are the new dreamer, yes. But it was your father's items that allowed you to create on such a grand scale. So grand that you tore the walls. The woods will not allow you that opportunity again."

Tore the walls. *Is that what allowed me to come back in time? Allowed the Dark to follow me?*

"But I still have…" Aleksander paused, fishing in his pockets. He frowned, checking another pocket. "Where's my compass?"

"Gone," said Tokala. "For now."

"You can't do that!" said Aleksander.

"Leave this corner of the woods," said Tokala. "Let us rebuild by hand, not your imagination. Go explore the world you created. Once you learn to stop controlling everything, the woods will allow you to take control again."

"You just want me out so you can take over." Aleksander stepped nose-to-nose with the guardian. Without the stoop of old age, Tokala's height easily matched Aleksander's, and he drew himself up even taller.

Aleksander did the same, moving closer until the air quivered between them.

"I bet you're proud of yourself," snapped Aleksander, right in Tokala's face. "I bet that compass makes you feel powerful. What are you going to make with it first?"

Tokala shook his head, slow and weary. At once, he looked like the ancient version of himself that Leonardo knew. "You're still the dreamer. Your father's items only work if you are in the same corner of the woods. If you leave, this watch is no more powerful than that twig on the ground."

That's why John's hat didn't work for him, Leonardo realized. *Aleksander was nowhere near him when he had it, out on The Forever.*

Pinch, in contrast, was in the same corner of the woods as Leonardo every time he created something.

Tokala slowly turned and gazed into the shadows, directly into Leonardo's eyes.

Leonardo gasped. Time stutter-stepped, and he blinked around at the Cove. Waves crashed on the beach as Aleksander stood before a group of kids, speaking emphatically. He looked older, a teenager now. A pirate ship rolled along the horizon, black sails billowing as it dipped over swells.

Leonardo was shaking. He slipped into the crowd before Aleksander could spot him and forced down his shock. He remembered the first time he'd met Tokala. The guardian knew exactly who Leonardo was, and his cryptic questions had pushed Leonardo on the path to where he stood now. *How much, exactly, did Tokala know?*

That was an answer Leonardo doubted he'd ever learn the answer to. And he didn't have time to ponder it. He focused on Aleksander. His brother was pitching the idea of seizing control and ruling over the other kids of the Cove.

331

"We can take the fortress," he explained. "Look."

He grandly removed a silk sheet from a pile on the sand. Underneath, piles of weapons glinted in the sunlight.

Time skipped again, and a group of girls in golden armor beat back Aleksander's army on the steps of Lion Clan's fortress. Their weapons were more advanced, and Aleksander's clan fell back with every ringing crash of steel. This was the original Lion Clan, the warriors of legend, long before Mishti's time.

The woods—or Lostwoods, here in the Cove—*favored them from the beginning*, he realized.

Just to prevent Aleksander from gaining power?

It also didn't slip past Leonardo that Lion Clan was named after an animal Aleksander specifically brought to the woods.

Insult to injury?

Or...suddenly, everything began to make sense. If the woods were inherited, then Aleksander's successor would be Leonardo. All the lion clues, how Leonardo was led to lion clan...it wasn't about the lions, it was about Leonardo. The woods simply had to use a symbol Aleksander had already put in place.

Another twist in the timeline, and now an even older Aleksander marched into the Darkwoods. He crouched on the riverbank, arranging stones in the dirt before him.

Those are his rocks. Back in Raven Clan, Aleksander had organized all his thoughts and strategies with rows of river stones. A raven swept past, heavy wings carrying it low over the water. A thick, militaristic beak jutted from a face slick with black feathers.

Aleksander paused to watch it.

"Raven Clan," he mumbled under his breath. He nodded. "That's good. Powerful."

Leonardo crouched between berry bushes up the bank from him. He edged forward, straining to hear.

"The woods will bring Leonardo here," Aleksander said to himself. He pulled a new stone from the water. "That's the only way to get rid of me while keeping itself alive."

He's right. Leonardo looked down at his hands. *Was I brought to the woods just so Aleksander could be vanished?*

And what about the twins?

If they were babies when he was six years old…*They could be pulled into the woods any time now.* And then Leonardo would be unnecessary. But he couldn't forget that time didn't behave right in the woods. Aleksander looked like a teenager now, but Leonardo wondered how many years it took to get him there. After all, Aleksander was older than the pirates.

Suddenly, Aleksander jumped to his feet. Leonardo flinched back, startled.

"*Yes!*" Aleksander clenched his fists. He advanced toward a maple sapling sprouting from the bank. "I'll beat you at your own game."

Then he stomped on the sapling, snapping it in half.

Leonardo winced. Aleksander's insanity was reaching its maturity. But he'd spent his own childhood learning to navigate Aleksander's antics, and he followed his brother's train of thought easily. Beating the woods at its own game meant using Leonardo—the one person the woods could use to get rid of him—to instead conquer the woods. He knew that the future manifestation of Leonardo would oppose the fight, so he needed to change Leonardo. Turn him into a conqueror.

"I'll have to lie to him," mumbled Aleksander, pacing. "I'll lie to everyone."

Time skipped, and Leonardo stood beneath the boughs of a pine as Aleksander carved raven faces into a tree trunk. Leonardo's stomach lurched, and stars crossed his vision. He kept his feet and forced himself to focus on Aleksander's work.

The leader tree. But if Aleksander created Raven Clan, then he was the only leader to have ever ruled it. He carved feverishly, glancing over his shoulder every few seconds.

It was all a lie. When Aleksander spoke of past leaders, no one would question him since they could see a tangible record on the tree.

Time corkscrewed into another rapid sequence of visions.

John standing on the deck of *The Forever*, talking about the Highland.

"It's boring, really," he told Kate and the other pirates. "A lot of hills. The clans there are dull."

Then Leonardo was standing among the dry, sandy cliffs of Hawk Clan territory. He ducked behind a rock as a boat rounded the river.

"You've returned," shouted a voice Leonardo recognized from his early days at Raven Clan. Lorenzo—Hawk Clan's leader before Gallus.

"Yessir," replied Gallus. From his spot behind the rock, Leonardo couldn't see either boy, but they spoke loudly enough that he didn't need to get any closer. "My valiant patrol has returned from the mysterious Highland."

"Cut the dramatics, Gallus," said Lorenzo. "What did you find?"

"It's boring, really," replied Gallus. "A lot of hills. The clans there are dull."

Leonardo caught his breath, then his surroundings changed, and he watched Aleksander talking to a group of young boys in the Raven Clan clearing.

"It's boring, really. The clans there are dull."

He had vivid memories of Aleksander telling him that exact description.

This isn't one of Aleksander's lies. This was the woods protecting its heart. They already knew the woods altered the memories of kids traveling from one corner to another, but this was the first time he'd witnessed it directly.

There were never clans in the Highland. Which meant that Leonardo had effectively united every kid from every corner of the woods.

We did it.

The world tilted, whooshing past in a blur of green and blue.

Leonardo woke up flat on his back in the Highland. The woods had revealed its last secret to him, and he knew that the vision was over. A gust of wind blasted him in the face, and Leonardo scrambled to his feet, grabbing for his sword. But this time, he wasn't facing the Dark. Pinch strode among the ranks of sleeping kids, a backpack slung over his shoulders, with an accordion hose attached to a jumbo-sized leaf blower. He blasted away the dream fog, and other kids began to wake, stumbling to their feet.

The racket of the machine drowned out any chance to speak,

but Pinch tipped his cap to Leonardo and continued blasting. The cliff's edge became visible again, but clouds of Darkness shrouded the woods below.

Sophie grabbed his shoulder.

"Leonardo," she pointed at the sky, "It's here."

Lion Clan is no different than any other clan. Leonardo saw it clearly for the first time. *I was guided to the Cove to fight the Dark. Lion Clan was just another lion sign.*

The lions were Leonardo's symbol. Aleksander brought them to the woods for him. All of it was one giant clue that Leonardo was the new dreamer. He'd needed every hint the woods could offer him to figure it out, but he saw it now. He had the compass, the pocket watch, the rock, and the hat. And he knew how to save the woods.

CHAPTER 43

Everyone listen closely," yelled Leonardo. He stood before ranks of Ravens, Hawks, Lions, Tigers, Dragons, Snakes, pirates, and Redwoods kids.

"The woods are made of imagination," he told them. "My father and brother created it all. Now it's my job to keep it alive. This is the heart of the dreamworld. We can create whatever we want, and we're going to create everything."

"What are you talking about?" called Caliban.

"Trust me," said Leonardo. He'd said that a million times to Mishti. *And look where it got her.*

He shook it off. *Focus.*

"Pinch, use your hat, make something big. The biggest thing you've imagined yet. Viola, your grandfather's pocket watch is just as powerful. Moth, I'm going to need your compass."

Moth fumbled in his pocket and threw it to Leonardo. Leonardo caught it, gazing at its weathered casing.

I hope this works.

"What do the rest of us do?" asked Puck. He stood with a new sense of confidence. He'd led the clans in Leonardo's absence and gotten everyone safely to the meet-up point. He spun his sword, eyes narrowed at the Dark.

"Start imagining things to protect us," shouted Leonardo. "We're in the heart of the woods. Use its magic."

Individually, they might not hold the same power as those carrying his father's possessions, but he'd witnessed kids in the woods' infancy using their imaginations to create. If they were to survive this, they needed every collective drop of creativity they could muster.

Overhead, the last of the fog dissipated, revealing an inky sky that spanned as far as he could see.

Pinch was the first to start imagining. A fleet of army tanks appeared, spread out for a mile across the field. They looked like children's toys, dwarfed in the distance, until their guns tilted up to the sky and fired at once, with a crack that vibrated Leonardo to his bones.

Leonardo flipped open the face of the compass. The needle spun. *It will always guide you to the door,* their father had told Aleksander.

Leonardo had used it as a regular compass before, but now they were in the Highland. In the heart of the woods, and it behaved nothing like a regular compass. The needle spun wildly for at least a hundred revolutions, then stopped abruptly, pointing to Leonardo's right.

Here we go.

"Follow me!" yelled Leonardo. He shoved the compass in his pocket and drew his sword. He sprinted hard over the short grass, every kid from every corner of the woods behind him.

Tank fire filled the sky as the Dark descended, hurtling in columns toward them. Viola ran next to Leonardo. She shut her eyes, and a second later, a thousand geysers burst from the earth, launching gallons of water at the Dark.

It worked! Leonardo caught his breath.

The Dark exploded outward, dispersing into millions of ribbons.

More water.

Leonardo closed his eyes and visualized the first thing he could think of. When he blinked at the field ahead of them, a brigade of firetrucks blinked into existence, their hoses mounted to the roofs and throwing a cascade of water a mile high. The mist reached him in seconds, spattering his face and speckling the front of his shirt.

But they'd already learned that water was losing its effectiveness on the Dark. Smoke poured from where ribbons of the Dark dissipated against the spray, but millions more made it to the ground, and they converged into ghostly limbs and legs.

Oh shit.

Pompey let out a gasp, sprinting madly on Leonardo's right. Charley fumbled with a high-powered water gun, the contents of its overfilled tank sloshing as hundreds of more nightmares manifested from the sky.

"Oh my god!" yelled someone from the mass of Dragons and Tigers.

Nothing looked quite human-shaped, but the shadows could run, and an army of misshapen creatures tore across the field toward the kids.

Screams and terrified voices collided as the army of kids scattered.

"Stay together!" yelled Leonardo, but his voice disappeared in the chaos. He shouted louder. "Stay to—"

Then the Dark was upon them.

The screams sharpened in pitch as kids fell under the phantom surge. Leonardo swung his sword and sliced through the first shadow, then the next, then the next, twisting and gasping as they grabbed for him. He never broke stride, thundering over the short grass as hard as his legs would pump. One misstep would send him barrelling into the dirt, but his heart raced too hard to slow down.

Kids struck the ground and vanished instantly in explosions of black smoke. Leonardo's heart wrenched with every lost child. Cleopatra and Sophie fired arrows, clumsy and off-target in their mad sprint, but the volume of shadows ahead of them meant that even poorly loosed shots found a mark, and puffs of smoke rose from the hoard.

Puck fought with every ounce of Raven Clan training he'd spent his days perfecting, his sword a blur. Hawks and Ravens alike flanked him, long-standing rivals turned allies.

A splash of cold wetness struck the back of Leonardo's neck.

He whipped around. Snake Clan charged in tight formation, palms splayed as shields of icy water sprayed before them. Caliban's hood flew back, his scar glowing black as he pulled magic from the air.

Leonardo stumbled around again as Demetrius ushered his clan together, their blue robes glinting through a whirlwind of darkness. He yelled instructions that Leonardo couldn't hear, then every member of Dragon Clan snapped their gaze upward. A winged beast streamed over their heads, a hundred times bigger than the dragons from their island.

It unleashed a roar that pierced Leonardo's skin and bones and vibrated him to his core. A blast of pure energy decimated ranks of the Dark's army.

Every surviving kid fought and dreamed as one, united for the first time. A parade of bizarre items flew around Pinch; winged chainsaws and giant vacuum cleaners that sucked up the Dark, and his high-powered leaf-blower, clenched in rigid fingers.

Moth hacked through creature after creature with his sword, running harder than Leonardo had ever seen him. His face drew tight with intensity, and his curls plastered flat with sweat. He was a different person than the scared kid from Aleksander's clan.

Juliet, Viola, Pompey, and Charley ran side by side, weapons and water guns flashing, and Leonardo's Ravens battled with the ferocity of the old days. Cato swung a sword in each hand, cutting a path of destruction through the Dark. Electrified air stung Leonardo's nostrils and throat. Bitter soot coated his tongue as he stumbled over churned-up earth, the sweaty leather grip of his sword fused to his palm. In the battles Leonardo grew up fighting, his enemies were tangible, blade-wielding kids—corporeal and vulnerable. This howling swirl of shadows kept him hacking and ducking at a full-tilt sprint without a sliver of a window to breathe.

The bangs, screams, roars, and rattling grind of laboring machinery beat on Leonardo's eardrums, lancing like a needle into his mind. White-hot pain seared his arms and torso as he missed slashes, and the Dark ripped at him. The smell of burning flesh cloyed heavy and sickening over the field, and Leonardo's ankle rolled unnaturally as he dodged a falling body. Scalding smoke singed his back as the Dark claimed another victim.

Shit. They couldn't sustain this.

The general and his Red Flags fought alongside Iris and the Blue Flags. A life of tree-climbing left them the fittest of any clans, and they began to pull ahead, hacking the shadows away. Leonardo gritted his teeth and pressed harder, running so fast that the creatures flashing past him were nothing but a blur. Another kid dropped. For a moment, he thought it was Bates, and his heart froze. But the kid's face was unfamiliar, and Bate's furious raven call cut through the chaos to Leonardo's right.

Leonardo swung his sword wildly, shouting as claws scraped his skin and more clouds of gritty smoke exploded in his face.

Imagine something, dammit, he cursed at himself. He was the only living descendant of the woods' creator. And he carried both the compass and the key. A possession from each of the first two dreamers. He needed to think bigger than anyone else had.

Out ahead, Demetrius' giant dragon crashed to the earth, smothered in darkness. The impact nearly threw Leonardo off his feet. In the same instant, inspiration struck him.

Before the idea was even half-formed, Leonardo whipped around and carved his sword in a stiff arc, the tip pointed at the horizon. The Dark parted as a hard seam cut across the sky.

Instantly, the sky folded like slack fabric, and a surge of iridescent, shimmering energy dumped out of the gash. Air escaping a sliced balloon. It struck the field with the thunder of battle drums, sparks spraying violently as a shimmering mass hurtled over the dry earth.

Leonardo's mouth fell open. *It worked.*

The Dark retreated into the sky with the yank of puppet strings. Leonardo staggered and fell to his knees, slamming palms-first into the grass. His chest heaved as he sucked in breath. Legs gave out as clan kids collapsed around him. Blood and raw skin gleamed everywhere. Throbbing wounds bled freely down Leonardo's face and arms. The deafening crash of the spilled magic grew louder, and the ones who kept their feet shouted a warning. Leonardo pushed upright, eyes wide as he faced the pearly rush.

What did I do?

The surge leveled them. A battering ram of ancient magic drove into Leonardo's chest, flipping him head over heels and propelling him under pounds of force. It smelled like pine tar and sea breezes and dusty cliffs and marshland. The essence of the woods concentrated into the humming flood of its lifeforce.

Leonardo struck the ground hard, tumbling in a high-speed barrel roll. He squeezed his eyes shut, shoulders, hips, and knees bouncing repeatedly off the earth until the contents of his stomach threatened to eject. He twisted awkwardly, breaking his violent ride enough to get his limbs under him and launch dizzily to his feet. He blinked at a storm of iridescent colors, weaving around him and shrieking like a banshee wind. The rushing magic propelled him forward as it snapped at his clothes.

The shapes of other kids pinwheeled and rolled past him, ghosts in the glittering wind. A hard gust lifted Leonardo off his feet and threw him flat on his chest. His breath expelled, and he skidded face-first in the grass. He came to a stop as the last of the magic whistled past him, tousling his hair.

Leonardo lay motionless for a long moment. His ribs ached. His face stung. His lungs dragged air into his limp body. He tenderly pushed himself up. Rag-dolled bodies lay scattered around him. The pearly mass thundered away, a rogue wave in a sea of grass.

"Holy shit." Pinch rolled onto his back. "That sucked."

Leonardo scanned the coughing, wheezing survivors, running a desperate tally.

*Viola, Moth, Pinch, Charley…*They were all still with him. For now.

Then he spotted it. Up ahead, a wooden door loomed among the rocks and flattened grasses. Hope swelled in his chest. He fished his father's compass from his pocket and gazed down at the face. It pointed straight ahead.

It's the door.

He struggled to his feet and leaned back. The Dark gathered overhead. His lungs burned, his leg muscles felt ready to snap, and his sword weighed three tons, but fresh motivation pushed him onward.

We're almost there.

"Here comes round two," yelled Puck. He grimaced, rising to his feet.

"Let's go!" Leonardo winced, laboring into a run. He grabbed hands and arms and dragged kids off the ground. Grunts of pain and exertion filled the air as the clans struggled into motion, clutching at sprained shoulders and hips.

A wrenching, skin-crawling grind blasted over the field, so loud that Leonardo's ears popped.

"Go, go, go!" he yelled.

The Dark hit the ground behind them with a boom that charged his veins with pure, fear-stricken adrenaline.

He sprinted harder, the thundering footsteps of his friends behind him. He shoved the compass in his pocket and grabbed for the rock, throwing it and catching the key on the run.

The door drew closer and closer, and the Dark gained on them by the second, and Leonardo's lungs burned, but he kept running until red blurred the edges of his vision, and the door drew closer, closer.

Leonardo stopped hard against the riveted wood, gasping for breath as he jammed the key in the lock. It clicked, and Leonardo threw the door open.

CHAPTER 44

Woodland awaited them. A clean, untouched sanctuary.

"Go!" he yelled, shoving kids through the open doorway. Viola stopped against him, twisting to look at the Dark.

"Leo," she gasped. "There's not enough time."

Leonardo could barely breathe as the Dark rolled closer.

"Move it!" yelled Pinch. "Go, halfwits, go!"

"I'm going, halfwit!" Puck threw himself over the threshold.

Kids in their tattered, multi-colored robes and torn shirts raced across the final meters of the field. The Dark barreled after them. Leonardo shoved their blood-stained backs as they passed, forcing the stampede through. Finally, the last ones rushed past him, leaving only Kate at the rear. Leonardo pulled the key from the lock and tossed it back into a stone, then wound up and threw it as far as he could. He wouldn't be needing it again.

"What's through that door?" Kate staggered to a stop.

The fear that filled her voice surprised him for only a second. *Dammit.*

"A new woods," said Leonardo, eyes locked on the wall of shadows fifty feet away. Forty feet. Thirty.

"Come on!" said Viola. "Let's go!"

"I can't," said Kate.

"What?" demanded Viola.

Leonardo opened his mouth, but the certainty hit him before he could utter a sound. Kate came from the first breath of Aleksander's woods. The pirates were the first living things created from it, and they loved it in a way that no one else could.

"I know," said Leonardo.

Viola whipped around to look at him, incredulous.

"A hundred years is long enough," said Kate. "If I'm dying, I'm doing it in my woods. It's my duty."

Viola blanched, and Leonardo's blood went cold. Viola was the last of the guardians.

If it's Kate's duty to stay, he thought, an iron tang of panic on his tongue, *then is it also...*

The Dark hurtled toward them.

"No," he told Viola. "You're coming with me."

Leonardo tugged her arm, and Viola followed him through the doorway. The Dark shot toward them, twenty feet away. Kate glanced back at Leonardo and all the others, standing just across the threshold.

She drew a breath and smiled. "Until we meet again."

Then she whipped out her sword and kicked the door shut.

It locked with a quiet click, but Leonardo felt it like a punch in the stomach. Viola let out a shocked sob, and silence spread over the new woods. There was no thump on the door, no impact as the Dark reached it. They were in a new place now, an infinity of time and space away. For a long time, no one said anything. The minutes dragged as they all stood staring at the door.

Finally, Leonardo turned to face the massive crowd of kids, slumped against moss-covered trees and laying where they had dropped in the dappled sunlight. As he watched, the wounds and gashes on their skin began to heal, erasing the last traces of the old place.

We did it, thought Leonardo. Not everyone had survived the journey, but their sacrifices were what allowed the rest of them to make it out. Leonardo's clan—his *family*—was here, and the Dark was locked out for good.

As if to prove that point, Nym stepped over an arched root, smiling bigger than Leonardo had seen since they first left Raven Clan.

"It's gone," said Nym. He tipped his head back as if a chain had been cut loose. "I can feel it. It disappeared when that door closed."

And just like that, a flood of relief and victory washed through their ranks. Someone cheered, then someone else took it up until the treetops rang with the sounds of their celebration.

Viola pulled Leonardo behind a tree and kissed him. They were safe now. Together. All of them were together, and they would never have to run again.

He breathed in the smell of Viola's skin, her hair, as she rested her head on his shoulder. Life pulsed through her fingers, grasping his shirt, and Leonardo held her against his beating heart.

I caused the first Dark attack. Right at the birth of the *Dark*woods. *Which explains the name*, he realized.

"I had a vision," said Leonardo softly. "Back in the Highland."

"What do you mean?" She looked up at him. "Like my visions?"

"Not exactly." Leonardo struggled to put it into words. *If I brought the Dark to the past from the future…*He frowned. *How did it get into the future in the first place?*

"I went back in time," he said finally.

They had been trapped in an endless loop. His father's woods may have started as a dream, but Aleksander's version was a nightmare. A mirror facing a mirror.

Viola waited patiently for him to elaborate. After everything they had experienced, he wondered if anything could surprise them ever again.

"I spoke to Aleksander," continued Leonardo. He studied the patterns of dappled sunlight on her face. "I warned him not to fight the woods. I thought I could change the timeline, but I think I just fueled it."

He had spurred Aleksander's paranoia, and his sharp bitterness toward Leonardo, and his desperate grip on his youth.

No. That part wasn't entirely Leonardo's fault. That most likely stemmed from their father's fate. But Leonardo foretelling Aleksander's demise was the final straw.

Behind Viola, an iridescent squirrel tore up the trunk of a gnarled tree.

"Fueled it, how?" Viola tilted her head.

"Aleksander tried to build an army. At first, he imagined kids, and then he started pulling real ones out of their lives and into the woods. I don't know if he meant to, or if it happened by accident."

"He created a black hole." Viola's eyes widened, reflecting the vibrant green of Leonardo's woods. "He imagined too big."

"I think so." Leonardo nodded. "And then the woods took control of everything he created."

The Natives, the fairies, the sirens. The woods turned them into guardians of its three corners, to keep all its new children in line. The pirates, being the first kids—and favorites, if he knew how the woods worked—were guided together and given The Forever as a gift.

My father's pirate hat was on The Forever.

Which meant that the woods had actively stolen items which belonged to Aleksander. Even if he started as the writer, by the time the Dark arrived, Aleksander was nothing but a character in the story.

"And these woods…?" asked Viola slowly, gazing around. "Will they do the same?"

"I don't think so." Leonardo plucked a translucent leaf from the tree. "If we respect the woods, it will take care of us."

Aleksander's mistake was that he took his first loss too seriously. He associated success with defeating Lion Clan—and the woods by extension. Any maybe the woods knew that, and by elevating Lion Clan's status, it led him down a rabbit hole of raven carvings and lion hunts. Which explained his anger when Moth spotted the lion years later. It meant his hold on the Darkwoods was fading.

A fairy flitted past, and Leonardo tilted his head. Moth had found his compass in the dirt the day he arrived in the Darkwoods, just before he spotted his first fairy. Moth had kept that compass in his pocket every day since he arrived. The understanding flooded Leonardo's mind; *the old magic lets Moth hear the fairies.*

But only if Leonardo was in the same corner of the woods. And maybe the magic behaved a bit differently for everyone. He'd used the compass plenty of times and never heard a fairy speak. And Pinch's hat gave him totally different abilities.

The true nature of his father's magic—and the woods' influence on it—was a mystery, but Leonardo didn't care to master it in the way his brother had.

"I think the woods figured out Aleksander's plan," he told Viola, leading her back onto the path. "But rather than facing him directly, it made the plan its own. Right from underneath him."

Leonardo remembered multiple conversations with Tokala, where he urged Leonardo to make some kind of choice. To deviate from his brother's path.

"What do you mean?" Viola ducked under a low branch, covered in tiny flowers.

Around them, curious voices mingled as the survivors explored their new surroundings, moving over mossy rocks and gentle hollows.

"When I arrived," said Leonardo, "the woods began to drop lion signs in my path. Everything that guided us to the Cove was put there to lead me to Lion Clan. But instead of conquering them like Aleksander wanted, I chose to unite the woods."

Kate and Adriana were made of the woods. Maybe their attempts to seduce him were really the woods making Aleksander's plan its own.

Trying to ensnare Leonardo.

Or maybe…

Maybe him being the dreamer was what drew them to him, even without their realizing it. Maybe they were as innocent as everyone else in the fight.

*And Viola…*Leonardo's stomach dropped. She frowned, sensing his shift.

"What is it?" She stopped on the trail, edging backward to see him clearer.

No. Viola had come to him before he was the dreamer. Everything between them was real. Poignant relief washed over him. He didn't even know how to vocalize his thoughts. He turned in a circle, gazing at the kids exploring the new woods. Then he stopped on Pompey and Charley as the last puzzle piece fell into place.

He couldn't believe he hadn't seen it before. They were far from identical, but they looked similar enough, and they were the same age, and not all twins looked alike.

Charley was brought to me, and Pompey was placed in Lion Clan. Again, to bring us together. Because the woods' only chance to save itself was to make Leonardo realize he was the dreamer.

Charley threw a pinecone at Pompey, and he dodged into the trees, laughing.

"We have a lot to figure out," he said finally. "But everything will be ok now."

"I know," said Viola quietly. She took his hand, then stretched for another kiss.

A short walk later, a gurgle of water carried over the birdsong, and Leonardo called everyone together. He had imagined this world in the split second that he opened the door, but he knew it as well as if he'd been walking it his entire life.

"This is a simpler world," Leonardo told them, leading the way over a low rise. He glanced at Moth and Pinch, and Pompey and Charley, and Caliban and Sophie and all the others. "We're not going to fight for territory in these woods, and we're not going to try to control it."

These woods would be what they were always meant to be; a sanctuary.

Overhead, hundreds of treehouses nestled in the branches, connected with rope bridges and ladders, while up ahead, a stream wound through the trees, filled with smooth stones.

"Everyone take a stone." Leonardo waded into the cool water and bent to pick one up. It looked a lot like Aleksander's.

Quizzical, Viola bent and picked one beside him.

"You still have the pocket watch, right?" he asked her.

"Of course." Viola reached in her pocket.

"Good." Leonardo recalled his father's words; *never lose track of how long you're away.* "Hold onto it."

"Do these unlock that door?" Pinch tossed his stone in the air and caught it as a key. He stepped up the far side of the bank toward a new, ivy-covered door between a pair of willow trees.

"Yes." Leonardo moved past him. He slipped his fingers into Viola's as Moth and Juliet crossed the stream, picking their own rocks, then Charley and Pompey ran, splashing through the water.

Leonardo smiled. He would have to tell the kids the truth. But not now. There would be time for everything later. He gazed up at the treehouses, dappled in the afternoon sunlight.

"What does it lead to?" asked Viola.

"Outside," said Leonardo. He smiled at the surprise on her face. Then he slipped his key into the lock and pulled the latch.

THE END

ACKNOWEDGEMENTS

Well, here we are! This trilogy has been an adventure and a half, and I feel so fortunate to have such an amazing team around me. My editorial partner in crime, Fiona, I have no idea what I'd do without you. Thank you for always pushing me to delve deeper into the characters and world of the Darkwoods, and for all the advice and support you provide above and beyond your edits. To Stephen Dafoe, thank you for covering this trilogy so extensively over the past few years. Your interviews and news stories have been a huge contributor to the public success of Lost Boys, and your support as a fellow author and friend means a lot to me. Sofia, I'm thrilled that I got to work with you again. Thank you for your time and artistry on another beautiful map. To the Dramallamas, this acknowledgements page would not be complete without a shoutout to you guys! I still love every second I get to spend in the theatre with all of you. As a writer, it's a major creative recharge whenever I step through those doors and see so many hard-working performers and artists. To my amazing family and friends, thank you from the bottom of my heart for all of your support. I couldn't do this without you. And of course, thank you to my readers for sharing in Leonardo's world with me. Your enthusiasm for these books drives me forward. Lost Boys may be coming to a close, but the journey is only just beginning!

RILEY QUINN is a Canadian author and musician. He grew up in Western Canada, dividing his time between the Prairies, the Rocky Mountains, and the shores of the North West Coast. When he's not writing, Riley can be found performing and teaching music in his local community.

To learn more, visit: www.rileyquinnofficial.com

CPSIA information can be obtained
at www.ICGtesting.com
Printed in the USA
BVHW030037220521
607898BV00002B/2